Night Sights

a novel by

Charlie Fernandez

ACKNOWLEDGEMENTS

Several people were kind enough to advise me in areas outside my expertise. Thank yous go to John Del Nero for his help on police and criminal matters, Kindra Freedom for her help on medical matters, and Brad Newhart for military questions. If there are failings of accuracy in the story, they are solely mine for not paying attention to the advice I was so generously given.

This book would not have reached its final form without the patient efforts of my three critique partners: Heather Howland was instrumental in the story development; Diane Steiner's insights brought greater dimensionality to the characters; and Lila Ekstrom schooled me regularly in grammar and punctuation and any errors remaining I have no excuse for.

For the cover art, I am indebted to Linsey Fuller who took a picture and a concept and make it real.

Lastly, I would like to thank my wife, Marilyn, who has kept me both grounded and focused for forty years.

Charlie Fernandez
Phoenix, AZ

Chapter One

No Barking

I turned off Polk expecting my house to be burned to the ground. You know the image: the chimney, standing amidst the smoking ruins, the inevitable result of war.

The war was with Monica, my next-door neighbor. Gaia, as she styled herself, taught holistic drumming through the community education program. Her students, mostly aging hippies and Indian wannabes, were nice enough. They celebrated Fridays with an impromptu recital in Monica's back yard followed by a soak in her hot tub.

Actually, I didn't mind the drum sessions. They reminded me of old cowboy-and-Indian movies. What pushed me into the red zone was her dog, Shaman. The war was about the barking and the collateral damage to my nerves. She left Shaman in her back yard when she wasn't home. Otherwise he'd chew her furniture. Did a

1

good job, too, very thorough. Unfortunately, being outside alone made him anxious, jumpy. He barked at everything. When he stopped barking, he howled, sitting on the hot tub cover like the lone coyote on a mesa.

I suspect Shaman was why the previous owner gave me such a good deal on the house.

Silly me. Fresh from the hospital and loopy with post traumatic stress counseling, I assumed Monica would intuit the savaging effect a barking dog had on a nervous system as frail as an autumn leaf. But when I mentioned Shaman's penchant for vocalizing, the spittle from her rebuke pelted my face like a summer thunderstorm. Now we discussed noise issues through public services.

So I was a little surprised that the one-story, craftsman-style bungalow was still standing. Aside from the lawn needing to be edged and mowed, the place looked none the worse for wear: a quiet house in a quiet neighborhood, quiet except for the incessant barking of Monica's stupid dog.

I backed my pickup into the driveway steering from the side mirror. When the brake lights turned the pale gray garage door purple, I shifted into park and relaxed for the first time in a week. I took my cap off and scratched at my hat-hair with both hands. The rear view mirror told me I needed a shave. It also said I looked tired. Not surprising. It's a sixteen-hour drive from Pahrump, Nevada. And I still needed to clean the camping gear, put it away, then wash and wax the truck.

As I stretched, the hardness on my right hip reminded me I was still packing. I had worn my Glock four days straight during defensive handgun training and all day again today traveling. It was almost comfortable. But then, I was new to handguns. The numbness on my hip might be nerve atrophy from the long ride.

I got a concealed carry permit after I moved back to Eugene, after the shooting. If there was ever a next time, I wanted to be prepared. That's what the training in Pahrump was about, being prepared. What I hadn't anticipated was how self-conscious carrying a hidden handgun felt. My Glock was the compact model chambered in .40 caliber, a good carry gun because of its light weight and low profile. But in a college town like Eugene, it felt like a howitzer, like I was hiding something that couldn't be hidden, a soul stained by mortal sin. That's why the training was good for me. It reminded me it wasn't my sin.

I turned the engine off and sank further into the seat, surprised at how good it felt to relax.

"Yoo-hoo, Bobber."

I opened my eyes. My neighbor on the other side was standing next to the truck. I could just see her forehead.

"Mrs. Batty." I sat up. I must have dozed off. "How have you been?"

Mrs. Batty was the first neighbor I had met. She was a bit forgetful since her stroke, and she needed a cane to get around, but at ninety she still walked every afternoon. I imagined pioneers setting out from Independence, Missouri on the Oregon Trail with that same determination.

"I'm fine, but you look like you could use a good night's sleep. You must have caught a lot of fish."

"Yes I did," I lied. "And so did my clients. We all had a great time."

The counselor they gave me said it was important to avoid stressful situations during recovery from PTSD.

And four days of firearms training was stressful enough without explaining the why of it to the neighbors. So I was taking a pass, telling everyone I went fishing instead. The salmon fly hatch was on in central Oregon and I guided for the Copper John Fly Angling Shop. It was the best kind of lie, discreet.

"Did you take the dog with you?"

"The dog? I don't have a dog, Mrs. Batty. Remember?"

"Not your dog." She corrected me. "You don't have a dog. I'm talking about Monica's dog."

"Shaman?" I listened. No barking. The silence was beautiful, but odd. "Where'd he go?"

Mrs. Batty reached up and touched my arm knowingly. "I bet you want to unpack and shower. You look exhausted." She turned to leave. "Your secret's safe with me."

"Mrs. Batty, what secret?"

"I know you found him a good home."

"Mrs. Batty!" But she was gone.

A well-kept, dark blue van with ladders bungeed to the top-rack slid to a stop in front of the driveway. The white script on the side panel said "Jimmy Dean Electric."

"Hey, Bobber, you just get back?"

"Hey, Jimmy Dean, how you doing?"

"I've been waiting on you, boss." Jimmy Dean DuChien slipped the van into park and hung through the driver's window, primping his mullet of reddish-blond hair like a fox admiring its tail. Style was not an issue with Jimmy Dean.

"How come?" I was halfway down the driveway before I remembered the Glock holstered inside the waistband of my jeans. My vest covered the grip. It would be okay, I told myself. Get used to it.

I knew Jimmy Dean from high school. We'd been friends until his older brother, Floyd, got kicked off the football team and his father lost his job. Then they moved to Texas and we lost touch. Actually, it was me who told the coach someone was stealing from the lockers. Turned out it was Floyd.

"Find out how's the fishing. A couple of my electrician buds are hot to trot for a couple days on the Deschutes."

Jimmy Dean wanted to guide professionally. I was trying to get him on at the Copper John.

"They're still hitting salmon flies."

"Anything in particular?"

"No. Sofa Pillows, Norm Woods, Dan Garbers, they liked them all. But you gotta be on the surface."

"Yeah?"

"The hatch is almost over, so they're real picky."

Jimmy Dean shook his head, then looked up and down the street.

"Hey ah, boss," he said in a low voice, smiling. He lifted his chin toward Monica's house. "You didn't happen to take what's-her-name's dog, did you?"

"I wouldn't waste the gas on that piece of shit."

"Oh-ho!" Jimmy Dean grinned, his eyes gleaming demonically. "So he's here?"

"No, no." I shook my index finger at him. "Don't start talking like that. I don't know what happened to that dog. I've been gone all week."

"Then why are you smiling? You're grinning like a goddamn Cheshire cat."

I tried to hide my smile. Truth was, sure, if the dog was gone, I was glad.

"I knew it, boss! You offed the dog, then went fishing. You cold motherfucker, you. Stone cold!"

A screen door slammed. He looked past me. "Oh-oh, don't look behind you."

"Okay, Robert." Monica's voice chipped the air like flint. "You've had your little joke. Now give him back."

She advanced across her front lawn wearing a plaid work shirt with the sleeves cut off, her Indian braids bouncing at the waistband of her sweat pants. I thought about shouting, "armed citizen, stop or I'll shoot," like they taught in training, but didn't.

"I heard he was missing," I told her calmly. "But I don't know where he is."

"Who's this?" she demanded, looking at Jimmy Dean.

"I'm an electrician friend of Mr. Mulligan's, ma'am," Jimmy Dean said politely. "I'm working in the area."

"You can't park here," Monica told him, then turned to me. "I'll ask you one more time, then I'm calling the police. Where is he?"

"I'll tell you one more time, then *I'm* calling the police. I heard he was missing, but I don't know where he is."

"I know you took him," she insisted. "I watch the Crime Channel. You never liked Shaman to begin with; that's motive. You conveniently go on some fishing trip; that's opportunity." She stopped.

"Capability, ma'am. The third one is capability," Jimmy Dean prompted. He grinned. "He has that, too."

"Jimmy Dean, stop clowning around."

"If you don't give him back, I'm calling the police. You can suffer the consequences." Monica marched back across her lawn, climbed her front steps, and slammed her screen door.

"That's okay, boss," Jimmy Dean said. "What with the overcrowding at the jail, you'll be out in no time."

"That's not funny."

"You don't have to play sly with me, boss. We go way back." Jimmy Dean stopped for a moment to light a cigarette. "You know what your neighbors think, don't you?"

I looked at him. "I had nothing to do with it."

Jimmy Dean giggled merrily. "They think it's you. They're glad you got rid of the fucker."

Chapter Two

Animal Control

"I don't mean to rush off." I backed away from the van. "But I got to get on my gear. You know how it is."

"Let me guess." Jimmy Dean grinned. "You're dog tired."

"Funny." I walked back to the truck, climbed into the camper, and shut the door. I didn't want to think about that goddamned dog.

Since the shooting, I forgot things if I got rattled. That's why I didn't go back to work. I was a product manager and product management was a rattling kind of job. So I made lists. It was the counselor's idea, probably his only good one. Lists made me feel organized, in control, prepared, like my handgun. I found my unpacking list and got busy. The first item was to move the cooking gear from the camper to the kitchen for cleaning. That's where I started. It didn't take a lot of thought. It took repetition. I realized it didn't matter if it was camping gear or handguns. It was about repetitive training to build muscle memory. That's what developed good habits. That's what got you prepared.

I wasn't prepared for the shooting. I didn't have good habits. I was living in what the training called the white zone. Maybe that's why I didn't duck when the shooting started. It was a convenience store robbery gone bad. I was dead by the time I hit the floor. That's how quick it can happen.

The EMTs brought me back. They went to shootings all the time. They were prepared. They knew what to do. In the hospital, I decided to be prepared too, to live in the yellow zone so, if it ever happened again, I'd have the option to shoot back.

I checked off "cooking gear to house" on my list. Next item, "clothes to laundry."

I was in the laundry room dumping my dirty laundry into the washer when I heard a knock at the front door.

"Hey boss, you in here?" It was Jimmy Dean. "I got somebody wants to talk to you."

I crossed through the kitchen to the living room. Out the picture window a truck from Animal Control was parked in front of Jimmy's van. On the front porch, an older guy in a tan uniform shirt and shorts stood next to Jimmy Dean. He looked like the ticket taker at Safari Land.

"Mr. Mulligan?" the guy asked. "Spellman from Lane County Animal Control."

"Yeah, hi." I opened the door and shook his hand. "What can I do for you?"

"We just got a report of animal cruelty. We take that pretty seriously. I happened to be in the area on another call, so I thought I'd stop by and check it out. Is now a good time?"

"Monica Hoffman, right? My neighbor, she called it in."

"All calls are confidential, Mr. Mulligan," Spellman replied.

"I don't know what happened to Shaman," I said. "I just got back from a week-long fishing trip. I guide for John Ogle at the Copper John Fly Angling Shop. I'd just like to unpack and take a shower."

"Like I said," Spellman repeated. "We take animal cruelty very seriously."

"Boss." Jimmy Dean looked at me over Spellman's shoulder. "You should talk to the gentleman. I'll help you unpack." Then he grinned. "I ain't going to help you shower though."

"Thanks, Jimmy." I sighed and shrugged at Spellman. "You mind? You can sit on the deck and ask your questions. We'll just be walking back and forth unloading stuff from the camper."

"Works for me," Spellman said.

"Come on in, then. You want a glass of water or something?" I asked as we passed through the kitchen. "Hey, Jimmy Dean, grab that list off the table, will you, and read me the next thing after laundry."

"Propane tanks."

Spellman surveyed the back yard as I stepped off the deck and climbed back into the camper.

"You say you were on a fishing trip?" he asked.

"Yeah." I detached my two small propane tanks and passed them to Jimmy Dean. "Set these on the deck, will you? I'll get them refilled tomorrow."

"You got the good life, Bobber," Jimmy Dean said. He turned to Spellman. "He's got the good life, don't he? I'm getting me some of that. He's going to get me on at the Copper John. Ain't you, boss?"

I nodded.

Spellman seemed wistful. "What do you do with all the fish?"

"Release them. Sometimes a client on an overnighter will keep one for dinner."

"Nothing better than fresh fish." Jimmy Dean nodded agreeably. "Up here it's trout. Down home, we had bass."

"How long were you gone?" Spellman asked.

"Six days total. I just got back. What's after propane?"

"Sleeping gear."

I handed my sleeping bag to Jimmy Dean and grabbed my air mattress. "Hang it on the deck railing so it can air out." I led the way across the deck and draped the deflated air mattress over the railing.

"So, if you've been gone all week, how come you know about Shaman?" Spellman asked.

"That he's missing?" I tried to sound unself-conscious, like I wasn't hiding anything, but I knew this wasn't a social visit. It's hard to sound honest when you really want to. "Jimmy Dean here filled me in just before you got here."

Jimmy Dean nodded.

"Mr. Mulligan, does it seem strange to you that you leave town and Shaman disappears?"

"I bet you would have left sooner, hunh?" Jimmy Dean joked.

"Shaman's gotten out before, but it is a little coincidental. I mean, what are the odds?"

"Exactly," Spellman agreed. "You're also the only neighbor who complained. What are the odds of <u>that</u>?"

"He's always been a complainer," Jimmy Dean offered. "Got my brother Floyd kicked off the football team complaining. Remember that?"

"That dog was a nuisance barker," I said, about to shoot Jimmy Dean DuChien if he didn't stop. "I don't know why no one else complained."

"We ask people to keep a log in nuisance barker disputes. Did you keep a log like you were requested? For two weeks, all the times Shaman barked more than fifteen minutes. If you did, I'd like to see it. It would really help."

"I kept it for a couple days," I admitted. "Then I stopped."

"May I see what you have?"

"I threw it out."

"Oh-oh." Jimmy Dean's eyes flicked from Spellman to me and back like he was watching me lose a chess game.

"Why is that?" Spellman asked.

"Because I got mad. Why should I track Shaman's behavior? Monica should do it. It's her dog."

"By Monica you mean your neighbor, Gaia?"

"Yes, god damn it! Gaia! Monica! Same thing. Why do I have to do all the work? Why don't you hold her accountable for something? It's her fucking dog." I realized too late how loud my voice sounded, how agitated I was getting.

Spellman continued as if he hadn't heard me. "If Shaman is so terrible, why are you the only one who's mad about it?"

"I'm not mad!"

"You're shouting," Spellman replied calmly. "What emotional state would that indicate to you?"

"I'm frustrated," I admitted. "The dog barks. My neighbors know the dog barks. We talk about it all the time. I was just the one who talked to Monica about it. Maybe everyone else was afraid. You talk about anger, she's the one with issues."

"Do you know anything about a poison meatball?"

"She accused me of poisoning Shaman." Earlier in the spring, Shaman had gotten sick. The vet thought someone might have slipped him a poison meatball. Monica thought it was me.

"And?"

"And if I'd done it, I would have used more poison."

Spellman jerked upright and stared.

"Look, Spellman," I said. "The dog eats anything he can reach. I know because I've heard her complain about it. It was Valentine's Day. I think he got into some chocolate. That's what poisoned him."

"And vandalism?" he asked.

"She blamed me for that too," I said curtly. About the same time as the poison incident, someone marched through Monica's newly planted flowerbed. It made her cry.

"Bobber is a sitting duck for trouble," Jimmy Dean explained to Spellman. "Matter of fact, it's like he's the only duck on the pond."

"Back to your fishing trip for a moment," Spellman said, ignoring Jimmy Dean. "Who did you go with?"

"I went with clients from the Copper John."

"Can I get their names?"

"Our client list is confidential."

"If I called the Copper John, would they verify the trip?"

"Yes."

John Ogle was an ex-policeman. I told him I was taking the handgun training and I told him why. He'd vouch for me, no problem. Still, it pissed me off. My one well-intentioned white lie was now a matter of public record and reflected poorly on my character as well as his. Meanwhile, irresponsible Monica was held blameless. I guess that's why the road to Hell is paved with good intentions.

"So your story is that Gaia's dog, Shaman, is a nuisance barker, but you have no proof. You were specifically requested to keep a log of Shaman's barking, but can't supply it." Spellman looked from his notepad to me, then back. "You admit you don't like Shaman, but say you wouldn't hurt him."

I wanted to add something, but I didn't know what. His facts, however brief, caught the gist of it. I kept my mouth shut and just nodded at him.

Spellman continued. "People in the neighborhood believe you had a motive for taking the dog. But you deny doing it. You went on a fishing trip at the exact time Shaman disappeared, but you think that's a coincidence. You won't divulge who you were with, but you say your employer can verify your story. Is that a fair summary?"

"That's about it," I said.

"Well, I think that's all I need. Thanks for your time."

I walked Spellman back through the house. He said he'd be in touch. I could hardly wait.

When I got back to the deck, Jimmy Dean had a weird expression on his face.

"Hey, boss," he said. "I don't care if you bullshit somebody else, but would you bullshit me?

"I didn't bullshit that guy."

"I don't care about him. Would you bullshit me?" he insisted.

"No."

"Then let me ask you this," he said, holding up my list. "The next item after sleeping gear is fishing gear."

"So?"

"I don't see any fishing gear."

Jimmy Dean DuChien, ace detective, had me by the balls.

Chapter Three

Just a Dog

"Didn't need any gear," I mumbled. "They brought their own, the clients, a couple lawyers from Portland. Nice stuff, top of the line. I just rowed and cooked. I didn't even fish."

"I got to get back to work," he said, the weird expression still on his face. "See you around."

He stepped off the deck. A moment later, the van engine revved loudly, then the tires chirped as he put the van in gear. I winced at the sound. I was exhausted and it wasn't from the long drive. Being a liar took a lot of energy, even for a little lie. That asshole counselor hadn't told me that.

I crossed out fishing gear and moved on to the next item on the list, then the next. It was all muscle memory.

I was washing cooking gear when the doorbell rang. I thought Jimmy Dean had come back, but it was some guy in a sport coat and slacks. His dark hair was close cropped and he was chewing gum.

"Can I help you?" Another lie. I didn't want to help this guy. I didn't even open the screen door in case he was selling insurance or something.

"Detective Cadanki, Eugene Police." He introduced himself. "Are you Robert Mulligan?"

"Yes."

"May I come in?"

I unlocked the screen and opened the door. One little lie, I thought. That's all it took. "Is this about the barking dog?"

"You're good." He stopped chewing, surprised. "You complained about the dog?"

"Yeah, my neighbor's dog, Shaman. I didn't think the cops came out for barking dogs."

"We don't." He chewed his gum with sharp ferret-like bites. "This is something different. Where's the dog now, do you know?"

"No. It disappeared," I said. "I was out of town." I was afraid to tell the truth, but unwilling to lie again.

"Mr. Mulligan, do you think someone could have taken that dog?"

"You mean did I take it?"

"No. I mean one of your neighbors. Someone else in the neighborhood."

"No," I answered. "Why?"

"Do you have any enemies? Someone who would want you to look bad?"

"Besides Monica?"

"That's the Monica next door?"

I nodded.

"I talked to her yesterday." He bared his teeth like he was trying to smile. "I dated a girl like that once."

"How it'd go?"

"She dumped me."

"Yeah?"

"Yeah, I told her I had an incurable venereal disease. What about friends? You got any friends would do you a favor?"

I shrugged. "What kind of favor?"

"Steal a dog."

Jimmy Dean DuChien came to mind, but if he stole a dog for anyone, it'd be to help John Ogle. He didn't need to do me any favors.

"Can't think of anyone," I said. "Why do you keep asking dog questions if this isn't about dogs?"

"I'm honing my technique." He stopped chewing and bared his teeth again.

"You ever hear of the KISS principle, detective?"

"Keep it simple stupid?"

"That's it. Maybe the dog just ran away."

"I'll remember that. Thanks for your time." He flipped a business card onto my coffee table. "Your neighbor's dog comes back, give me a call," he said and left.

After I finished washing the cooking gear, I made a gin and tonic and sat on the deck as the sun set. Somewhere between sips, I noticed Shaman's absence and decided to celebrate the quiet night and replenish my flagging spirit with a cigar. Then I remembered Cadanki's card and retrieved it from the coffee table.

Detective Cadanki worked in the Violent Crimes Unit.

I sipped the gin and tonic and watched the gray cigar smoke drift leisurely into the back yard. All the while I kept wondering why a Violent Crimes detective was so interested in a missing dog. By the time I finished my drink and the cigar, I still didn't know.

When it was completely dark, I went in, took a shower, and did my security routine. I circled clockwise around the house checking the locks on all the doors and windows ending at the front door. As I pushed the deadbolt home, my eye caught movement. A large shadow moved slowly through the darkness under the trees. It was a van rolling down the street with its lights out. As it approached, a faint orange glow silhouetted the driver. He was smoking a joint.

I wanted to yell something. "Hey, dipshit" came to mind. But the door was locked and I didn't feel like opening it. So I just stood there and watched. Finally, I just shook my head and I went to bed. It had been a long day. Nothing was making sense anymore.

I slept like the dead. Like I'd slept in the hospital after the shooting.

What woke me was pounding. It took a moment to focus on my watch. It was a little after two o'clock in the morning. Someone was knocking on my front door. I put on shorts and a t-shirt. The living room sparked and flickered with light. Through the picture window I saw an EMS ambulance. At first I thought Mrs. Batty had had another stroke, but it was parked in front of Monica's. Two police cruisers were parked in front of mine. All the vehicles had their lights going, lighting the street in a lurid, electric daylight kind of way.

I switched on the porch light, unlocked the door, and pulled it open.

"Sorry to disturb you," the patrolman standing there said. He shifted his weight so one foot was on the threshold. There was a second cop behind him. "I'm Officer Taylor. This is Officer Smalley."

"Officer, what's going on?" I squinted at their faces. The porch light made their badges shine.

"You're Robert Mulligan?" Officer Taylor asked.

"Yes, why?"

"You complained about your next door neighbor's dog?"

"Yes, it's a nuisance barker."

"And you're currently under investigation for animal cruelty?"

"Not that I know of. A guy from Animal Control stopped by earlier today. Yesterday, I mean. He was looking for the dog. It's missing. Why?"

"Do you know what happened to the dog?"

"No. Just that it's missing. Why?"

"And you've been home all evening?"

I nodded, suddenly afraid to speak, worried that somehow I'd said too much already. The training said to remain calm when talking with authorities. Immediately asking to see a lawyer was a red flag, a sign of guilt. I wondered if I'd waited long enough.

"Can you prove that?" the other cop, Smalley, asked.

"Do I need to?"

Taylor looked at Smalley. I guess the tone of my voice told them the easy stuff was over.

"Maybe you'd like to come down to the station to explain," Taylor hinted. The threat was clear.

"About that goddamned dog?" I asked.

"Not the dog," Smalley said.

Taylor eyed me like I was playing dumb. "About trying to murder your neighbor."

Chapter Four

Volunteering

I stiffened. The rear door of one of the patrol cars was open, yawning at me like the gates of Hell. The more I stared, the bigger and darker it got. My alibi blinked through my mind with the flashing patrol lights: I was asleep. Somehow three words didn't seem like enough. I wondered if that counselor would tell me to lie again.

Someone came up the walk and pushed past Smalley and then Taylor. It was the detective from yesterday, the one from Violent Crimes.

"Hot enough for you?" Cadanki looked at me, calmly chewing his gum.

"Plenty," I croaked.

"What are you two doing here?" he asked Taylor.

"This is her neighbor, you know, the dog guy."

"I got that much, Sherlock."

"We were going to take him in for questioning."

"Don't waste the gas. You want to do something useful, go stand in the street. And take Dr. Watson here with you." He watched the patrolmen retreat to the street, then turned to me.

"Your neighbor lady's dog, what's-its-name, ever come back?"

"Shaman. No, not that I know of."

"Didn't think so." He nodded his head, then shook it. "Do you smoke?"

"No, why?"

"A little marijuana maybe?"

"No."

"You ever been in the South, Mr. Mulligan? Somewhere they talk with an accent?" He looked at the two patrolmen. They looked away.

"I did trade shows in the South as a product manager, New Orleans, Orlando, Dallas. Before I left. Why?"

"But you never lived there. You don't talk with an accent." He was still looking at Taylor and Smalley. They looked back, smiling, then turned to watch the EMS ambulance drive off.

"No, why?"

"Because, according to your neighbor, whoever assaulted her smelled like cigarettes and marijuana and may talk with some kind of accent, possibly Southern."

"Tell that to those two." I lifted my chin at the two patrolmen.

"I'll do that," Cadanki said. He leaned closer. "Everybody wants to be a detective."

"How is she? Monica, I mean."

"She's fine. Couple whacks on the head is all."

"They said it was attempted murder."

Cadanki shot Taylor and Smalley a look. They stopped smiling and walked away.

"Not even close."

"But the ambulance?"

"CYA. You know how it is. Everybody wants to sue everybody."

"So she's okay."

"Black eye." Cadanki shrugged and chewed his gum. "The perp might need medical attention, though."

I looked at him. He wiggled his eyebrows.

"You know anyone smokes, talks with a Southern accent?"

"No." I shook my head. "I got a friend from Texas. He's the only one I know still smokes."

"He talk with an accent?"

"More like a drawl. But, I mean, I can't see him . . . He's an electrician. I'm trying to get him on at the Copper John."

"You got a name and number?" Cadanki pulled out a note pad. "I'll check him out. Leave no stone unturned. Department policy. It's new." He stopped chewing long enough to grin.

"Jimmy Dean DuChien," I said, feeling guilty. I'd already lied to Jimmy Dean, now I was volunteering his name to the cops. What else could I do to the poor guy? "I don't remember his phone number. It might be in my cell phone. He lives over on Friendly around 24th."

"I can find him with that." Cadanki wrote in his notepad. "Remember to lock your door." He turned to leave. "Hey, call me if that dog ever comes back."

I locked the front door behind me, walked to the bedroom, and collapsed onto my bed.

By the time I got up, the mid-morning sun was warming the driveway. I did fifteen minutes of dry-fire practice, a simple routine to build muscle memory: draw, sight picture, trigger press, after-action drill. Then I made a cup of coffee, put on cargo shorts, and started washing the truck. I couldn't think of a good way to conceal my handgun, so I locked it in the safe.

The warm sun made me happy. I hummed to a Diana Krall CD. I thought about singing the words, but I wasn't that happy. And I can't carry a tune.

"Is that The Heart of Saturday Night?"

I startled. I'd drifted into the white zone, thinking about last night, washing the dirt off my truck like an archeologist burnishing a pagan relic, unaware of my surroundings. The training was about staying in the yellow zone.

A woman stood next to me in t-shirt and jeans. She looked about five years younger than me, probably in her late twenties. She was lanky in a tomboy kind of way. Maybe it was the t-shirt and jeans. I liked the look. Her hair was sun-bleached and very fine. A ponytail of it, like bronze steel wool, extruded from the back of her U of O baseball cap. I liked her eyes, too. They were light green and reminded me of the fresh sage that grew along the Deschutes.

"*Heart of Saturday Night*? Diana Krall?" She prompted.

"Yeah," I finally said, trying not to stare. "*Heart of Saturday Night*."

"I thought so." She nodded. "I have that same CD." She looked from me to the truck. I loved her eyes.

"It's so dirty," I said to make conversation.

She shot me a glance, frowning.

"The truck I mean. I've been gone all week." I wanted her to stay. I wondered if she liked washing trucks.

"I know," she said, shifting from one foot to the other. "I volunteer at Lane County Animal Control."

"Oh."

"It's okay. I'm not working. Yet. I'm on my way. I live behind you." She paused to catch her breath. "I thought maybe we could talk. Before I go in."

"Oh." I tried to sound a little more upbeat this time. "I thought you looked familiar."

"I'm right behind you." She pointed across my back yard. "Across the alley in the apartment complex: second floor. I moved in for summer term."

I followed her finger. Her picture window directly overlooked the back of my house. The curtains were open. Last night sitting in the dark with my gin and tonic, I had watched her unpack. It was like a drive-in movie watching her cross the window. The tenant before her used to do it topless. This girl was a little more circumspect.

"I've seen you in your back yard. My name is Amy."

I shook her hand. It was lean and delicately boney, but surprisingly strong. It matched the rest of her.

"Bob Mulligan. Somebody stopped by yesterday about my neighbor's dog. It's missing."

"I know. That's why I'm here." Amy from Animal Control seemed to assess the amount of road dirt remaining on my truck. "Can we talk? Unofficially?"

"Sure." I'd talk about anything if it got her to stay. "About the dog or about Monica?"

"The dog," she said, then her eyes widened. "Why? What about Monica?" She nodded, encouraging me to spill the beans.

"She got attacked. Someone broke into her house."

"Is she okay?"

"Don't know." I shrugged. "I think so. The detective said she got hit in the head a couple of times. He didn't seem worried."

We stood next to the truck, the CD playing in the background, each lost in separate thoughts.

"You wanted to talk about the dog?"

"Yes." She shook herself back. "What do you think happened?"

"Maybe the dog just ran away. Everyone wants this to be some big conspiracy, but maybe Shaman just took off again."

"Again?"

"It's happened before. Monica leaves for work. Shaman gets bored barking and takes off."

"But how? The yard's fenced."

I shrugged. "You'll have to ask him."

"And it's just coincidence he left when you left?"

"It would have to be." It sounded weak even as I said it.

"Did you know that animal cruelty is often a precursor of more serious anti-social behavior?" she asked. It sounded like she was quoting one of her textbooks.

"In young children." I tried to finish the quote.

"You think neighborhood kids took him as a prank?"

"Look, I don't really care what happened to the dog." I tossed my sponge into the bucket. A plume of fine white suds shot skyward. "All I want is to live a quiet life in a quiet neighborhood. That's it. That's all I ask."

I felt foolish for throwing the sponge. Here was this cute girl, woman I should say, trying to keep me off the ogre list, but truthfully, all I wanted to do was punch something. That god damn dog! Maybe I was still tired from yesterday. Maybe the counselor was right, accumulated stress would cause emotional outbursts.

"Sorry." I picked up my sponge and attacked my truck. Maybe I was afraid my quiet life in a quiet neighborhood was slipping away.

"You know, Mr. Mulligan." Amy touched my arm to get my full attention. She got it. "In the military, they train you to fight for what you believe in, that good things are worth fighting for, to never give up."

Never give up. They said that at the handgun training. Good things are worth fighting for and sometimes you have to. I guess I'd forgotten.

"You're right." I put the sponge in the bucket, carefully this time. "Thank you."

I looked directly into those lovely eyes. "Can you do me a favor?"

Amy nodded.

"If I came by later, could you get a list of dog complaints?"

"Anything in particular?"

"Barking dog complaints where the dog was later reported missing."

"I think I can. Why, what are you thinking?"

"If Shaman didn't run away, someone took him and they did it while I was gone."

"Coincidence?"

"That's what I want to find out."

Cadanki's visit yesterday wasn't a random house call either, a detective from Violent Crimes showing up before the violent crime was committed. I wanted to know what he knew about barking dogs.

Chapter Five

Neighborhood Gossip

We left it at that. I went back to work on the truck. She went off to do her volunteer thing. She promised to have the list when I got there.

Around noon, I quit for lunch. I picked the newspaper off the front porch and scanned it as I ate. No headlines about Monica's attack or missing dogs, no dogs in the obituary section. No Monica in the obituary section. Also, I saw no stories about dog fighters stealing area dogs for bait. The paper was quiet and, without Shaman, so was the neighborhood.

After that, I edged and mowed my lawn, then Mrs. Batty's. She came out to apologize: the cookies weren't ready. She paid me for yard work in chocolate chip cookies.

When I was done, I slipped my handgun into the holster inside my waistband and put on a short-sleeved shirt as a cover garment. Then I went over to Monica's and knocked. While I waited, I reviewed my training. If she came at me with a knife, I could shoot her. But if she just attacked me with her fists, I couldn't.

"What do you want?" she asked, hiding behind her front door. I've faced friendlier rattlesnakes.

"I wanted to ask if you're okay, see if you needed any help."

"Oh, fuck you. This is a cover-up, isn't it? I told the cops you took Shaman. Now you're over here trying to cover up."

Silly me, this war had no truce. Cadanki was right, it was the perp who might need help.

"Have you looked for Shaman at the animal shelter?" I asked.

"No."

"I'm going over there to get something. You want to go, see if someone turned him in?"

"Is this part of the joke, Robert? Act like you're trying to help?"

"Monica, I'm going to the animal shelter," I said. "Do you want to go and look for Shaman, yes or no?"

"Okay, yes." She stepped out from behind the door. It had hidden her black eye. Cadanki was right, aside from that, she looked none the worse for wear.

We took my truck to Lane County Animal Control.

"Did you take my dog?"

"No, I didn't take your dog."

"Where is he then?"

"That's what I'm trying to find out."

It took less than ten minutes to reach Lane County Animal Control but it felt like forever. To make matters worse, Amy wasn't there. She was out on a call.

We spent the next twenty minutes in the kennels looking for Shaman. He wasn't there. So we went over to the Humane Society's animal shelter. He wasn't there either.

When we got back to my place, Monica got out.

"Thanks for nothing," she said and slammed the door.

"You're welcome," I said.

I got out of the truck, got a beer from the deck fridge, and sat in my Adirondack chair to think. I was on my second Corona and not making much progress when I heard someone in the driveway.

"Hi, Amy from Animal Control, remember me?"

"Hey. I stopped by to see you this afternoon but you were out."

"I was mediating. That's what I do." She made a motion with her eyes, then bobbed her head, smiling. "I'm the volunteer mediator."

Amy stepped up on the deck. She was a cute-looking girl, with the lean muscled body of a Tai-Bo kick-boxer. She eyed my Corona.

"You look thirsty," I said and offered her a Corona from the fridge.

"I got you that list." She pulled a sheet of paper from her pants pocket and unfolded it. It was in spreadsheet format. "Barking dogs that go missing."

It was a short list, only five entries, one of which was Shaman. Somehow I had expected more. I stared at the rows and columns and my mind went blank. My former life in product development was all about squeezing meaning from spreadsheets, but now it seemed hopeless. I rolled the cold Corona bottle across my forehead. The coolness felt good.

"So, what now?" Amy asked, sipping her beer.

"A cop stopped by yesterday," I said, taking it in small steps. "He asked about Shaman." I went into the house and fetched my notebook computer.

"Why would a cop be interested in Shaman? That's Animal Control."

"That's what I want to find out." I handed her Detective Cadanki's business card.

"Violent Crimes Unit." Her eyes held a question.

I sat beside her and opened a browser to the City of Eugene Crime Statistics web page. It was one of the better uses of my tax dollars.

"What's the first address?"

She read me an address on Friendly Street. I typed it in, set the date for the month before the dog was reported missing, then hit the Find button. We looked at the crimes reported in a quarter mile radius: a low level of property crimes, mostly thefts, and one simple assault.

"That's our base line," I said.

I changed the date to the month after the dog went missing and hit the Find button again. The simple assaults didn't change, but property crimes were up by one and there was a rape.

We worked through the rest of the list comparing crime statistics before and after the dogs went missing. Assaults varied randomly, but property crimes increased and there were three rapes in a sample of four, excluding Shaman.

"You think that's what he's looking at?" Amy asked. "Missing dogs and rapes?"

Someone stepped onto the deck behind us. I jumped. I'd fallen into the white zone again.

"Yoohoo!" Mrs. Batty called, her cane in one hand, a plate of cookies in the other.

"Mrs. Batty!" I said. We stood up like she'd just caught us smooching.

"Is this your girl friend?" Mrs. Batty wanted to know. "Here, honey, have a cookie. They're fresh out of the oven."

"Thank you," Amy said. "Chocolate chip, my favorite."

"My neighbor," I corrected, and took the cookie she offered me.

"She's cute, Bobber, you ought to ask her out." Mrs. Batty smiled at Amy and grabbed her by the arm. "Honey, you won't find a nicer man than Bobber. Handsome, too," she said confidentially. "Isn't he handsome, honey?"

Amy was blushing, but I noticed she nodded her head.

Mrs. Batty leaned close to Amy, conspiratorially, like she was going to whisper something. "And he's not a homo."

"Mrs. Batty," I interrupted. "This is Amy from Animal Control. Amy, this is Mrs. Batty, my neighbor on the western front."

Amy and Mrs. Batty shook hands.

"We don't need any animal control around here," Mrs. Batty asserted pleasantly. "Bobber is our animal control. I'm so glad you took that dog, Bobber."

Amy from Animal Control shot me a look, her eyes firing like double-tapped hollow points.

"Oh, don't worry, honey." Mrs. Batty patted Amy's hand. "Bobber found him a good home. Didn't you, Bobber?"

"No!" I blurted, watching Amy's face harden in anger. "Mrs. Batty, please."

35

"Oh!" Mrs. Batty exclaimed. "Now I've told your secret. And I promised not to."

"Mr. Mulligan knows animal cruelty is against the law." Amy eyed me like she was deciding where to shoot me first, in the head or center mass. "Don't you?"

"Why, yes, honey." Mrs. Batty recovered her composure. "I'm sure he does."

"Mrs. Batty, Amy and I are worried Shaman's disappearance might mean an increase in crime."

"Oh, dear." Mrs. Batty sighed. "I hadn't thought of that. It makes me want a gun. When my first husband was alive, we always had guns. Everyone brought them home from the war, World War Two."

"It's probably nothing," Amy reassured her pointedly, still staring at me.

A snippet of training lecture flashed through my mind, the basic premise behind defensive handgun training. A barking dog can protect sheep from wolves, but it takes a handgun to protect yourself against society's wolves.

"Society has rules," Amy stressed. "That's what makes quiet little neighborhoods like this possible. We have rules we live by."

"Bless your heart, Amy, was it?" Mrs. Batty took Amy's hand like she was helping a small child across the street. "Like my second husband used to say, the one who fought in Korea, living by rules only works if everyone does it. Criminals don't live by the rules."

Chapter Six

More Bad News

"You should have left Shaman and taken Monica," John teased. "She makes twice what you make, doesn't save a dime, and votes for everything you don't believe in." He waited for a reaction.

"Maybe you should give me a raise."

We were in the Copper John Fly Angling Shop. I was helping John price fly tying material. He was lean and straight for a man in his seventies, but sometimes, like now, the arthritis in his hands acted up. Forty years of police work, too many fistfights.

"How do you know all this about Monica?"

"I got people." Copper John smiled at me over his bifocals, his eyes as blue as the sky. His bushy white eyebrows were like clouds. "You got to have people, you know."

"Hey, I met that girl. The one moved in behind me, across the alley."

"Did you ask her out?"

"No, I didn't ask her out! I just met her." I squirmed in my folding chair. "Besides, she works for Animal Control."

John made a face like a client had just fallen out of the drift boat. "So what'd you talk about?"

"What do you think, Monica and her damn dog."

"How'd that go?"

"Not so good. I convinced her I didn't do anything and we should work together."

"Well, that's good. What's wrong with that?"

"Well, then Mrs. Batty came over and thanked me for taking the dog. So now she thinks I'm a liar as well as a thief."

"Oh-oh." John shook his head. "And this was the girl you thought was so cute."

"I didn't say that."

"You did too."

I let it go. John's memory was better than mine, probably because he was a cop for forty years. And, like I said, the shooting messed up my memory sometimes. The counselor had said it would go away. He wasn't specific as to when.

"Hey, John, you know of any dog fighting going on?"

"No. Is that how you're going to fund Monica's pension or is that what you think happened to fido?"

I ignored him. "If he didn't run away, someone must have taken him and they must have had a reason."

"You'd think."

"I had a cop, a detective actually, stop by the house."

That got John's attention.

"I'm guessing, but I think he was looking for a connection between missing dogs like Shaman and sex offenses like rape."

"Sounds like a long shot."

"Why?"

"Rape is often a crime of impulse or opportunity. Kidnapping a dog first would indicate planning."

I thought about that. There went my whole theory.

"Was Shaman some expensive breed?" John asked like he was trying to cheer me up. "You know, valuable as a stud?"

"I don't think so, but he wasn't packing."

"That's right, testicles and handguns are the same thing to some people." John smiled at his joke. "Hey, not to change the subject, but my niece is in town. Actually, she's my great niece, my brother's son's kid. She's about your age. Since you botched it with this other girl, I could set you up."

"Something wrong with her?"

"No, I told you, she's related to me."

"You're supposed to tell me nice things about her."

"She's back from Iraq. Decided she wants to be a counselor."

"The first part's good," I said, unimpressed with the counselor part. So far, most of the advice I'd gotten from that PTSD counselor hadn't worked so well. "What'd you say these hooks were?"

"Tiemco package of 25." He moved his finger down his price catalog. "$5.25. Hey, I got more news about Monica and it ain't good."

"What now?"

"She was asking legal questions."

"What kind of legal questions?"

"How to get a restraining order, for one. Then she wanted to know if she could sue for injuries sustained as a result of her dog being stolen." John eyed me over his bifocals. "I got the name of a good lawyer I can give you."

"Yeah, thanks."

"You ought to just come clean."

"Thanks, Dad. I'll tell everyone I lied about the fishing trip because the real truth was too scary." The whole thing was making me mad. My business was my business.

"I'm not talking about the handgun stuff. That's between you and the Creator."

"What then?"

"Did you have anything to do with that dog disappearing?" John looked at me and waited for my answer.

"No, nothing." It's hard to sound truthful when an ex-cop asks you a question.

"Then you got nothing to worry about."

"Except that the whole neighborhood thinks I took him. Jimmy Dean thinks it's hilarious."

"Well it is, kinda."

"I thought he ran away," I said, "but he wasn't at the animal shelter."

"You think he'll come back on his own?"

I shrugged and hung a couple bags on the hook rack. "That's why I was moving on to dog fights and sex crimes. Suppose that detective is right? Suppose it's not just a missing dog?"

"Check with the police department. They could use someone like you."

I finished the rest of the pricing in silence. I couldn't think of anything to say, too busy talking to myself. Anger was gaining momentum, building like a snowball rolling downhill.

"God damn it, John!" I said finally, turning. John wasn't there. He was in his office.

"You say something?" he asked, coming through the office door.

"I said, 'God damn it.'"

"Life's a bitch," he replied. "Get used to it." He rang the till open, the bell emphasizing his point. It sounded like the end of round one. I wasn't looking forward to round two.

I finished loading the hook rack. It was next to the whiteboard we used to schedule fishing trips.

"What's this trip?" I asked. An unscheduled trip was on the to-do list.

"It's not an official trip."

"So it's an unofficial trip. What is it?"

"That's your buddy DuChien," John said. "What do you know about him?"

"We were friends in high school." I shrugged. "His father was a real asshole. So was his older brother, Floyd. The old man drank like a fish, couldn't keep a job. Junior year, they moved to Texas. I think that's where they were from. That's the last I saw of him until a couple of weeks ago. I ran into him at a brew pub."

I stopped. Copper John waited for me, like he was listening to a confession.

"He's an electrician. He has his own business. I think it's residential work mostly. He's in the neighborhood quite a bit."

"Military service?"

"Army, before 9-11. After that he worked for a big commercial outfit in Texas. He guided on the side, had a bass boat."

"What's he doing up here?"

"Lifestyle change."

I could sympathize with Jimmy Dean. After the shooting, I'd come back for the same reason. The fact wasn't lost on John.

"You trust him?"

"He'd make a good guide, if that's what you mean."

"Well, summer's coming on," John said, floating the idea to get my reaction. "Maybe we could use some help. Take the pressure off you. Let's give him a try."

I nodded. It was my idea all along. It just took a month to circle in the thought eddy and come back as John's.

"Run him down the McKenzie, will you? Make him do all the work. You're the client; he's the guide. See if he knows what he's doing."

"Suppose he tips the boat over?"

"That's why it's your trip." John smiled. "I don't want to get wet."

Chapter Seven

The Flirt

I took the trash out Tuesday morning around seven. The can was in the alley. The truck wouldn't be there until nine, but I had to work while John had his annual physical.

"You can tell a lot about a person by the trash he leaves behind."

I turned to see Amy from Animal Control, in bike helmet, khaki shorts, and a teal green t-shirt walking her mountain bike across the alley toward me.

"Hey."

"Hey." She smiled back.

"It's called garbology."

"You're making that up." Her eyes flashed like she was waiting for a punch line. "For real?"

"For real. I was in product development for a while. We used garbology to research customer behavior."

"Yeah? What kind of products?"

"Inkjet supplies."

"How come you stopped?"

"It's a long story. Where you headed?"

"My uncle has an appointment. He wants me to drive. Then school."

"No animal controlling today?"

"No, the consensus is there are no animals to control." She paused, smiling sweetly. Her big eyes were adorable. "But if someone wanted to reestablish speaking terms with their neighbor, I would make myself available to negotiate the peace treaty."

Was she flirting with me?

"How about you? What are you doing up this early?" she asked. "Besides taking out the trash?"

"Nothing special, just work," I admitted like my life was dull. "My boss has an appointment too, so I have to open the shop."

I thought about asking her out, but it was seven in the morning. It seemed a little early to, I don't know, bring up that type of thing. Amy looked down the alley, still smiling.

To break the silence, I put my trash in the can and closed the lid.

"Well," Amy finally said. "I gotta run. See you later, maybe."

I nodded as she stepped onto her bike pedal and coasted sidesaddle down the alley.

"Bobber, who was that?" Kara Kibble asked, nodding her chin at Amy's shrinking silhouette. The Kibbles lived on the other side of Monica. She opened the Kibble garbage can and tossed in a white plastic bag.

"That's Amy, she lives up there." I pointed to Amy's apartment window. "She's a volunteer mediator for Animal Control."

"Where boob-lady used to live?"

"Yeah, that would be the place."

Kara was Ken and Karen's teenage daughter, seventeen going on forty, lanky like Amy but with long dark brown hair. She was dressed in leggings, a skirt, three or four overlapping tops, and several necklaces. A large, heavy-looking daypack hung down her back almost to her knees. She was a junior at South, a good student, and a real competitor in track and cross-country.

"Did you ask her out?" she asked pointedly. She was also my self-appointed dating coach.

"No, it's too early in the morning for that. Isn't it?" I sounded like an old fogey. At thirty-five, I felt like one, too. Kara seemed to bring it out in me. "What are the rules on that, Coach?"

"Shoulda-woulda-coulda." Kara scolded me with her finger. "There's only one rule: wanna-haveta."

"Wanna-haveta?"

"Yeah, if you wanna mate, you haveta date."

"Got it."

A dark van turned into the alley and stopped short. Then it cruised slowly toward us and stopped.

"Well looky who's up this early." Jimmy Dean DuChien grinned from the passenger-side window.

"Hey, Jimmy Dean." I nodded.

"Hey, boss." He leaned out to shake my hand, then jerked his thumb at the guy silhouetted in the passenger seat. "You remember my brother, Floyd. He's up from Texas for a visit. Thought I'd put him to work."

"Floyd, long time no see."

"Bob." Floyd raised his hand like a pistol and fired with his thumb.

"And who's this lovely flower of womanhood?" Jimmy Dean asked, focusing his attention on Kara.

"This is my neighbor Kara. Kara, this is Jimmy Dean, an old high school friend."

"Jimmy Dean DuChien at your service. DuChien, that's French for 'the fox.'" Jimmy Dean reached out his hand and shook Kara's. "It's a real pleasure to meet a friend of the boss man. You have the prettiest eyes." He was still holding her hand. "That one blue top really brings out their color."

"Thank you." Kara blushed, turned to me for reassurance, then back to Jimmy Dean. "It's my favorite."

I watched as my dating coach melted under the warmth of Jimmy Dean DuChien's boyish charm and big Texas smile.

"Your daypack looks heavy," he continued. "School, right? You're a student?"

Kara nodded. "But only for another couple of days, then it's summer vacation."

"All those books, I bet you're a smart one."

"Well, Kara." I put my hands on her shoulders to break the spell. "You better get going or you'll be late for school."

I turned her toward home and gave her a little push. "Say hi to your mom and dad for me."

"Boy, ain't she a cute one." Jimmy Dean watched her disappear through the fence into her back yard.

"I'd like a piece of that, myself," Floyd snickered.

"She's young enough to be your daughter," I said, feeling like I needed to point that out.

"Old enough to bleed, old enough to butcher."

"You know, Floyd, you haven't changed much since high school."

"Hey, no offense, boss." Jimmy Dean smiled. "Floyd was just kidding. Weren't you, Floyd?"

"Come on, Bob. Don't be such a pussy," Floyd said. "That's just a little boy talk. We's all friends here."

As I stared down the alley after Kara, I wasn't so sure. But Floyd was like that. Jimmy Dean had the gift of gab. Floyd always got under everyone's skin. Actually, I wished I had some of Jimmy Dean's talent, not to make a seventeen-year-old blush, but to ask a thirty-year-old out. But the missing dog thing had me feeling more like Floyd.

"Hey?" Jimmy Dean asked, interrupting my thoughts. "What're you doing today? You got time to do a trip down the river? John says I need to take you down the river before he'll sign me up."

"I can't, I'm the only one at the shop today. Let's try next week. I'll see what my schedule looks like.'"

"Okay," Jimmy Dean said. "But don't bullshit me, now. You know I don't like that."

Chapter Eight

Night School

I got back from the shop late. Not that we had any customers. John kept trying to set me up with his niece. I pulled into my driveway just as Monica and a dozen of her toady students arrived with their drums. Monica gave me the finger when she saw me.

I opened the doors and windows to cool the house down, keeping the screen door on the front locked, then made a sandwich. Monica and company filtered through her house and drained into her back yard. I could hear snatches of their conversation. They had had a funeral for Shaman somewhere. Now they were going to finish off the evening with a drum session and a memorial hot tub soak. I still thought it was premature, police crime statistics notwithstanding, but then Shaman wasn't my dog.

I retreated to my den. It was a little quieter there. I was working on a watercolor. I have no talent for painting, drawing too for that matter. It was that counselor's idea, another bad one. I was repeating the beginner's class for the third time and had yet to paint a picture good enough to hang on my own refrigerator.

The drum banging was still hot and heavy as I left for art class at the community college. By the time I got back, it was around 10 o'clock. The banging and shrieking had given way to music, loud party talk, and laughter. A quiet night, all things considered. Quiet enough that packing a handgun felt unnecessary. A night so relaxed, it made me doubt I needed a handgun at all. I had to remind myself of my promise. After the shooting, I had promised myself I would never go unprepared again. So the answer always came back yes, I needed to carry a handgun.

I propped the front door open and locked the screen, grabbed a Corona on my way through the kitchen, and opened the back door to get a draft going. It was a little cooler on the deck. Except for the noise from next door, the night was as it should be, quiet, dark, and starlit.

My pot garden needed watering. Not a marijuana garden, but a bunch of plants growing in clay pots, maybe fifteen or twenty pots. So I left my half-finished beer on the flat arm of the Adirondack chair, uncoiled the hose from the hanger and started in on the big pots first, a Japanese Maple and a pair of miniature Italian Cypresses.

Someone screamed in Monica's yard, but it wasn't a good scream. Then everyone started shouting.

"There he is," someone yelled.

"In the alley."

"A peeping tom!"

I crossed the deck in three strides and hit the lawn at a run. Through the cracks in the ancient cedar fence I could see a shadow moving strobe-like down the alley toward me.

"Hey, you!" I yelled.

The shadow froze.

I reached for my gun. In the dark, with people screaming next door, the grip felt comforting. I let my hand rest there, unsure whether to draw, trying to remember my training. Was my life threatened? I couldn't tell yet. I wasn't sure who the shadow was or if he was armed. He seemed more threatened than I did. He was running away.

The moment passed. I didn't draw. It was a relief.

I worked the latch, pulled the gate open, and slipped into the dark alley. A cool breeze chilled me. I realized I was covered in sweat. The alley was empty, no figures silhouetted in the streetlights at either end. I looked for movement in the shadows. They tell you to have a light source with you at all times. I had an expensive tactical flashlight with enough lumens to blind a welder. It was sitting in my den next to my watercolor stuff.

I moved left down the alley toward Monica's. Wherever the shadow went, he went very quickly. Across the alley, the two-storey hulk of the apartment building stood in silence. The bottom, storage and covered parking, was a jumble of indistinct black and gray shapes. The walkway along the building to the next street over was empty. I moved closer to get a better view.

My eye caught movement. A shadow slipped between two cars. It was headed toward the walkway. I ran to cut him off. As the distance closed between us, I put my right hand back on the gun grip. I was going to draw my gun and yell when something slammed into me from the side. I put my hands out to break my fall and felt the sandpapery bite of concrete. A second attacker! I fought to breath through the panic. I hadn't even considered the idea. I scrambled to my hands and knees, but the attacker jumped on my back. His weight drove me hard to the ground. I struggled, surprised a knife didn't slide into my flesh or a gun barrel touch the back of my head. I hadn't drawn my gun, now it was too late. It happened just that fast.

"Got him!" he yelled. It was Ken Kibble.

"Ken." I gritted my teeth, the side of my face pressed to the concrete. "It's me. Get off, you're breaking my back."

"Oh my God, Bob? I was chasing the peeping tom."

"He went that way," I said. "Toward 10th." I looked down the walkway to the next street. "He's gone now."

"I'm really sorry. I didn't mean to . . . I saw you and thought . . ."

"Yeah, that I was the guy." I knew Kara. I didn't know Ken or his wife that well. "You said a peeping tom?"

"That's what somebody yelled. I was in the back yard with Karen. She wants it to be more like yours, you know, tidy. All of a sudden, everyone next door was screaming. So I ran through the gate. You started running toward the walkway. I thought you were trying to escape."

"Yeah, the guy made a break for it. I tried to cut him off." I didn't tell Ken I had a gun and that I was prepared to shoot any bastard that attacked me.

Monica and half a dozen other women were huddled by her back gate. They were dressed in a motley collection of beach towels and bathrobes that reminded me of an old Eddie Bauer catalog. Monica had chosen a sleeveless, plaid flannel shirt for the evening. But at least she had a flashlight.

"You!" She hissed. "I might have known you'd be involved." Her long hair, wet at the tips, was even more witch-like than usual.

"You don't know anything," I hissed back.

"That's why he got rid of Shaman." Monica confirmed to her friends. She sounded a little tipsy. "He's a peeping tom."

Monica's friends cooed like mourning doves.

"You don't know what you're talking about." I wanted to smack her, blacken her other eye.

"And it was probably one of his cowardly friends that attacked me."

"You're drunk," I said. All this over a goddamned dog.

"Monica," Ken Kibble interrupted. "Bob was chasing the guy you saw, the real peeping tom, but he got away."

"What about a peeping tom?" a new voice asked.

The flashlights turned to reveal Amy from Animal Control, slender to the point of gangly, stalking into the alley from the walkway. Spotlighted as she was, she reminded me of a National Geographic photo of a cheetah returning from the hunt. The flashlights caught the brass highlights in her brushed-back hair. She wore faded jeans and a sage-and-white plaid linen shirt-jacket with a sage tank top underneath.

"We were mourning Shaman with a drum ceremony." Monica smirk at me. "We were all very stressed, so we decided to have some wine and hot tub it. I kept smelling cigarette smoke. That's when I saw someone staring at us through the fence."

"He was just standing there in the shadows watching us," one of her friends said.

"It was creepy."

"He ran into the alley."

"Ken chased him," Monica said, "and came back with Robert."

"Ken explained that, Monica," I said.

"You took Shaman," Monica concluded for the audience, "so you could peep at us without being discovered."

"Do you smoke?" Amy asked me.

"No."

Amy turned to Monica. "Want to smell his breath?"

Monica folded her arms across her chest.

"Maybe it was the attacker," someone suggested. "He came back to watch us."

Everyone cooed again.

"I'm calling the police." Monica looked at me defiantly, then marched back into her yard taking her friends with her.

Amy from Animal Control looked at me. "Can we talk?"

"Sure," I said. I relaxed for the first time since the screaming started. I felt for the comfort of the gun grip hidden beneath my shirt. It wasn't there. The holster was empty.

Chapter Nine

Teaching Moment

"On second thought, this isn't a good time for me."

My handgun with a fully loaded magazine was missing, probably lying in the walkway. Thank God I hadn't racked a round into the chamber.

"Keep moving, partner," Amy from Animal Control whispered, poking me in the back. "And don't turn around."

I almost put my hands up, like she had the drop on me and was marching me off to the hoosegow. We walked back through my gate, across the back lawn, and climbed the steps to the deck, my anxiety increasing with each step.

"Look, I'm sorry. I've got to take care of something," I said finally. "You'll have to excuse me. There's something I need to do. Right away. It's urgent. Really, I'm missing something. I need to find it."

Amy reached a hand behind and under her coat. "Looking for this?"

It was my Glock. I could tell by the custom night sights I'd had installed. She turned toward the back yard, pulled the slide back, locked it in place to show the gun was clear, and handed it to me butt first, barrel down. From her coat pocket, she took the magazine.

"Mighty sloppy gun handling," she said pointedly, no trace of playfulness in her voice now. "You have a concealed carry permit?"

I nodded.

"You train or just blow it off?"

"No, I train. Dry-fire drills." I took the gun glumly. Too embarrassed to reload it, I released the slide lock, slipped the gun into my holster, and put the magazine in my pants pocket.

"You do? How often?"

"I just got back from a four-day defensive handgun class." It just came out. I couldn't stop it. I'd never be a good liar. It felt too good to confess.

"I thought you were fishing?"

"I kind of lied." I shrugged. "I just didn't want a lot of people knowing my business."

"Mind if I get rid of this coat?" she asked. She removed her coat and studiously arranged it on the back of the chair.

On her strong-side hip was a Kimber 1911.

"So did you sleep through training?" she continued. "Because I'm pretty sure your instructor said to maintain control of your firearm at all times."

The warm June evening felt a whole lot hotter.

"Look, Mulligan." Amy from Animal Control made eye contact, lifting her chin slightly to make her point. "I'm not here to give you a bunch of crap, but if you're going to carry, do it responsibly. I think this is one of those teaching moments. I'm hoping you can learn something. If you want to."

I nodded, flushing. I screwed up. I didn't like the idea, but I couldn't deny it. Amy from Animal Control was right, the best I could do now was learn something.

"I also noticed you didn't have a round in the chamber," she said. "Was that on purpose? Or did you forget that, too?"

"I haven't been carrying that long," I admitted. "I'm working up to it, but I'm not there yet. It feels safer."

"Safer for the threat." She looked at me doubtfully.

"All things considered, it was probably better unloaded." I joked.

"No sense carrying a firearm if you're unprepared to use it." She was serious. "That guy could have had a gun or a knife. If he'd turned on you, you'd be on your way to the emergency room right now."

"I pretty much messed up right from the start," I said, getting serious, too. "First, I forgot my flashlight. Then I gave away my tactical advantage by shouting at him. Then I couldn't decide whether to draw my gun or not. The guy was running away, so I didn't."

"I think you did that part good," she said. "It's not like you're hunting. You're trying to reduce a threat. If you can do it just by shouting, that's better than drawing your gun."

"Yeah, but then Kibble tackled me. I thought there were two threats. That's when I really wanted to draw, but it was too late."

"You couldn't get it up."

A blush flickered across her cheekbones, like she was thinking of some erectile dysfunction joke she didn't know me well enough to tell.

"It was all so quick," I said, not giving her time to think more about it. "One minute I was here on the deck, the next I was fighting for my life in the walkway."

"The gun owner's dilemma." She sat in my Adirondack chair. "When bad shit happens, it happens fast. You can't legally draw your gun until the threat is imminent, but by then, it's too late."

I nodded, enjoying the company. Maybe I should get a second Adirondack chair? In case this ever happened again, I'd be prepared.

"You carry extra magazines?" Amy asked, breaking the silence.

"Two in a double mag pouch."

"You might try one of these." She turned to the left, showing her weak-side hip. On her belt was a double mag pouch containing a spare magazine and a small black canister the size of a tactical light. She slid the canister out and tossed it to me. It was pepper spray. "Unless you're in a shootout, you don't need more than one spare mag. And if you are in a shootout, you don't need an extra mag, you need an AR."

"If this dog thing escalates, I might have to get an AR."

"You think tonight was the next step?"

"I don't know." We looked at each other. I tried not to look worried. "I hope not."

"You still hoping Monica's dog ran away?"

"That's what I'd do if I were Shaman."

She snickered.

"The funny part is, now he's gone, I actually want him back."

"So, you do think tonight's the next step," she repeated, her smile fading.

"If Shaman ran away, he'd be back by now," I admitted my worry.

"You're thinking someone took him, then?"

"That's the most reasonable explanation. And it's not because they wanted a pet."

"So there goes your quiet neighborhood." Amy reached for her coat. "You know that part in the movies when you know something bad is going to happen, but you don't know when? I'm getting that kind of feeling."

"Yeah, me, too."

"What about the cops? You think they'll be much help?"

I shook my head. "Average response time is too long. Like you said, when bad shit happens, it happens fast."

"Well, then, I'm glad I'm not the only one carrying." Amy stood to leave, then stopped. "Mind if I ask what got you started?"

"No." I slide the palms of my hands back and forth like I was wiping away a prayer. The counselor said this would happen. People would ask, want to know. "The short version is I got involved in a gunfight."

"You're kidding."

"No. And I didn't have a gun. I walked into a store just as the cops and robbers decided to have a shootout."

"Really?"

"Yeah, I got caught in the middle."

"What was that like?"

"It was a teaching moment." I stopped, smiled. That was the end of the short version. I wasn't ready to tell the long version. Still I felt the icy finger of Death slide across my soul again. "I learned I should be prepared the next time."

Chapter Ten

No Missy

The weather turned hot. I finished my after-action drills one night and was watering the smaller plants in my pot garden for the third time. It was almost dark, but the heat didn't let up. Potted plants on a deck with a southern exposure isn't a very bright idea. It showed a lack of awareness and foresight, totally white zone. I should have designed it with a drip system on a timer. A trip to Jerry's and $100 for hose, drip heads, and a timer could fix that.

"Missy, here Missy." Kara's voice interrupted my reverie. The back gate rattled and Kara poked her head through.

"Bobber." Kara, dressed in shorts and t-shirt, saw me on the deck and walked into the yard, searching with her eyes as she crossed it. "Have you seen Missy?"

"Dust mop?" That's what I called her little dog. It was one of those short-legged, long-haired, white things. I can never remember the breed. She loved the fluffy little creature with all the affection of a favorite stuffed animal. I joked about shoving a broom handle up its butt, an image that always made her wince but laugh. Missy was a nice dog though. It even liked me. "Did you check your broom closet?"

"It's not funny," Kara insisted. "She's gone."

"She's probably just wandered off."

Kara started to cry.

"Hey." I hugged her, patted her on the back.

She hung on to me and cried for a moment, sniffling softly. I think she just needed a little support. It's tough being a kid sometimes.

"What happened?" I put my arm over her shoulder and turned to the gate. "Come on. I'll help you find her."

"I was in my bedroom writing on my Facebook wall and doing homework. Missy wouldn't stop barking, you know how she does when she sees a squirrel."

"She's a tiger." Missy would bark if you even spelled the word "squirrel."

"So I let her out, but she never came back. And now she's gone."

"We don't know that." I corrected, trying to dispel Kara's worry. "Let's check your yard."

"I did that already."

"Every corner?"

"Not every corner."

"Where's your mom and dad? Are they home?"

"They just got back. Daddy is walking around the block clockwise. Mom is walking around the block counter-clockwise."

"Good." We walked down the alley to the Kibble's gate. Their property was a corner lot, wide and shallow, that fronted on Polk Street and abutted the east side of Monica's lot at the back. I could see the whole length of the alley, but no Missy.

Kara pushed on the gate latch. It made that sharp, metallic click like they do, but in the stillness of the evening, it sounded ominous.

"Missy?" Kara called.

We started searching the back yard along the fence line. We worked together, more for Kara's sake than for efficiency. I pulled my keys from my cargo shorts. I kept an LED there now. I flicked it on.

"Here, shine this along the fence as we go." I handed her the small light with its cold, bluish-white beam. "Dust Mop, Missy, here girl."

"Are there any places where Missy can get out of the fence?"

"I don't think so. My mom made my dad nail chicken wire to the bottom of the fence and buried it in the ground to keep the possums out."

"Right, he told me that." That was the project he was working on last summer when I moved in. Something was coming into his yard in the middle of the night and wreaking havoc. It didn't work for that, but it kept Missy in.

We traced the edge of the yard, alternately calling and shining the light into the darkness gathering around the overgrown shrubs. The place looked neglected.

"Your dad needs to do some pruning."

"That's what my mom says."

Searching seemed futile, but maybe Missy had been attacked by a raccoon and was lying somewhere unable to move.

About half way across the back of the house, the LED light reflected something white behind a stand of ornamental grass. It wasn't moving.

"Missy?" Kara whispered fearfully. It still didn't move.

"Stay here, Kara." I was afraid we'd found Dust Mop. "I'll see what it is."

I stepped into the shrub bed. The ornamental grass was some bamboo relative. Zebra grass, I think Ken called it. The mature fronds were striped. The name was a slick marketing ploy to sell an invasive specie to unsuspecting homeowners. Whatever it was, it was badly overgrown, blocking the view into the back yard from a pair of double-hung windows just visible over the frond tops.

I pushed the fronds out of the way with my forearm. The white thing lay in the narrow space between the plant and the foundation. It was an overturned 5-gallon bucket.

"Is it Missy?"

"No," I said, relieved. "It's one of your dad's buckets."

"Kara, she's not on the street." Ken Kibble walked into the yard from the patio on the right. "Have you found anything out here?"

"Hey, Ken." I stepped from the bed holding the bucket by the wire handle.

"Bob. What's that?"

"One of your garden buckets. It was up against the foundation."

Kara started crying, slowly at first, then building. Her mother stepped onto the patio behind Ken.

"Let's go inside, honey." She hugged Kara and directed her into the house.

"That shouldn't be out. I keep them in the garage. Where was it?"

I took Ken to where I'd found the bucket. His flashlight beam made the contours of the bed stand out, a mix of mulch and shadow. It was easy to see the circular pattern where the bucket rim had cut into the mulch.

"Somebody was looking in your window."

"That's Kara's bedroom," he answered my unasked question. "Son of a bitch! I can't believe it. Some son of a bitch was looking in Kara's window. It's that peeping tom. The guy from the other night."

I didn't reply. Ken's comment summed it up. I took the flashlight and started looking around again.

"Who? Who?" He stood there, squeezing his hands into fists. "I'll kill the son of a bitch."

"Boyfriend?" I asked. "Does Kara have a boyfriend?"

"No, she's too busy with sports and school."

"An admirer, someone who sends her stuff, tries to get her attention?"

"You mean a stalker. No. I think boys find her a little intimidating."

I lit the window frame. "Does this window open?"

"No, not the bottom. It was painted shut when we bought the place. I never got around to fixing it. I don't think I will now."

"Good plan. Get rid of this grass thing, too. Open the area up."

"I should call the police," he said.

I nodded, thinking about the possible connection between missing dogs and rapes and hoping it wasn't true. "Has Missy been barking more with Shaman gone?"

"Hard to tell with Missy, but maybe. I don't know."
Ken frowned, looking at me for an explanation.

"I'd call the police. Let them know what's going on."
Even if it wasn't true, it was better to be prepared.

Ken reached in his pocket and withdrew his cell
phone.

I followed him to the patio as he made his call. I just
stood there with nothing else to do. Beyond the patio
light, the world was all shadow and darkness and the
evening sounds of quiet lives in a quiet neighborhood. A
chill breeze blew across the yard like air conditioning. It
reminded me of the convenience store before the shooting
started. Death stood behind me again and whispered my
name then laughed with an icy breath at some secret joke.
The hair on the back of my neck stood up.

"I will not be a victim again," I whispered back. "You
can not make me."

Chapter Eleven

Rockets Red Glare

The next day was the 4th. I worked in the shop, but it was slow, like I told John it would be. I used the time to clean the place and tie a few flies. John used the time to pester me about his niece. So I pestered him back about shop security. He had his six-shot service revolver, but hadn't shot it in a decade. When the pestering ran out, I quizzed him on peeping toms and prowlers and such. By 3:00, we were out of things to talk about.

"You're losing money."

"You're surmising."

"I'm looking at your empty cash drawer. Let's close up early. Have happy hour at my place. I'll make you a martini."

"Will I be able to drive home?"

"You won't remember you have a home."

"Sounds good to me."

We closed up, hung the "Gone Fishin'" sign on the door, and John followed me the short distance to my place. We arrived right at Happy Hour.

"Hendricks or Tanqueray?" I asked as John made his way to the deck.

"Tanqueray. Mind if I invite my great-niece? She doesn't get out much."

"She's not one of those loud drunks, is she, likes to pick fights? Garlic, jalapeno, or double-stuffed?"

"That's what I want to find out. Jalapeno."

I had just finished making our martinis when a knock rattled the back gate and Amy from Animal Control slipped into the back yard. She was dressed for the weather in white shorts and orange tank top, both of which seemed to make her summer tan glow.

"John, this is Amy from Animal Control that I was telling you about."

"Hello, darling." John kissed her on the cheek. "That was quick."

"Hey, Uncle John. Yeah, I live right across the alley." She pointed.

"Animal Control isn't your last name?" I joked as embarrassment heated my cheeks like a powder flash.

"Ogle." She smiled sweetly.

"Maybe you can get your money back on that training." John snickered. "It hasn't improved your awareness any."

"All right," I said, regaining some composure. "How long?"

"Since my physical." John chuckled. "We finally got a chance to chat. Hey, make Amy a martini or she'll feel left out."

"Tanqueray, if you have it."

I went to the kitchen to fix the drink. When I came back, Ken Kibble was telling John and Amy about Missy's disappearance and the discovery of the peeping tom. I made another martini for Ken.

"How'd your conversation with the cops go?" I asked.

"A detective came out right away. You hadn't been gone more than a couple of minutes."

"A detective?" John asked doubtfully. "Are you sure?"

"That's what his business card said." Ken nodded. "Detective Cadanki, Violent Crimes Unit."

Amy and I exchanged glances.

"He asked about you." Ken stopped and looked at me. "Did I know you? Did I think you took Monica's dog? It was odd. He seemed more interested in the missing dogs than the peeping tom."

"It's odd they didn't send a patrolman." John frowned and sipped his martini.

"That's what I thought," Ken agreed. "I thought detectives only investigated murders and rapes and that. Violent crimes."

"I think that's what he is investigating," I said, looking at Amy, then John and Ken.

"Bobber and I put together a list of missing dogs," Amy told them. "Out of four incidents, three were followed by an increase in violent crime. Rape."

"Yeah, but that's a small sample," Ken objected, "statistically, I mean."

I nodded. "But is it any easier to believe Shaman and Missy disappeared by coincidence?"

"And you've already had an assault and a peeping tom in the neighborhood." John looked at Ken. "What are the chances of that?"

"I think Bobber's right," Amy said flatly. "I think this Cadanki believes there's a connection."

"So," Ken said slowly.

What they said in training was suddenly all too real. The police may catch the criminal, but it's always after the crime, always too late for the victim.

"Suppose the neighborhood is at risk," I said. "Things could get worse."

"I can't afford it getting any worse." Ken said, half to us, half to himself. "I've got a wife and teenage daughter. If anything happened to them, I don't know what I'd do."

"The city offers that crime prevention program, Neighborhood Watch," John answered. "Start your own group."

That was the reality of it. Just like the training said. Ultimately, you're on our own. It's not the police who prevent crime. It's everyone's responsibility. I looked at Amy. She was nodding. God, I loved the way she looked, even if she was related to John.

"I'm leaving while I can still see straight," John said, finishing his drink.

After he left, we talked about improving security in the neighborhood, but nobody took any notes. It was almost dark by the time Kara came to fetch her dad for the fireworks.

"How long's it been since you've seen fireworks?" I asked Amy after they'd left. I didn't want the evening to end.

"Not counting Iraq?" Amy smiled wryly. "Since I was a teenager."

"Come on, then. Let's go. They have a pretty good show at the U of O football stadium."

I locked the house, we climbed in the truck, and I drove to a spot where we could see the action without getting stuck in the crowd. It was a small park down river from the stadium. I brought a blanket from the truck and spread it on the lawn. The river looked beautiful: silver, black, and blue in the evening light.

"There they go!" I pointed through the tops of the scattered trees at the sudden sparkle of lights.

"Ooh!"

The sparkling sky faded to black, followed by a series of loud bangs. I listened to them echo into the night. My heart raced. From the dark edge of the past, images fired into my memory. Now I was sweating. That counselor at the hospital had said to be prepared, that feelings, memories could come back unbidden.

At least he got that much right. I tried to smile at Amy, to return to the good time. But I was slipping away, my memory as out of control as a gunfight.

More sparkling lights, bright and white and high up. Another series of bangs, like gunshots. And another, returning fire. Spent brass cases bounced on the hard linoleum floor. I shook my head. The thumping was only loose rocks tumbling along the riverbed. or was it? I couldn't tell.

Another burst of gunfire, the same pattern. Boom boom, boom. A double-tap followed by a headshot. I had to move, but my clothes caught me in a sweaty grip.

Boom boom, boom boom. Double-taps. Return fire. My eyes burned. My mouth tasted of salt. I had to get down, get on the ground.

"Bobber?"

I was falling, my chest burning. I couldn't breath.

Boom boom boom.

"Bobber? What's wrong?"

I hit the ground hard, candy bars and packages of M&Ms fell around me like autumn leaves.

Boom boom.

"Bobber? Are you okay?"

"I have to go."

"Wait I'll get the stuff."

"No. Take the keys."

"Bobber! Wait!"

"I have to go."

"Bobber!"

Chapter Twelve

Gates of Heaven

I sat in the dark trying to wash away the panic with a sparkling water. I wondered about my counselor, what he would be thinking, as I rubbed the ice-cold can across my forehead to kill the heat.

The truck pulled into the driveway. Amy cut the lights and crept slowly toward the garage. When she reached the side of the deck, she slipped it into park and cut the engine.

My truck is a comfort. I got it after I got out of the hospital. It's bright red like the blood I left on the convenience store floor. I wanted to thank Amy for bringing it back. I also wanted to cry. But that would be stupid. If you want to be a survivor, you can't act like a victim. That's what the training said. My counselor would disagree.

"I drove around for a while looking for you." Amy walked across the deck and placed the keys on the arm of the Adirondack chair. She sat on the steps. "I like your truck."

"It's nice," I said, but couldn't go farther.

"It's the shooting, isn't it?" Amy spoke softly, looking into the darkness of the back yard. "The fireworks or something brought it on. You've got PTSD, right?"

I nodded. "Post Traumatic Stress Disorder." I rubbed my head into the sparkling water can. I felt lame.

"You want some water?" I asked.

"Yeah. I'll get it." Her passing to the fridge and back cooled my skin.

"Can I ask you something?"

"Shoot," she said, then, "sorry, bad choice of words."

"You're going to be a counselor. Am I a nut-job?"

"Honey, I know you're a nut-job." Amy rolled her eyes. I couldn't see the sage in them, but I knew it was there. "PTSD has nothing to do with it. Uncle John can't keep a secret."

"Uncle John?"

"Spilled his guts the minute I asked about you."

"That easy?"

"Didn't even get to use my water board."

"How much did he tell you about . . .?"

"He said you'd been in a shooting," she said. "I recognized the PTSD from Iraq. That's why I want to be a counselor. A lot of things trigger memories. Very few trigger memories that powerful and that debilitating. But they're still just memories."

"He just said a shooting?"

"Yeah. He said you'd tell me if you wanted me to know. I'd be interested in knowing."

I hesitated. "I'll tell you on one condition."

"What's that?"

"Tonight hasn't been much fun for you. I'd like to make it up. Take you out to dinner sometime?"

"A date?"

"Yeah."

"Okay, sometime, if you ask." Now Amy seemed flustered, fidgeting on the step. "But this better be good."

"I was in product development for Hewlett-Packard, a product manager. That's the guy who reminds the engineers they have customers. I worked in the Inkjet division."

"In Corvallis?" Amy asked, referring to the small town an hour north of Eugene where HP had a large facility.

"In San Diego. I was in commercial inkjet. Corvallis is the consumer side."

I waited for Amy to ask another question, but she didn't.

"So this gunfight I was in. My program was having a major checkpoint meeting. I'd promised the engineers that I'd buy doughnuts if they met their specs and I could tell they were going to. So I knew a convenience store near the site that sold Krispy Krème doughnuts on the side. Like a franchise or something. I figured that would be a good treat. So I get a company car and off I go.

"Only problem is, I walk into the store just ahead of a couple of gangbangers who want to stick the place up. But I didn't know, I just walked in and went to the back where they kept the doughnuts and started putting my order together.

"I heard some loud talking, like arguing, but I didn't think anything of it. So I fill two boxes and go to pay.

The gangbangers are arguing with the clerk. I didn't realize what was going on until one of them walks up to me and jabs his gun at me, sideways like they do in the movies.

"The one is yelling at the clerk to give them the money. The other is yelling at me. The clerk is yelling he gave them all the money. They're yelling to open the safe. He's yelling he doesn't have the combination. And all of a sudden the front door opens and there's two cops standing there smiling at the thought of fresh doughnuts.

"Everyone freezes. The cops see what's going on, so they draw their guns and they start yelling, too. The gangbangers back into the store. They're jabbing with their guns and yelling back. And then the shooting starts. I don't know who started it. It just exploded. Boom, boom boom, boom. I'm looking back and forth like I'm watching a tennis match, but I'm in the middle! I see the muzzle flashes, the smoke, the guns jumping with the recoil. Pop cans rolling across the floor.

"Then my chest starts to burn. I look down, my shirt is changing color, a dark red stain flowing down. I put my hand on it. It feels warm and wet. When I look at my hand I realize it's blood. I remember thinking, 'Oh, shit! I can't give a presentation with blood on my shirt.'"

I looked up. "How's that for awareness?"

"I can see why you took the training." Amy bobbed her head.

"So then I'm falling. Everything is in slow motion. I hit the candy rack, bounce off, and land on my back. I stare at the fluorescent ceiling lights as M & Ms and beef jerky fall on me."

I stopped again, wondering if I should tell the rest.

"That doesn't sound too nut-jobby," she said matter-of-factly.

"So I'm lying there and I'm dead."

"Dead?"

"Yeah, for almost fifteen minutes. The EMTs had to revive me."

"Okay, now we're getting somewhere."

"So I'm dead. Maybe technically I'm still dying, but I'm on my way out. Then I hear bagpipes."

"Bagpipes?"

I nodded. "Bagpipes and drums. So I turn and there's the Black Watch, like in the Thanksgiving Day parade. They're following me. I feel, I don't know, comforted; it's comforting, comforting. Sometimes I'd go to a meeting and have the same feeling. Sounds odd, doesn't it? But I figured it out. I always carried my planner or slides or whatever tucked under my arm, like a bagpipe, and sometimes I'd walk down the corridor with a slow cadence like a marching band. It was muscle memory taking over as I was dying.

"So I'm leading this column and we stop at the gate. A wall stretches to either side and this is the only way in. And there's Saint Peter standing there.

"He looks at me and shakes his head.

"'But. . .' I protest. I'm thinking, I'm dead, what else is there?

"'No,' he goes like it's not even up for discussion. I can see his lips shaping the word.

"So I get angry and I shout at him, 'You dick head!' and I turn around and marched back the way I came."

I stopped and looked at Amy.

"And here you are," she said.

"And here I am."

"Did you really called Saint Peter a dick head?"

I nodded.

She clinked her sparkling water against mine. "Well, Bobber, I'll say this. You got a lot of nerve."

Chapter Thirteen

Criminal Enterprise

Friday, the 5th, I had a half-day trip on the McKenzie with one of our regulars, a lawyer friend of John's. His wife liked to come along for the ride. Fishing was slow in the July heat, but the river was as cool and enticing as an emerald.

"Not a bad day," Bill said as we took out at Armitage Park, the boat landing north of Eugene. He had hooked and released three nice rainbows in the fifteen-inch range and a dozen or so cutts around twelve inches. Caddis flies were fishing well in a #16 size.

Carol, in the same amount of time, had brought me up to date on her entire family, her two married children, their four children, only one of whom had turned out badly and was still living at home with his parents, someone called Annette, and her own latest volunteer adventure, training as a Community Emergency Response Team member so she could better prepare the four other rich folks in her neighborhood for a disaster. She had also extracted a promise from me to look into community volunteering and promised she would check up on me.

When I got back to the house, there was a police car parked in front of Mrs. Batty's, so I went down to see if everything was all right.

Mrs. Batty was sitting in her living room recliner, a cop was sitting at the dining room table writing, and the young couple who rented the house on the corner were sitting on the living room couch. Everyone but the cop seemed a little upset.

"This is my neighbor, Mr. Bobber." Mrs. Batty introduced me to the cop. We shook hands. He was a young guy, dorky bristle-cut moustache, firm grip.

"Officer Berry, Eugene Police."

"Bobber Mulligan." I introduced myself and turned to the renters. "I'm Mrs. Batty's neighbor on the other side."

"Tim Calloway," said the guy. He was maybe twenty-something, long reddish hair, wearing jeans and a Peace-sign t-shirt like he was in graduate school or something.

"Nancy, Tim's wife," the girl said. She had short, two-toned hair, a professional cut. She was wearing a white uniform, a dental assistant or nurse.

"What's going on?"

"Someone broke into our house," they said together.

I looked at Tim Calloway.

"When I got back from campus, both doors were open. We don't lock them. I thought they'd just blown open or something."

"What'd they take?"

"My Xbox, both iPods, and our wireless house phone."

"We had to come over here to call the police."

"Small electronics," Officer Berry summed the damage. "Easy to convert to cash."

"We were thinking about a new flat panel for the Duck games this fall," Tim said.

"I'm glad we waited," Nancy said.

"Have you got renter's insurance?" I asked. "Or does your landlord have insurance that would cover you?"

"No." Nancy looked at Tim to show who was to blame for that decision.

"I didn't think we needed it. I'm in school. Nancy works at the hospital. We're poor as church mice. Who'd steal from us?"

"You'd be surprised." Officer Berry looked at the Calloways. "With the overcrowding in the jail, small-value property crimes are essentially a pass. Even if we catch them, they're not off the street long enough to do any good."

"It's the drugs." Mrs. Batty tapped her cane on the floor.

"Yes, Ma'am. More drugs, more crime. That's the way it works."

"Why, I'm scared to death half the time."

"It looks like an army marched through my flower beds." Nancy sighed.

"Oh, honey, and you worked so hard. They were so pretty."

"What's the next step?" Tim Calloway asked the police officer. "Is there any chance we can get our stuff back?"

"Did you mark your property so you can prove ownership?"

"No."

"How about serial numbers?"

"No."

"Then, I'll be honest with you, it's not very likely. But it's not out of the question either. Something could turn up in the next crack house we bust."

Officer Berry closed his notepad and moved to the door.

"What's the next step?" Tim Calloway repeated a little more urgently this time.

"I'll file the report and we'll see what happens."

"That's it? You're not going to investigate the crime scene? Dust for fingerprints or something?"

"Unfortunately, no." Officer Berry stood at the front door. "This isn't like the CSI shows. It's a matter of resources. Besides, fingerprinting will leave you a bigger mess to clean up. Here's my card, if you think of anything else, give me a call and I'll see it gets added to your report."

"Officer, crime in the area seems to be increasing." I knew he couldn't do anything, but since he was here, and I was paying his salary, he could at least answer a few questions. "I understand about your resources. But what do you recommend we do?"

"The basics still work. That's why they're the basics. Lock your doors and windows. Keep your shrubs trimmed. Mark your property and make a list for insurance purposes. We have etchers you can borrow. And, if you don't already have one, form a Neighborhood Watch. There are no guarantees, but every little bit helps."

He handed me another card. This one was for Neighborhood Watch.

"What's going on here? Is this typical of other neighborhoods?"

"Statistically, you're in a higher crime area. Transients, many of whom are substance abusers, congregate in the parks along the Willamette River. Your neighborhood borders that area. And it's summer. There's always a little more activity with the nicer weather. What other things have been going on?"

"A couple of dogs have disappeared. My neighbor was assaulted. Vandalism like Nancy said. And now this."

"All in the last few weeks," Mrs. Batty said.

"So," I asked, "what does your experience tell you?"

"Hard to say for sure." Officer Berry sounded like he was trying to be honest. "If it were just one crime, I'd say it was a random doper. But with this other activity in the neighborhood, I'd guess an I-5 gang."

"An I-5 gang?" Mrs. Batty and Nancy Calloway both questioned.

Officer Berry nodded. "They move up and down the I-5 corridor. They come up from California working the cities as they go. They hit two or three neighborhoods in each city, then move on to the next city. When they get to Seattle, they spend a couple of weeks working the suburbs, then do the same thing heading south. Have you noticed an increase in door-to-door solicitations in the neighborhood?"

Nobody had.

"Sometimes they case locations that way or scam a little pocket change. You know, 'please buy a magazine subscription so I can go to college.'"

Officer Berry looked at us.

"I realize that's probably not what you want to hear, but there it is. All I can say is forewarned is forearmed." He shrugged at the simple fact. "Call me if you think of anything else."

After he left, we didn't say anything for a while.

"There's something I didn't tell him," Nancy said finally, then answered our unasked question. "I wasn't sure so I didn't bring it up."

"What?" Tim asked.

"I think whoever it was went through my underwear drawer," Nancy said in a low voice. "I think he took a pair of my panties."

Chapter Fourteen

Hard Targets

Saturday I got up early, practiced drawing from concealment and after-action drills, had breakfast, then started in watering my pot garden. I was thinking one trip to Jerry's hardware store and my problems would be over when the phone rang.

"Hey," Amy said. "Can you help me with a homework assignment?"

"Sure," I said, wanting company, her company.

"I need to mediate a discussion."

"Yeah, sure, no problem."

"Okay, then. I'll be over shortly."

I hung up, patting myself on the back for being so lucky. I could give a progress report to Kara Kibble. I'd finished the watering and was mentally designing the new drip system when the back gate banged opened and

Monica charged into the yard like the next event at a fiesta.

"You!" She bellowed, lowered her head, and came straight at me.

My Glock was in the gun safe. I'd put it there after my drills. Defenseless again, I thought ruefully. It's just that quick.

"Come in, Monica," I said, exaggerating the 'm' as Amy slipped through the gate behind her.

The buttons of her sleeveless work shirt strained as Monica shouldered past me and flopped into the deck chair as gracefully as a sack of grass seed tossed off a speeding truck. Burlap would become her.

"Gaia," she hissed. "My friends call me Gaia."

"What does that have to do with me?"

Amy rolled her eyes, then motioned with her head to the steps. "Sit."

It was my deck and my deck chair, and I didn't understand why, but I sat on the steps like I was told. "This your homework assignment?"

Amy smiled innocently. "Okay, Gaia, you want help from Bobber so you need to initiate the discussion."

"No I don't."

"Yes, you do," Amy insisted. "You wanted to ask him a question. Remember? That means you have to start."

Monica glared at me from the Adirondack chair.

"Start by saying something nice," Amy prompted.

"You mow Mrs. Batty's lawn for her."

"Now, Bobber, you say something."

"She pays well."

Amy eyed me with a smirk. "Wasn't that easy? Now, Gaia, go on."

"You haven't been attacked."

"You don't know a thing about me."

"Whoa!" Amy shouted like I'd just pulled a gun. "Don't assume you know what she's going to say. Let her finish. It may not be what you think." She nodded at Monica.

"I talked to the Calloways yesterday. Someone broke into their house."

"I know."

"I know you know."

"Everyone take a deep breath," Amy directed. "We're making great progress."

I was sitting on the deck leaning away from Monica, every muscle tense. I was fishing the Deschutes one time and accidentally sat down next to a rattlesnake. It was the same feeling. I exhaled and tried to relax.

"Gaia."

"Karen Kibble said someone stole their crappy little dog and was peeping in her daughter's window. But it wasn't you. It's because her husband is lazy and doesn't do the yard work like he should. It's his responsibility. She says the reason you haven't been robbed is you made your house safe against attack."

"Very good," Amy said. "You've got his attention. He's listening. Now would be a good time to ask your question."

Monica moved her mouth. She was either going to say something or spit on the deck.

"How do you do that?" she asked. "Make your house safe?"

"I lock my doors and keep the shrubs pruned."

"I know all that, but what's your trick?"

"There's no trick," I said, wondering if my handgun would count as a trick.

"See," Monica said to Amy, "he wouldn't tell."

"He did tell," Amy said. "You asked how he did it and he said he locked his doors and pruned his shrubs. Then you asked if there was a trick and he said no."

I liked the way she handled things. I wished she'd been my PTSD counselor. I'd be cured by now.

"But he's hiding something. I can tell."

Amy looked at me doubtfully.

"No I'm not," I said, glad my handgun was in the gun safe and not poking out of the waistband of my pants.

"He wants the rest of us to be attacked so he isn't."

"Nonsense," I said.

"Bobber, do you want the rest of the neighborhood to be attacked?" Amy asked.

"No, of course not."

"Then what are you hiding?" Monica snapped.

I loved the color of Amy eyes. She smiled and nodded that everything was okay. I never got that feeling from the other counselor.

"I have a concealed carry permit," I said, "and a handgun."

"See! I knew he was lying." Monica looked at Amy and pointed at me. "That's why he hasn't been attacked. He has a gun."

"How, if nobody knows I have it?" I asked.

"Then why have it?"

"So I can protect myself."

"From attack."

"It doesn't stop the attack, it's a defense for when it happens."

Monica squinted at me, her eye as vacant yet menacing as the nozzle of a flame-thrower. "I'm against guns."

"Up to you." I shrugged. "Find another way."

"Alarm systems are too expensive."

"Start a Neighborhood Watch group."

Monica stood up. "You've got your gun and to hell with the rest of us. Is that it?"

"Gaia, you're missing his point." Amy stepped forward, but Monica backed away.

"Owning a gun doesn't make me the neighborhood safety officer," I said.

"I got his point." Monica backed across the deck to the driveway. "I'm safe so fuck you is his point."

I stood up, too. "You're against guns. Alarms are too expensive." I flapped my arms in exasperation. "What other choice have you got besides safety in numbers?"

"You've made your point, Robert," Monica hissed. "And that's just what I'll do." She glared at me one last time, then disappeared around the corner of the house.

Her footsteps echoed down the driveway. A moment later hinges squeaked as she yanked her front door open. Then there was a single bang like a rifle shot as she slammed the door shut.

"That went well, don't you think?" Amy sighed and slid into the depths of the Adirondack chair.

"Come on, you did good." I patted her knee.

"I guess mediation is like Mrs. Batty said the other day. It only works if everyone wants to be mediated."

"You'll be a hell of a counselor. You were just playing to a tough crowd."

"Thanks. By the way, I could use your help."

"Mediating?"

"No. I've had enough mediating for one day, thank you very much."

"You need your shrubs trimmed?"

"I'm on the second floor."

"You need a gun?"

"I've got a gun, remember? What I need is a lock on my storage unit."

"I'm heading to Jerry's. I'm going to drip system the deck. Come with me and you can help me pick out another deck chair."

"Sounds like fun. When you going?"

"As soon as I check on something Monica said." I started examining the windowsills on the back of the house.

"Whacha looking for?"

"Tool marks."

I'd painted the house the previous summer. If someone had tried breaking in recently, they would have left tool marks in the paint.

"You think someone tried to break into your house?"

"I don't know. But it's true what Monica said: I haven't been robbed. And it's not because I have a gun. So either they haven't tried or they tried but failed."

We moved counterclockwise around the house. It didn't take long, there weren't that many windows. Everything looked normal until we got to the two windows on Mrs. Batty's side. They were double-hung like the rest. The first looked into the living room, the second was the window in my den. Both sills had cracks in the paint and slight depressions in the sill where a flat bar had been used to pry against the lower window frame. I kept both windows locked.

"Well." Amy looked at me. "There's your answer."

"I feel so much better."

Chapter Fifteen

Confession

"Knock, knock."

"Hey, Jimmy Dean. What are you doing up this early?"

"I was in the area." Jimmy Dean sat on the edge of the new Adirondack chair. "Thought I'd stop by, see about our fishing trip."

"I got time this week. Let's do it." I adjusted the mister over one of the ferns.

"Dang, boss, that's some pretty smart shit you got going on." Jimmy Dean traced the black drip tubes back to the feed line and from there to the timer.

I tossed the dregs from my coffee cup into the boxwoods that hedged the deck.

"Want a cup?" I headed to the kitchen.

"Yes, sir. That would be fine." Jimmy Dean settled deeper into the chair. "Now Floyd, he don't ever drink coffee. He's a little restless as it is."

"Hey," I said, coming back. "I have a confession to make."

"About fishing?"

"Yeah, but not like you think," I said. "The other day I lied to you about that fishing trip on the Deschutes."

"I figured you was keeping secrets, boss." Jimmy Dean grinned. "Truth is, you ain't much of a liar. I just figured you didn't want to own up about the dog."

"It's not about the dog."

"See, there you go again." He pointed his coffee cup at me, but he was smiling.

"I just didn't want people knowing where I really went."

"We all have our little secrets." He waited. "So, where'd you go?"

"I took a defensive handgun class."

"Dang, boss, you gonna shoot somebody?"

"That's exactly why I lied about going."

"Sorry, boss. I was just funning," Jimmy Dean apologized. "That's great. I'm into guns myself. I think everyone should have one. You learn anything?"

"Yeah." I launched into the different drills they had us do to build muscle memory, the lectures they gave, the shoot-house scenarios they put us through. Talking about it brought back memories. The only memory I left out was why I wanted a handgun in the first place.

"And you carry?" Jimmy Dean asked, surprised. "You got a permit and everything?"

I nodded.

"What's this about a permit?" Floyd stepped onto the deck from the driveway. "What are you two magpies squawking about?"

"Fishing permit." Jimmy Dean winked at me, then looked at Floyd. "We was planning that fishing trip. I'm the guide and Bobber is supposed to be new to the sport. So I asked him if he had a fishing permit."

"You want some coffee, Floyd?" I asked.

"Never touch the stuff." Floyd sat in the other Adirondack chair. He was wearing a holey camo-colored t-shirt, cut-off jeans, and sunglasses.

"Something else? Sparkling water?"

"Beer if you got it."

"A little early, isn't it?" I asked, glancing at Jimmy Dean.

"Not for the night shift, it ain't." Floyd looked at me with his sunglassed eyes and smiled.

I smiled back, wondering if he was on something. Maybe it was just the sunglasses.

"Better get him a beer, Bobber. He'll be easier to live with."

I handed Floyd a Corona from the deck fridge.

"You watch your mouth," Floyd barked. "Just because you got a fancy truck and all don't make you better than me."

"That so?" Jimmy Dean sipped his coffee.

"Jimmy Dean's going to guide for the Copper John," I interrupted, wanting my Sunday morning back.

"Jimmy Dean don't need no fancy truck," Floyd scoffed. "And he sure as hell don't need no Copper John." Floyd turned to me. "He'll be guiding for me soon as I get my business going."

"The hell I will."

"You're starting a guide service, Floyd?"

"I am." Floyd nodded between sips of beer. "Had one in Texas."

"Yeah, and you can count me out." Jimmy Dean eyed his brother coldly.

"You mind your mouth!"

"Hey, Jimmy Dean, when we going fishing?" I asked.

"Anytime," he said uncertainly, glancing at Floyd. "Things is slow. I'm free all next week except for Thursday."

Floyd took a slug of beer and smiled.

"How about Tuesday?"

"You ain't bullshitting me, are you?

"He don't like that, when you bullshit him," Floyd said.

"I'll put it on the calendar tomorrow. Lets fish the afternoon. We can go from Hayden Bridge to Armitage Park."

"Works for me, boss."

"You're the guide," I said. "What time you want to meet? And what do you want me to bring?"

"Let's meet at Armitage at noon."

"Bring your fishing pole." Floyd grinned beneath his sunglasses.

"Fly rod, not fishing pole," Jimmy Dean corrected.

"I'm used to fishing in Texas," Floyd drawled in reply. "We only had poles there."

"Is that all you want me to bring? No flies, no waders? You have life jackets? What about lunch?"

"I got you covered, boss. Don't worry about a thing."

"Noon then," I said, glad the trip was finally on.

"Hey, ah, Bob?" Floyd sipped on his beer. "That bitch next door ever get her dog back?"

"How do you know about that?"

"Don't listen to him," Jimmy Dean said. "He's just trying to get a rise."

"Jimmy Dean can't keep a secret is how."

"No," I said. "He's still gone."

"And you didn't take him?"

I shook my head.

"You ain't bullshitting? I can't stand a bullshitter either."

I shook my head.

"'Cause it sure looks like you took him."

I opened my mouth, but Jimmy Dean said, "Don't let him get you, boss. He's just teasing."

Floyd raised his forearms like a boxer protecting against a right cross. "Okay, Bob, Bullshit Bob. Whatever you say."

No one said anything. We just sat there in the Sunday morning sunshine.

Floyd drank the last of his Corona and held the bottle upside down. "What about that other dog?"

"God damn it, Floyd!" Jimmy Dean said.

"Missy?"

"Yeah, that kid's dog from the other day in the alley. How do you explain that?"

I looked at Floyd. "Will you get off it, Floyd?"

"Sorry, Bob." He raised his hands in surrender. "I was just curious to get your take is all. You know, 'inquiring minds need to know.' That's all I'm saying."

I shrugged. I wanted another cup of coffee, but I didn't want Floyd to stay for another beer.

"Come on, Bob, don't leave me hanging." He patted his t-shirt and pants pockets, looking for something. "I'm dying. If you didn't do it, who?"

Jimmy Dean was looking at me, too, now.

"It's not just the dogs," I said. "Monica, next door, was assaulted and the Calloways down the street were robbed. The cops think it's a gang up from California working the I-5 corridor."

"The cops?" Jimmy Dean asked in surprise. "What'd they do?"

"Took a report and filed it wherever they file that stuff."

"Hey." Floyd grinned at us. "They taser anybody?"

"Not this time." I had to grin. It was kind of a local joke.

"Come on, Jimmy Dean," Floyd stood, patting his pockets again. "Give your old brother a ride home in your fancy electrician truck. I'm dying for a smoke and I'm all out."

"So, Bob," he turned to me. "You ain't lost nothing, have you?"

"No."

"How you explain that?" He slapped me on the knee before I could say anything. "Just teasing, Bob, you know, cause you're so sensitive about them dogs."

I made another cup of coffee after they'd gone and tried to relax. I wanted to get my Sunday morning back. I didn't want to think about anything except my new sprinkler system and Amy Ogle, but Floyd had me started. I couldn't think of anything else except being a target for a gang of out-of-state thugs.

Finally, I went in, got my handgun, and did some trigger control drills. I drew the gun, aligned the night sights, and pressed the trigger until the gun went click. Only then did I start to relax.

Chapter Sixteen

Taking Out the Trash

The next day, I woke up jumpy. All day at work I imagined some shadowy gang of thugs prying at my windowsills, tearing my house apart, scattering my possessions on the front lawn. John kept asking me what was wrong. I kept saying nothing, but each time the meaning changed as the stress wore deeper on my nerves.

When I got home, the house was just as I left it, but hot as a pistol. I gave up and opened the doors and windows. If anyone came in, I'd just have to shoot him. Castle doctrine would be my defense. I grabbed the mail from the mail slot and went out on the deck to let the house cool.

It was warm but shady on the deck. A late afternoon breeze chased gently around the yard, cooling the sweat on my arms and legs. I released a Corona from the deck fridge, sat in the older deck chair, and used my pocketknife to slit the first envelope from ear to ear. It was a bill, so was the next.

The gate latch rattled.

"You home?" Amy Ogle poked her head through the gate, saw me, then came all the way in. She was dressed for the weather in an orange t-shirt, putty-colored chino shorts, and white sneakers. "Mind if I hang out a while? My place is an oven."

"No, come on in." The tan that her clothes revealed was a lot easier on my eyes than looking at bills.

"I've been locking my windows when I leave. It's like a sauna when I get back until I get a cross-breeze going."

"Same here." I jerked a thumb at my house. "Beer? Wine? There's a Pinot Gris in there."

Amy looked through the fridge, extracted a Corona, and sat in the other chair. I slit open another envelope.

"Instructions for a nuclear reactor?" she asked, nodding at the pages.

"Idiot's guide to understanding my new phone bill." I tossed it onto the garbage pile then took the pile into the recycle bin. The pantry felt like Arizona in the summer.

"Still too hot?" Amy asked when I came out.

"It's nicer outside."

She finished her beer, set the empty bottle on the arm of her chair, and looked at me with a what-now expression.

"Feel like a walk?" I asked, sure Kara Kibble would be proud of me.

"Sure. I haven't seen the neighborhood. You can give me a tour."

I locked the place back up and we started down the sidewalk.

"I see Monica and Ken got right on their shrubs." I nodded at the overgrown plants that crowded their front windows.

"Maybe they're waiting for the weekend."

"Maybe."

We crossed Polk heading east toward downtown. Amy marveled at the vintage bungalow-style homes and mature street trees that shaded us against the late afternoon sun. But it was the overgrown landscape shrubs that caught my attention. They were easy cover for anyone wanting to look in a window unobserved. I could see why we were infested with crime.

We walked as far as Monroe Street, to the small park, and sat on one of the benches on the periphery. The block-sized lawn was surrounded by tall trees and hedges. At one end was a small hill, at the other a playground, sandbox, and restrooms. The park was virtually empty.

"This is so nice." Amy's gaze panned the length of the park.

We watched the half dozen people that were there. Two teenage girls in shorts and bikini tops idled away time on the swings. A young couple by the sandbox slipped their two-year-old into a stroller and headed home. Two panhandlers sprawled on the lawn smoking. They took turns drinking from paper bag-covered containers. An old man with a cane passed us walking gingerly around the park.

As the old man got closer, one of the panhandlers said something. He shook his cane at them and walked on.

A dark van that had seen better days pulled up. The panhandlers said something to it, too. The van drove toward the playground and the transmission clunked as the two girls walked over to it. The side door slid open, the girls got in, and the door slammed shut as the van's transmission clunked again and the van took off in a cloud of burning engine oil.

Mrs. Batty came trudging down the sidewalk like she was hiking the Skyline Trail. She joined us on the bench, resting her hands on her cane.

By the time we left, the first yellows and grays of sunset were beginning to concentrate in the western sky.

"We used to call them bums." Mrs. Batty looked at the two panhandlers. "Now you have to call them homeless people."

As we approached, they looked up.

"Hey, can ya'll spare some change?" the first one called to us.

I shook my head at him.

"No," Mrs. Batty snapped. She turned to us. "Don't give them any money. They just use it for beer and cigarettes."

The first panhandler mumbled something under his breath and snickered.

"We're veterans," the other one said.

"I'm a veteran," Amy said. "What outfit?"

"Nice going, dipshit," the first panhandler slapped the second and lifted the bottle to his lips.

"They're nothing but trash." Mrs. Batty waved her cane at them. "I'm going to call the police when I get home."

"Fuck you, you old bag."

"Hey," I warned him, "watch your language."

"Kind of spoils the ambiance," Amy said.

"Fuck you, too, bitch," the first panhandler said, louder this time.

"I said watch your language," I repeated.

"Fuck the both of you and your mother." He stood up and came toward us, bottle in hand.

His partner stood up behind him.

"Let's go." Amy touch my arm. She reached for Mrs. Batty's elbow to steady her. "Mrs. Batty, let's go."

I didn't move. I couldn't take my eyes off the panhandler. I didn't want to. I watched his hands. That's what they teach you in training. Always watch the hands. That was one mistake I had made. When the gangbanger came toward me, I didn't realize he had a gun. I wasn't watching his hands.

My handgun made me feel less threatened. I wondered how threatened I needed to feel before I drew it. Here it was again, the same dilemma as the other night. So what was the lesson?

The two men came closer still, one behind the other.

"Mrs. Batty," I said. "Can I borrow your cane?"

She looked surprised, but gave me the cane.

"Oh, ya'll want a piece of me, do ya?" the first one asked. "C'mon. I'll whip your raggedy white ass." He spit saliva as he spoke. Oddly, it reminded me of Monica Hoffman.

He turned from us to wave his partner forward. As he turned back, he pulled a large hunting knife from his belt.

I stepped forward. Amy came up to the side, her hand on her pepper spray.

"Ain't so tough now, are you, hunh?" he sneered. He crouched and jabbed at me with the shiny knife blade. "C'mon, let's get it on."

He lurched forward and slashed with the knife.

Amy brought her pepper spray up.

101

I sidestepped and smacked his calves hard with the cane.

"Ow, fuck!" The panhandler fell to his knees. "What'd you do that for?"

He slashed with the knife again.

Amy hit him in the face with a burst of pepper spray.

I came up behind him and clipped him a good one on the back of the head, sending him facedown into the lawn.

His partner held up his hands and backed away, then turned and ran.

"Nice shot." Amy nodded at the panhandler.

"You, too." I smiled like we did this for a living. I looked at her, her short, brassy hair and long, tanned legs.

"What?" she asked.

"Nothing."

"Let that be a lesson." Mrs. Batty took her cane and smacked the groaning panhandler on the back.

Chapter Seventeen

Overboard Guide

I was at the Armitage Park boat ramp at noon as curious as John to find out what a Texas bass guide knew about trout fishing in Oregon. Jimmy Dean wasn't there.

I waited until 12:15. Maybe he was hung up in traffic.

By 12:30, I was thinking either I'd gotten the day wrong or he'd been in an accident or something.

At 12:45 I was ready to head back to the shop. That's when Jimmy Dean's work van came roaring into the parking lot dragging a rusty trailer and a sorry-looking, kidney-colored wood drift boat.

Jimmy Dean leaned out of the driver's side window, a big smile showing beneath his mirrored sunglasses. "Hey, who wants to go fishing?"

"Noon, Jimmy Dean. You said noon."

"Now, boss, don't go getting your shorts in a wringer. Last I knew noon was between 12 and 1. Least it was in Texas." He looked at his watch. "So actually I'm fifteen minutes early." He grinned from ear to ear.

A beat-up looking dark blue van pulled up behind Jimmy Dean's rig.

Floyd leaned out of the window. "Hey, asshole, you going fishing or not?"

He was wearing sunglasses, too. I couldn't tell if he was talking to Jimmy Dean or me.

"Floyd won't let Vicki run shuttle unless he comes along," Jimmy Dean explained. "Don't worry though, he ain't gonna fish."

"Vicki?"

"His girl. He brought her along from Texas."

Behind us the van swung into a shaded parking space and the transmission clunked into park. Floyd got out, then Vicki. He was wearing the same outfit as the other morning. Vicki was a skinny girl with a bad complexion and dirty-blond hair. She was in shorts and a bikini top. She looked young.

"Hop in, boss, we're burning daylight."

I got in, still unsettled about the way things were going, but not knowing what else to do.

The side door slid open and Floyd and Vicki climbed into the back.

"Boss, this here is Vicki." Jimmy Dean introduced us. "Vicki, this is the boss man, Bobber Mulligan."

We shook hands. She looked even younger at arms length. Her eyes were red and she was sniffling like she had a runny nose.

"Summer cold?"

"Yeah, kind of. Allergies or something."

"Christ, a person could break their neck back here," Floyd said, as he scrambled over electrical conduit and wiring and sat on a big white cooler. Vicki sat beside him.

"We are going to have fun today!" Jimmy Dean swatted me on the knee.

We roared out of the parking lot and headed up river, catching glimpses of the water we would drift in the distance through the trees. We talked fishing on the way and by the time we reached the Hayden Bridge boat ramp I was again looking forward to the trip.

Jimmy Dean backed the trailer expertly down the boat ramp, hopped out, and put the boat in the water. He didn't want any help, so I rigged my fly rod.

"You gonna work on your suntan today, darlin'?" Floyd asked Vicki. He kissed her on the lips, brushing her breast with his hand as he did so.

"Everybody ready?" Jimmy Dean asked. He looked at Vicki. "You know how to get back? Just follow the same road."

"She ain't stupid," Floyd said.

"Yeah." Vicki said. She climbed into the van and took off.

"In the boat if you're going." Jimmy Dean directed. "We're burning daylight."

Floyd and I got in and sat in the two front seats.

"Whew, it's gonna to be a scorcher," Floyd said. "You bring plenty of beer?"

"Naturally," Jimmy Dean said. He reached into the white cooler and tossed us each a beer. "Here, boss, put one of these little things on."

He handed me a #14 Elk Hair Caddis, a good choice for a lazy July afternoon on the McKenzie.

I caught the first fish of the day, a 10-inch cutthroat, on my third cast as Jimmy Dean slowed the boat to drift past a nice section of overhung bank.

"I thought you had an aluminum boat, a guide model?" I asked.

Floyd looked at Jimmy Dean.

"I did, but I sold it." Jimmy Dean gave me his grin. "I ain't had a chance to replace it yet."

"Working too hard?"

"Every minute of every day."

"This one here ain't his," Floyd said, grinning, too. "He borrowed it."

A little further down, Jimmy Dean said, "Get ready, we're coming up on my favorite spot in the whole river."

"I think I know where you mean," I said. "The old Barclay place. It's great water."

The stretch of bottomland we were approaching was named after the family who had homesteaded the land. They used to pasture cattle there. The river slid past a huge backwater that curved out of sight into a stand of savannah oaks. There was an overgrown dirt track down into it from the highway and an old campsite hidden in the trees.

"We call it the Fox Hole," Floyd said.

Sure enough, I hooked a nice rainbow. Jimmy Dean pulled the drift boat deftly into the eddy and beached it on the downriver side so I could bring the fish in without boating through too much of the good water.

"Let's stop for lunch, boss," Jimmy Dean said. "Give you a chance to fish the eddy a bit. Lunch'll be waiting on you when you get back."

"I need a beer." Floyd pulled his t-shirt over his head, exposing a tattoo high on each shoulder, a shamrock with a twelve in the center on one shoulder, a crucifix on the other. Below the shamrock was the word "love," below the crucifix was the word "hate."

"I didn't know you had tattoos, Floyd."

"Yeah, got these in the army." He grinned. "Jimmy Dean's got some too."

"Beer and a sandwich is in the cooler," Jimmy Dean said.

"What a guide! This is all good water. I might just work down along the bank a bit."

"That's what I figure."

The eddy line ran a good two hundred feet down river. I took my time and fished the whole length of it, something I rarely had a chance to do. I caught and released five nice rainbows.

I got back to the boat about an hour later. Jimmy Dean and Floyd were yammering at each other farther up the backwater. I grabbed a beer and sandwich and headed in that direction. The beer tasted mighty good. The peanut butter and jelly sandwich looked like it'd been in a fishing vest most of the season. But I ate it anyway and, as hungry as I was, it was pretty good too.

"How'd you do?" Jimmy Dean asked when he saw me.

"Five nice ones." The gravel beach gave way to sand. Jimmy Dean and Floyd were sun tanning. I thought at first Floyd was naked, but when he stood to dress, I saw he was wearing a thong. I like thongs and lace panties on girls. On guys, it's weird. When I was a product manager, somebody always wanted to dress like a girl for Halloween. Some of them did a pretty good job, too, but it was still weird.

"What you looking at?" Floyd asked. "Ain't you never seen a thong before?"

"Not on a guy."

"Vicki gave it to me."

"She said it was European," Jimmy Dean explained.

"It looks French, kind of," I replied. I didn't like the French that much either.

"Hop in, gents, we're burning daylight," Jimmy Dean said when we got to the boat.

"Who wants another beer?" Floyd asked, reaching into the cooler and handed us each a can.

Jimmy Dean spun the boat in the eddy and pushed toward the current. The bow hit the current and twisted downstream, rocking the boat gently. A couple of six packs worth of empty cans rattled across the floor behind the rower's seat. Most of them were Floyd's, but Jimmy Dean and I had drunk our share.

The fishing stayed good the rest of the afternoon. Jimmy Dean stopped a couple more times so I could fish more of his hotspots. They were all good, I'd fished them before. I think, though, he probably just had to piss. He hadn't brought anything to drink but beer. I guess that's how they fish in Texas.

Just above Armitage, we stopped one last time. I fished a long gravel bar for about fifteen minutes.

"One for the road," Jimmy Dean said, opening three beers. We tapped our cans. "Here's to fishing."

When we pulled into the boat ramp, Jimmy Dean's van was right there.

"See," Floyd said to Jimmy Dean. "I told you. Vicki does good work."

"It ain't that," Jimmy Dean said.

Floyd threw up his hands and rolled his eyes. "I don't see why you're so goddamn determined to nigger down to that ex-cop." Floyd turned to me. "No offense, Bob."

I shrugged. It was none of my business.

"There's more boats coming in." Jimmy Dean ignored him. "I got to get this tub off the ramp."

"You need any help?" I asked.

"No, sir! Against the rules."

"How's that?"

"The rules, boss, remember? I'm supposed to do all the work, you're supposed to have all the fun."

"Well, I sure had that, Jimmy Dean. Thanks."

We shook hands.

"No problemo."

Floyd held out a beer questioningly.

I shook my head and got my rod out of the boat. He opened the can and took a long swig. When he was done, we walked up the ramp.

"Well, alrighty then, boss, I guess I'll see you down at the store," Jimmy Dean said.

He stuck out his hand and we shook again. He leaned close, his back to Floyd, almost whispering.

"Come on, boss, give me a hint."

"What can I say?" I shrugged. "We caught a bunch of fish, drank a bunch of beer. Nobody fell out of the boat. It didn't tip over. I had a good time."

"You ain't shitting me are you, boss?" Jimmy Dean looked at me, his head cocked to one side like he was sniffing my words for truth. "Because you know I don't like that."

"No," I said, "I'm not." And I headed off to my truck.

Chapter Eighteen

Petty Theft

I was prepared to be grilled about the Jimmy Dean trip, but John was busy hatching some plot with Bill to do a trip with some of Bill's lawyer friends. I waited around, rang up a few sales from customers that wandered in, then headed home a little disappointed.

Seeing Bill reminded me about Carol, so I made a note to look into CERT training. Then, feeling foolish, I crossed it out. What were the odds of being in an earthquake?

Better than being in a gunfight according to Carol's statistics. And if I really wanted to be prepared for any emergency . . . So I wrote the note again, then showered and changed into a clean pair of shorts and a fresh t-shirt.

The phone rang. Ken Kibble wanted to come over and talk. He sounded upset. I took a can of sparkling water from the kitchen fridge and waited, barefoot on the deck, for Ken to arrive.

When the gate latch rattled, I looked up to see all three Kibbles come single file into the back yard. I knew Ken and Karen to wave to when I saw them. Ken did some kind of management work for a grocery store chain. Karen taught 3rd grade. And Kara was Kara, my seventeen-year-old dating coach.

`I got three lawn chairs from the garage and everyone sat down.

"Were you at the fireworks?" Ken asked.

"Yeah, I took Amy Ogle." I looked at Kara proudly.

The Kibbles looked at me, waiting for more. I didn't know them well enough to tell them what had really happened.

"We didn't stay that long. I had an early trip," I said and left it at that.

"Did you see anyone when you got back?" Karen asked.

"No, why?"

Ken swallowed and looked at Karen. "We think someone burglarized our house."

"What? What do you mean 'you think'?"

"Our digital camera is missing," Karen explained.

"We can't find it anywhere," Kara said.

"Did you take it to the fireworks?"

"I don't think so," Ken sighed like he'd answered that question before.

"You don't sound too sure."

"He'd been drinking." Karen frowned at him disapprovingly.

"I set it on the table so I wouldn't forget it," Ken said, exasperated.

"And then you forgot it." Karen shot back. "You were drunk."

"I wasn't drunk. I had one martini."

"You can't hold your liquor. You never could. I don't know why you even try."

"Are you sure you set it on the table?" I asked.

"Yes. I think so." Ken motioned to Karen to keep still. "We didn't have it at the fireworks. But when we got home, it wasn't there."

"And they took a pair of my panties."

"Kara, they did not take your panties," Karen insisted. "You're underwear isn't worth stealing."

"Then where are they?"

"Have you checked the laundry?"

"Honey," Ken said. "Burglars take things they can sell to buy drugs."

"Are you sure it was stolen?"

"We've looked everywhere," Karen said.

"How did they get in? Did you call the police?"

"In the morning, after we couldn't find it." He didn't sound happy about the experience.

"Essentially, they said they were too busy," Karen explained. "Our camera wasn't important enough."

"They took a report over the phone," Ken said.

"Does someone have to get killed?" Karen asked. Her voice wasn't hysterical, but it wasn't far from it.

"Nobody's going to get killed." Ken's voice was a mix of frustration and irritation.

"Have you talked to the Calloways recently?"

"The Calloways?" Ken and Karen both asked.

"They were burglarized the same night, small electronic stuff. Phone, iPods, stuff like that."

"Do they know who did it?"

"No, but a cop came out."

"What'd he do?"

"Nothing. He took a report. He said it was probably one of those I-5 gangs passing through."

"I guess it's true, what we were talking about the other night," Ken said. "We have to be prepared. We have to protect ourselves."

"You mean buy a gun?" Karen looked from me to Ken. Her voice was high and had an edge. "You know how I feel about guns, Ken."

"I'm not going to shoot anyone for stealing Kara's underwear, Karen." Ken shot back. "Give me a little credit."

"That was the other thing," I said. "Nancy Calloway thinks the burglar took a pair of her underpants."

"It's the same bunch then, an I-5 gang," Ken said. "It must be."

"They waited until we were at the fireworks." Karen looked around. She seemed distressed that someone had planned and watched and waited and then attacked.

"Looks like it." I felt the same way, under attack. "I found pry marks on my windows."

"They get in?" Ken asked.

"No, I keep things locked when I'm not home."

"That's how they got in," Ken admitted. "Our back door was unlocked."

"This has always been such a nice neighborhood," Karen said, proud of the fact. "We've never had to lock our doors."

"Now would be a good time to start," I told her. I turned to Ken. "You can get your house inspected you know, for security."

"They still do that?" Ken asked.

"It's worth a call to find out," I said. "And there's Neighborhood Watch like John mentioned. The cop mentioned it, too."

"But that's the whole neighborhood." Ken rolled his head like he was getting dizzy. "And having meetings and who knows what else."

"I think you should do it," Karen told Ken. "Why do you always avoid things?"

"I'm not avoiding anything, Karen. So don't even go there." Ken looked to me for support. "I just don't have time."

I shrugged. "If that's too much, you can still improve the security around your house. Get rid of that big grass thing. I said I'd help and I meant it."

"That I can do," Ken said. "I just have to make the time."

"You should trim the rhododendrons while you're at it," Karen told him. "Everything looks so overgrown. It looks awful."

"Yes, Karen," Ken snapped. "I should do a lot of things. But I can't afford to quit work to do them."

"You always say that," she snapped back, "but you never do anything. Even when you have the time."

"Look," I said. "You've got to do something. Missy's gone, you've had a peeping tom, now someone's inside your house. What if they come back? Can you afford that?"

"I'm really scared," Kara said to her parents.

The Kibbles looked at each other, then at me.

"Why would they come back?" Ken asked.

"For more," I said, stating what I thought was obvious. "The camera was easy pickings. They just walked in and took it."

"But aren't they on their way to Seattle by now?" Ken asked.

"Maybe," I said, "but they could come back on their way to California."

"God," Ken said. "I feel like I'm under siege."

"You are," I said. "So you have to do something different, something that makes it harder for your enemies to attack you."

"Our enemies?" Ken and Karen asked, surprised.

"Yeah, whoever's doing this isn't your friend."

Chapter Nineteen

Blind Date

John arrived at the shop just as I was pouring coffee from the first pot of the morning. It was perfect timing; he brought fresh-baked doughnuts. It must be true what they say about cops and doughnuts, jelly doughnuts in particular, judging by John's preference. We alternated sound bites with food bites for the next ten minutes while I filled him in on yesterday's trip with Jimmy Dean and Floyd.

He made a face when I mentioned the thong and wasn't too happy about the tattoos, but he was most concerned about the beer. He said drinking like that in front of clients was unprofessional. When I reminded him Jimmy Dean and I were old friends, he still wasn't that happy. He needed time to think it through.

Things were slow. A couple old timers came in looking for flies. The UPS guy dropped off a special order, waders for one of the doctors in town. His wife had ordered them as a surprise for his birthday. John went back to the office to make a few phone calls.

"Hey, you want to give some casting lessons?" he asked, poking his head out the door, his hand over the phone. "I got someone wants to learn to fly fish."

"Sure, when?"

"Armitage Park around noon?"

"Sounds like a plan."

I was tying #14 Yellow Sallies to kill the time when an older gentleman came through the door. He'd been in the shop before a time or two. He was a retired plumber or something, Ed Gressin or Grisham, something like that.

"Long time no see," I stood and shook the hand he offered. "Ed, right?"

"Yeah, Ed Grissom. I come in every once and a while. Used to fish with John quite a bit when we were younger.

Just then John came out of the office. When he saw Ed, a big smile lit his face.

"Dang, Ed. I though you'd be dead by now."

"I'm trying, but it ain't as easy as it looks."

I motioned at the coffee pot and Ed and John both nodded. They moved over to the tying table and sat down.

"Reason I came in, you know that old boat I used to have?"

"Yeah, that wood one, sixteen footer?"

"Yeah. That's the one. I don't use it much anymore. Most of the time it just sits in my driveway."

"Yeah, that's the way it is."

"Well, it's gone. I think somebody stole it."

"How'd that happen?"

"Well, I went to meet some fellas. Tuesday's is our brunch day. It was gone when I came back. I thought my son took it, but he said no. My niece, she's good with computers, so she made up some fliers to put around. I thought maybe I could put one up here on your lost-and-found board in case anybody sees it around."

"Sure thing. Bobber, hand Ed that tape from behind the counter there. Then you better get your gear together for your date."

By the time I finished rummaging around in the storeroom for a couple rods and the rest of the gear for the lesson, Ed was gone. On my way out the door, I looked at his flier. It was nicely done in slide presentation format, all the words centered. I flashed back to life as a product manager. It was a lot of slide work and presentations to upper management. I let it go.

"Lost Drift Boat," the flier said in title-sized letters across the top. Below was a brief description on one side and a color picture on the other. It showed Ed and another guy standing at a boat ramp next to an old, kidney red drift boat.

"You know." I looked at John. "That looks an awful lot like the boat Jimmy Dean had yesterday, the one he said he borrowed."

"Do tell." John scratched his chin. "You better head out. I'll mind the store in case anyone happens to stumble in."

I took off. The drive to Armitage was maybe twenty minutes. In the parking lot, I took the annual-fee permit off the visor and flipped it onto the dashboard, another example of the government's hand in my pocket.

I was getting the rods rigged when Amy Ogle pulled up in her Outback.

"Bobber, hi. Where's Uncle John? He was going to give me a fishing lesson."

"Well," I said, thinking how devious John was for an ex-cop. "That old bastard couldn't make it. He sent me instead."

At least John had seen fit to have her dress for the occasion: ball cap, Polarized sunglasses, old running shoes, cut-offs, and a faded tank top.

I handed her one of the rods, grabbed the small soft cooler, and we followed the trail from the parking lot to the river and then downstream to the riffle. It was a popular spot being so close to town, but it didn't get much pressure on the weekdays. During the height of summer the water was low and easy to wade to a bar run island. The channel water on the far side was a good place to learn to cast since there was almost nothing to hit with your backcast.

Amy caught on like she was a natural.

"It must be in your genes," I said.

"What about my jeans?" she blushed.

"I said you have good genes."

"They're just an old pair of cutoffs." She blushed even more.

I was going to say something stupid, but a good-sized rainbow rose to Amy's caddis fly. Amy pulled back at the sudden splash, setting the hook nicely; the genes at work. The line straightened, the rod tip bend, and line screamed off the reel as the fish turned in the current and raced down stream.

"Tip up, keep your tip up. Let him take it."

We were at the bottom of the island. Amy fought the trout, reeling line only to have the trout drag it out again. As the fish tired, I nudged Amy forward, downstream, a little deeper into the tail water to make it easier to land the fish.

We were in up to mid-thigh before the trout tired enough for Amy to reel him all the way in. Still, he came in splashing, a nice sixteen-inch male, determined to fight to the end. By the time I was able to get my thumb in his mouth to hold him still, we were both dripping wet. I removed the hook and kept the fish in the water as Amy took a victor's look at her catch.

"Want a picture? I've got my camera in the side pocket of the cooler."

"Sure, I'll need proof for Uncle John."

We moved back to the shallow tail water and I had Amy kneel, holding the fish just out of the water while I snapped a few quick shots, before we released it.

"Nice fish," I said again. "Let's eat lunch then fish some more."

"Good idea. Let's see the pictures, too."

We sat together in the sun, drying off a bit. While I got out the sandwiches and drinks, Amy cycled the pictures on the camera's screen.

"Ham and cheese today with a little bit of lettuce to give it some crunch.

"Sounds delicious. We may have to show Uncle John pictures of the next fish, though."

"Didn't I get him?"

"Yeah, you did." Amy handed me the screen. "And that's not all."

I flipped through the pictures. Amy's smile was radiant as she held the fish to the camera. It was nicely centered.

"Stop looking at the fish," she hinted.

Behind the fish, Amy's wet t-shirt left nothing to the imagination. They were all like that.

"You're right," I agreed, unable to look back at the fish. "It's too distracting."

The sharp knuckles of her fist jabbed into my upper arm.

"Didn't you notice?"

"I was looking at the fish."

"Thanks! I thought guys got hornier in the summer."

I considered the question. "Hornier is such a relative term."

"Oh, brother!" Amy rolled her eyes.

"Hey," I said to change the subject. "Are you packing?

In answer, Amy turned slightly and raised her tank top. In the small of her back, the grip of a semi-automatic showed just above the waistband. It was tucked into an inside-the-waistband holster.

"Kimber Ultra Carry II in .45 ACP."

"That's the three-inch barrel?"

Amy nodded. "What about you? Don't tell me you're not carrying."

"No, I've got my Glock." I patted my right hip.

"And you're training? No sense carrying if you're not training."

"Yeah, I'm training." I hesitated. "But you know, I'm still not comfortable carrying with a round in the chamber."

"So you've got a magazine in the gun, but no round chambered? What are you going to do when a threat approaches?"

"I'll draw the gun. The bad guy won't know."

"He's a bad guy, what if he doesn't care?"

"I've thought about that. You're supposed to shout 'armed citizen, stop or I'll shoot.' I'll rack one into the chamber then. That will show him I'm serious and give him a chance to back off."

"Just don't forget," was all she said.

Chapter Twenty

Silence and Screams

Thursday was busy at the shop. Between customers John tried grilling me about the fishing lesson, but I gave vague answers. Finally he gave up.

After work, all I wanted was dinner. It was too hot to cook so I made a ham sandwich and called it good. Most of the evening I spent preparing for my next art class. I had this idea for a still life, but instead of a bowl of fruit, it would be an old wicker creel, a wood-handled net, an old reel, and the sections of a bamboo fly rod just kind of angled across things. It sketched out beautifully, but painting it in watercolors proved way over my head. After the third failure, I gave up and I turned in.

When I awoke, it was full-on dark. I wasn't sure what woke me. Half asleep as I was, I thought it might have been a distant scream. But then it could have been a dream. The second time I heard it, I sat up. It was a real scream!

I slipped into my cargo shorts and sneakers, grabbed my gun, ran through the living room, and scrambled to unlock the front door. On the sidewalk, I stopped to listen. The air was cool across my bare chest. The night sights on my gun glowed like landing lights in the darkness as I stood in the quiet thinking it was a dream after all.

Then chair legs scrapped across a wooden floor, the chair tipped over, and something heavy thudded against a wall.

I ran to my left, past Mrs. Batty's. It was coming from the Calloways'.

I looked in the window beside the front door. A light was on, but it was funny. It came from a shadeless table lamp lying sideways on the floor. The furniture in the front room was tipped over and in disarray.

I pounded on the door once, twice, three times. Nothing. Once, twice, three times. Nothing. The knob turned, but the door didn't open. Locked from the inside.

I ran around the side to the back door off the driveway. The Calloway's car was there, the door open, the dome light on.

A bag of groceries and a woman's shoulder bag lay on the ground.

The back door was ajar. It opened slowly to the touch on a squeaky hinge. The overhead light was on; a kitchen table and chairs pushed rudely to one side. Something white, either sugar or flour, spread along one counter. On the floor, it heaped amidst the clear shards of a broken jar.

It was as quiet as the inside of a coffin.

I came back to myself, tried to still the raging adrenaline, the pounding of my heart, to remember my training. My gun was out, my finger off the trigger. That was good. I racked a round into the chamber. I had forgot like Amy said I would. That was bad.

I looked through the crack between door and frame, no hidden threat. I tucked the gun to my chest and crossed the threshold.

Scan left, scan right; no threats. Advance across the kitchen to the archway. Pie into the living room. I forgot my flashlight again. Stress reduced peripheral vision. The lamplight wasn't enough. I wanted floodlighting.

Front door to the left, hallway to the right, three doors in the hallway. Front door locked, clear. First hallway door, on the right, bathroom, no threat in crack, pie the room, enter, nothing behind the shower curtain, clear. Second hallway door, on the left, office space, no threat in crack, pie the room, enter, scan left, scan right, closet, door open, no feet visible, nothing under the desk, clear. Third hallway door, on right, bedroom, no threat in crack, pie the room, a mess, enter, scan left, scan right, closet, sliding door open, no feet visible, motion in the mess of sheets, bedspread, and clothes on the far side of the bed against the wall. Moaning as something tried crawling under the bed.

I slipped my gun into my shorts at the small of my back and dug into the layers of cloth.

"Nancy, is that you?"

Nancy Calloway lay in the shadows between the bed and wall, bruised and bleeding, her arms and legs moving slowly and without coordination.

"It's me, Bobber from down the street. I'm your neighbor."

She made a sound I couldn't understand and looked up at me. Her bottom lip was split open and bleeding, her left eye swollen shut. It looked like her nose was broken. Her uniform top was ripped open, her brassiere hung from one shoulder.

"We have to call 9-1-1. Have you got a phone? Did you get your phone replaced yet?" I didn't bring mine. I had forgotten it, that and the flashlight. "I've got one at my place."

Nancy shook her head with a vacant motion, still dazed. I got a nylon windbreaker from the closet, helped her stand up, and helped her put it on. Slowly, together we went back through the house and out the back door.

By the time we got to my house, the shock had started to wear off and Nancy was crying softly. I sat her down on the couch with a glass of ice water while I dialed 9-1-1. I didn't know what else to do.

"Are you hungry? Do you want me to fix you a sandwich or something?"

"No," she shook her head. "He didn't get me. He was going to rape me. The pounding on the front door scared him away."

"That was me."

"I'm glad you got there when you did."

"So am I. If you want, I have a girl friend that lives right behind me. Maybe she can come over. She could help. Until the police get here."

"I would like that." She nodded and I called Amy. By the time I finished telling her what had happened, I heard the back gate rattle, and watched her cross the back yard still folding her cell phone.

Amy didn't wait for me to finish the introduction. She went right over and hugged Nancy Calloway like they were sisters. Then sat with her on the couch, her arms around her, their heads together. I stood in the open front door, looking down the street for the lights on a cop car.

"I was coming home from work. Tonight was my first night working swing shift. It pays better than days. We're trying to replace the stuff that got stolen the other day. I stopped at the store on my way home. When I was getting the grocery bag out of the car, he grabbed me. When I turned around, he hit me in the face. He was wearing a mask, one of those knit ski mask things."

"Balaclava."

"Yes, a balaclava. I tried to scream, but he kept hitting me and pushing me into the house. I tried to hit him, but he kept blocking me and hitting me back. He ripped my uniform. I think he had a knife. He could have killed me. I think he would have. But he heard the pounding on the front door and ran away."

"Thank God," Amy said.

"He just disappeared. I tried to hide under the bed. Then Bobber was there."

"I must have just missed him coming out the back door."

"Bobber said you have a husband, were is he?"

I hadn't even thought of that, that Tim Calloway might be lying injured in the house.

"Tim's pulling an all-nighter. He's on a team and they have a project due tomorrow."

"I can call him," I offered.

"That's okay. He's not very good in emergencies. It would probably be better if he just finished his project."

I looked at Amy, then back to Nancy, unsure what to do.

"It's okay, really. I feel a lot better now. My face hurts, I think he broke my nose, but I'm okay."

A patrol car pulled up at the curb. A policewoman got out and came to the front door. She introduced herself as Officer Grover. She said a detective was on his way.

Officer Grover took one look at Nancy and radioed for an EMT unit.

"Mr. Mulligan will you be available later? And you miss?"

"Ogle, yes."

"Mrs. Calloway, I want you to come with me. I need to secure your house. The EMT will be there shortly."

After they left, I took Amy in my arms and gave her a long, tight hug.

"Thanks," I whispered. It was all I could say.

I stayed up after she left, working on a watercolor for art class, as the adrenaline slowly drained away. It was replaced by utter exhaustion and I went to bed, the watercolor only half finished. Later, I woke again. It was still dark. I was alone. I had been dreaming that something dangerous prowled outside in the darkness while I slept. What woke me was the certain realization that it was not a dream.

Chapter Twenty-One

TGIF

Friday at work I was exhausted. Even John noticed. After I'd told him what happened, I'd catch him watching me from across the room. Around two he said I should go home and take a nap. I guess he finally got tired backing wrong sales amounts out of the till.

I went home, but I wasn't tired. I was restless. I got my watercolors and spent the rest of the afternoon working on things for art class. It made me focus. The concentration was good. Maybe the counselor was onto something.

Around seven, I put everything away and was scanning the fridge for dinner when the doorbell rang.

"You <u>are</u> home." Amy smiled. "I thought you would be."

"I was catching up on my watercolors."

"Monica had her first Neighborhood Watch meeting."

"How'd that go?"

"A police safety officer gave a presentation. There were only six or seven people. I only knew the Kibbles. He sounded like he talked mostly to middle schoolers."

Amy went on explaining what the safety officer said. It was basic preparedness, stuff I already knew and had done except for engraving. I objected to scratching up all my valuables hoping then no one would want to steal them, even if the scratches were my initials. So my mind had time to race ahead and I decided to make my move.

"I'm getting hungry," I said. "Ever been to the Ducktail?"

"The little brew-pub next to the New Deal Market?"

"That's the place. I'll buy you a beer and a burger."

"You're on, mister."

"Let me gear up." I stepped into my den. Amy followed me in and watched as I put on my inside-the-waist-band holster and slipped a magazine of hollow-points into my gun.

"Rack one into the chamber."

I did. We made sure the doors and windows were locked and then walked the four blocks to the tavern. It was a nice night, just starting to get dark, the temperature cooling down.

As we walked, Amy filled me in on the Kibbles. They had sniped at each other continually for what had happened. It had made everyone uncomfortable. They way she described it they both had a point. Ken needed to take a more active role; Karen needed to be more responsible.

When we got to the brew-pub, Ray, the owner, was behind the bar. He was a big guy with a shaved head and drooping moustache. He looked like a retired wrestler. The place was half full: a couple girl couples dancing, four or five college kids playing pool.

"Let's sit outside," I said. "Two Hefeweizen's, Ray."

"I'll send them out with Fancy. She'll set you up."

Amy picked a small table in the front yard near the sidewalk where we could feel the breeze and watch the cars and foot traffic.

"I read The Decline and Fall of the Roman Empire," I said. It came out of the blue. I wasn't trying to be funny. I used to read it on business trips. "What's going on here reminds me of what happened back then."

"Being taken over by Vandals, Visigoths, and Huns?"

"The weak leadership and abdication of responsibility that led to the fall of a once-great society."

"Interesting thought, the decline of society."

Fancy, the waitress, came, a blond with Hooters-sized breasts. She wiped the table clean, set our beers down on coasters, gave us napkins, pretzels, and a menu.

We relaxed into our chairs.

"This is good." Amy sipped her beer. "He makes it here?"

"Yeah, he's got a garbage can in back, stirs it with an old broom."

"Get out!"

Two girls went by dressed like hookers. They looked like the two girls from the park the other day. They were on their way to Sixth and Seventh streets. That's where that type of action took place. For a moment I thought I recognized them, high school friends of Kara Kibble's. But no, close up they were too old. It was just the makeup and clothes.

A dark van pulled around the corner, slewing to the outside on bad springs. The brake lights came on as it passed the girls. They talked a little. Exchanged something through the passenger-side window, then the girls giggled and walked off. The van came up the street and stopped just short of the tavern. The transmission clunked into park and the sliding door opened with a rumble, but no dome light came on. A man and woman got out. They stood there kissing like he'd just returned from World War II. Then he put his arm over her shoulder and they staggered closer.

It was Floyd DuChien and his girlfriend from the boat ramp, Vicki. They looked like they'd been bar-hopping most of the afternoon. Floyd was wearing cut-offs and a sun-faded blue tank top that showed off his shoulder tattoos. Vicki was wearing pink jogging tights and a yellow bikini top. The last thing they looked like they needed was more to drink.

"Son of a bitch, Bob Mulligan! Fucking A man, how they hanging?"

"Hey, Floyd." I nodded at him and then at Vicki. "Vicki, this is Amy. Amy, Vicki and Floyd."

"Floyd DuChien at your service." Floyd bowed like a tipsy courtier and reached to kiss Amy's hand. Amy grabbed her beer instead. "DuChien, that's French for the fox." He brushed his fingers through his hair like he was fluffing his tail.

"No it's not," Amy whispered to me from behind her Heferweizen. "It means 'of the dog.' Reynard is 'fox.'"

I don't think Floyd heard. He was watching Fancy approach.

"Well, darling." Floyd eyed her and smiled. "What's your name?"

"Fancy. Can I get you anything? A cup of coffee maybe, something to eat?"

"Fancy indeed." He held out his hand. "Floyd DuChien at your service." He took her hand and raised it to his lips. "DuChien, that's French for fox."

Vicki had been wobbly even with Floyd's support. But when he let go to focus on Fancy, she backed against the next table, tried to sit, missed, and landed on the ground.

"You fucking little whore," Floyd berated her as he grabbed her arm and lifted her bodily onto a chair. "Look at you, you're a fucking mess." He dropped into the other chair. "Do you hear me?" She flinched like he was going to slap her. "Sit your ass in that chair and don't say another word."

"Ray, can you come here a minute."

"Aw, fuck darling, now what'd you go and do that for? I was just funning. I wouldn't hurt her. She's my girl."

Ray came out from behind the bar.

"Hey, I was just fucking around."

"I don't allow no swearing around here," Ray said.

Floyd reached into his pocket and pulled out a pack of cigarettes, stuck one in his mouth, and patted his pockets for a light.

The big guy took the cigarette and crushed it in his big fist right in front of Floyd's face. "I don't allow no smoking either."

"God damn you, Vicki, see what you done now?" Floyd shoved his palm against the side of Vicki's face.

"And I don't allow none of that."

"Hey, all I want's a beer. Sit with my friends here and have a beer. Come on, man."

"Not tonight you're not," Ray said. He took a breath and seemed to get even bigger. "Here's what's going to happen. You're going to get your sorry ass out of my chair and off my property. And you're gonna take your girlfriend with you."

"You fat shit," Floyd said, but he stood up as he was saying it. "See if I ever come back here again. Come on Vicki. Let's find us a real bar."

Ray watched them all the way to the van. Floyd started the engine with a roar, dropped the transmission into drive, and floored the gas pedal. I could see the silhouette of his raised middle finger as he drove by.

"Sorry about that folks," Ray said and went back into the bar.

"That's your friend's brother?"

"And his faithful sidekick."

"Talk about the decline of society. And what was she on?"

"Probably the same thing as the other day."

"I wonder if she's a runaway?"

"Why's that?" I asked.

"She looks about Kara Kibble's age, but he's old enough to be her father."

I paid Fancy what I owed and we headed back to the house.

"Did you see his tats?" Amy asked.

"Yeah, he got them in the army."

"Did you tell Uncle John?"

"About the tattoos, yeah, why?"

"Because those look more like prison tats."

Chapter Twenty-Two

Panty Raid

I was sitting on the deck with my morning coffee trying to decide which chore to do first, mow the lawn or wash the truck. What I really wanted to do was try that picture again, the rod, reel, and creel still life.

"Our underpants are gone," Karen Kibble blurted.

I looked up. Ken, Karen, and Kara were advancing across my back yard like Israelites out of Egypt.

"It's like some big, cosmic joke."

Ken nodded to what Karen had said.

"They took my butt-floss," Kara grumbled.

"Your what?"

"My brand new thong. I got it at Victoria's Secret, pink with a smiley face. It cost $25. It was the only one they had."

"I thought you said the other day they didn't take any underwear? Just your camera?"

"They came back," Ken said. "Last night while we were at the movies. This time all they took was underwear."

"Mine and Kara's. They left Ken's."

I was going to make some remark about the condition of Ken's underwear, but didn't. It wouldn't have been funny. "That's what they took, just underwear? Nothing else?"

"That's all," Ken said.

"It's like someone is joking with us," Karen repeated.

"Did you call the cops?"

Karen looked at Ken. He nodded.

"What'd they say?"

"Same thing, an I-5 gang passing through."

"It's the party line." Karen smirked.

"Did they ransack your house? Were they looking for valuables?"

"No." Ken shook his head. "That's what's so strange. We came home from the movie and the house was just the way we left it."

"Everything looked fine, just the way we left it," Karen confirmed. "We went to bed. It wasn't until this morning that we realized we'd been robbed again."

"It was creepy." Kara shivered. "I opened my underwear drawer and it was empty."

"But how'd they get in?" I frowned. "Were your doors locked?"

The three Kibbles nodded.

"They have a key," Ken said. "That's what the police think. They took our spare the first time and we didn't notice."

"Ken promised to change the locks," Karen said. "You'll do that today, right, Ken?"

"I said I'd do it," Ken replied. He looked at me. "I'm going to take out the Zebra grass if you're still interested. And I could use your truck if it's available for a dump run. I'll pay for gas."

I thought I heard my coffee cup snicker.

"I'll be over as soon as I eat," I said. "Might as well get started before it gets too hot."

"Great. You and I can work while Karen and Kara go off shopping."

"We buying underwear, Ken," Karen snapped. "We're not wearing any."

"TMI, Mom." Kara rolled her eyes at her mother. "TMI."

"I was kidding," Ken said to Karen.

"I don't think you were."

"Bob, do you think I should get a gun?" Ken ignored her. "I've been thinking about it since the other day. Now might be a good time."

"You are not buying a gun." Karen spoke slowly, her words bullets she shot at Ken.

His face got red. I thought he was going to blow a gasket.

Kara looked at her parents nervously.

"Let's take out the Zebra grass first," I said.

"You own a gun, don't you?" Ken asked, not looking at Karen.

"I own a gun, yes. But I'll be honest, it's a lot of work."

"Meaning?"

"Meaning it's a lot of work. It's like a child. You're responsible for it twenty-four-seven."

Ken stiffened. "You don't think I'm a responsible parent?"

Karen smirked at him like I'd just made her point.

Kara looked at the deck and shifted from foot to foot.

"Ken, I know you're a responsible parent. Question is can you be a responsible gun owner?"

"Why wouldn't I be?"

"Do you want a new hobby?" I ran on before he could answer. "That's what gun ownership is, you know, if you want a gun for self-defense."

"How is it a new hobby?"

"Because you'll need professional training once a year. You should practice live-fire once a week and you should do dry-fire drills every couple of nights."

"Really?"

"Really."

"That's a lot of work."

"I told you so," Karen said. She took Kara by the shoulders, turned her around, and gave her a little push. "We're going shopping. We'll see you when we get back."

"That's what I'm trying to tell you," I said to Ken. "It's a big commitment."

"But the Second Amendment."

"You have the right to own a gun. All I'm saying is own it responsibly."

"Well, what then?" Ken shrugged, angry at giving up.

"Simple things first."

"Like what?" he asked dully.

"Pull the Zebra grass," I reminded him like he was a shock victim. "Trim the shrubs. Then you can look into guns or alarm systems if you want."

He nodded.

"I'd also make it a habit to lock your doors and windows when you're not at home; same thing at bedtime. Anything to make your home harder to attack."

"You think they'll come back?" Ken asked slowly. "That would be three times. What are the odds?"

"I don't know, but can you afford to take the chance?" I stopped, surprised at the urgency I felt. Then I understood why. "Suppose it's like the Calloways?"

"How like the Calloways? In what way?"

"They were robbed first, then Nancy was attacked."

"So?"

"Ken, they knew there was nothing to steal. Suppose they came back just to attack Nancy?"

"You mean suppose they come back for Karen and Kara?" A mixture of anger and pain tightened Ken's face. His hands clenched into fists.

I nodded. There it was. I felt better for getting it out, but I felt a whole lot worse, too.

Chapter Twenty-Three

Crime Scene Investigation

Ken did most of the talking. I did most of the sweating. His marriage was falling apart, had been for years. He'd hoped it would last until Kara was out of the house, but the burglaries had somehow accelerated the process. Now every choice he made exposed a character flaw and Karen questioned everything he did. Buying the gun was just an example.

I thought he didn't have any male friends, someone to talk to, because we didn't know each other that well. But he wanted to talk to me. I don't know why. I encouraged him to protect his family, to focus on that and not be overwhelmed. I said the things the counselor had told me. I'm not sure it did any good.

By 5 o'clock, we'd made two trips to the yard-debris recycling place, his house looked better, his spousal attitude had improved, and I was ready for a shower, a beer, and some quiet time. But the phone rang.

"We saw Amy at the mall." Kara's voice was excited. "We're coming over. We have a plan."

"Oh boy, a plan."

By the time I showered and put on clean shorts and a t-shirt, the girls were conspiring on my deck. They had a box in a shopping bag.

"Did you see all the stuff your dad and I did? Pretty good, hunh?"

"It's perfect," Kara said. "Mom was impressed. She says you're a good example."

"So, what's the plan?" I asked, sitting on the steps. The girls had appropriated both deck chairs.

"You know the Science Store?"

"Never heard of it."

"It's near Macy's," Amy said.

I didn't know, but I nodded anyhow. I didn't go to the mall much; too many people, too hard to identify a shooter, too hard to find an exit.

"Mom and I saw Amy and we were just talking and I looked in the window of the Science Store and there it was."

"What?"

"This!" Kara took a kid's educational forensic kit out of the shopping bag. "We can dust for fingerprints."

"What the heck, Bobber." Amy smiled at me mischievously. "If the police won't do it, at least we can give it a try."

"You know." I pounded my fist on the deck. "I agree. It's our neighborhood and we can defend it ourselves."

The kit focused on fingerprints. Not that I know a lot about forensics, but the kit seemed to provide all the fixings to do a pretty good job collecting and analyzing prints. And it came with a book. By the time Karen called Kara for dinner, we had made a plan to dust the neighborhood crime scenes for prints.

Amy stood up to go, too.

"I'll make you a cheeseburger," I blurted, then flushed at my shameless attempt to get her to stay.

Kara came up to me and put a hand to her mouth.

"We need to talk about the dork factor," Kara whispered in my ear. "But you get an 'A' for effort."

Kara left, but Amy sat back down. "She's a sweet kid."

I nodded.

"She's worried about her parents divorcing. She says all they do is argue."

"I know. Ken's worried, too. I think the burglaries have them stressed out."

"They have everyone stressed out."

I got two Coronas from the deck fridge.

"How long do these roving burglar gangs stay in town typically, do you know?" Amy asked.

"I'm not sure."

We went into the kitchen and I loaded Amy up with stuff to take out to the deck. I had a bag of cole slaw that I added some ranch dressing to. Normally I don't eat a lot of salads, but I wanted to make a good impression, get another 'A' for effort.

"I've been thinking about that." I lit the grill. "I'm not sure the police know what they're talking about."

"About the I-5 gangs?"

I nodded. "It's too easy."

"They say it's the season for these gangs to be passing through."

"That's what makes it too easy. It's the season. Two people call up from the same neighborhood to report burglaries. Oh, it's an I-5 gang."

"You mean when all you have is a hammer, every problem looks like a nail."

"Something like that."

Amy looked at me, waiting.

"A gang of professional thieves would depend on speed, don't you think? They'd find an unlocked house, ransack it for stuff to steal, and leave."

Amy shrugged. "Isn't that what happened?"

"To the Calloways, yes. It's not what happened to the Kibbles. The door was unlocked, yes, but the house wasn't ransacked and they only took a camera. The second time, they didn't even take anything of value. They stole underwear."

"How do you explain that?"

"I don't know. It's like Karen said. It's like somebody's playing a joke."

"The peeping tom?"

"Maybe." I thought about it. "That might account for the missing dogs, too. But not why Shaman disappeared while I was away."

Amy frowned. "Or why Monica was assaulted right after you got back. It's too coincidental."

"And Nancy's Calloway's assault, why was it more violent?"

"Aren't peeping toms supposed to be voyeurs, not rapists?"

"That's what I thought." I nodded. "Maybe that's where that detective comes in."

"Cadanki?" Amy supplied his name.

"Yeah. He's not investigating missing dogs."

I shaped the ground chuck into two patties and put them on the grill.

"And why would anybody break into a house and steal nothing but underwear?" I looked at Amy. "Even a $25 pair. Is a thong a pair of underwear? Can you say that?"

"Hmmm, I think a thong is just a thong."

"I can see a burglar taking small electronic stuff to resell. And a peeping tom might take a dog so he could look in a window undisturbed." I stopped. That's where the logic failed. "But why would a burglar take underwear instead of something more valuable and why would a peeping tom call attention to himself by stealing underwear? That's what I don't understand."

"Maybe they're not too smart."

"Crackheads?"

Amy nodded.

"Or maybe they just think they're smart."

I flipped the burgers and we watched the cheese melt. I toasted the buns off to one side. Amy sliced some sweet onion and a tomato, and got the coleslaw from the house. We made our plates up and sat down to eat.

"But then again," I said between bites, "what's the likelihood we know more than the police?"

"True, they do this for a living. This cheeseburger is delicious."

"How do you like the salad?"

"I don't usually eat rabbit food." Amy snickered. "Just kidding. But you do strike me as a meat-and-potatoes guy." She bit into her cheeseburger. "The police ought to know the difference between an I-5 gang and a bunch of crackheads."

"You'd think."

Amy thought a moment. "Maybe stealing the underwear was an afterthought."

"An impulse theft?"

"Yeah. Or maybe it was just for kicks."

"Still." I shook my head. "It doesn't make sense. If they wanted souvenirs, why didn't they take them the first time?"

"They did at the Calloways," Amy said.

"But they came back."

"That's right. What souvenir were they after the second time?"

I looked at Amy. "Nancy."

Chapter Twenty-Four

Among Friends

Sunday evening I ate early, Shaman still wandering around in the back yard of my mind. At least he wasn't barking.

I needed to do a watercolor for class and was idly glancing at my watercolor book. When I got to the portrait section, I thought of surprising Amy with a watercolor of her big fish, so I printed the photos from the other day to use as models.

My den was too hot and too isolated, so I set up in the living room on the coffee table. I was going to start, but the more I looked at the photos, the harder it was. I looked at my almost-completed sketch of the fishing gear. It wouldn't take much to finish it.

But I needed a watercolor for class. I looked back at the photos. I got a small picture frame I had lying around, polished the glass clean, and tried the pictures in the frame to get the look. The frame made the fish look small. To get the detail I wanted, the watercolor would have to be bigger, a lot bigger.

But I didn't have time to paint something that big.

I looked back at the sketch.

A bead of sweat ran down my forehead and across my cheek. It wasn't the heat. I couldn't make a decision. Ten years in product management and I couldn't decide between a painting and a sketch. It got hotter. I struggled against a sudden riptide of panic. I didn't know what to do. My heart raced. I looked around the room for something to anchor me, helpless.

I stood up and walk to the kitchen, got a can of sparkling water from the fridge, and held it to my head. I rolled it across my forehead. I never had a problem making product management decisions. I told the counselor that. He smiled kindly like he was talking to an idiot and told me those days were over, that I could expect to have occasional difficulties. What he didn't tell me about was the sense of failure and shame that came with the indecision.

I went back into the living room and worked on the sketch. I'd do the watercolor later. Right now, I needed simple, pencil and paper, black and white. A brush and a bunch of different colors were too much, the infinite variety possible. I didn't need infinite. I needed finite.

I worked on the sketch until I finished it, then held it at arms' length. It looked good enough to frame. I had captured the detail that showed the age and that hinted at the history of each piece, the wear on the edges: the silver edge where the black had worn off the reel, the oil-darkened cork of the rod handle, the lighter color of the wicker where the varnish had worn off. Each piece had its own presence, its own history.

I wondered about the sketch my life had become. My life was black and white now. After the shooting, I had made it that way and every day I worked to keep it that way. But Amy added color. I ran my finger along a photograph. Then I looked at my sketch. Really, what's the difference between a thousand shades of gray and color? They both revealed the presence and history of a thing. They just did it in different ways.

Maybe that counselor was smarter than I thought suggesting the watercolor class. I thought about that for a moment. No, he wasn't. And whoever thought it was funny to steal dogs and underwear wasn't that smart either.

I taped a new sheet of watercolor paper to my board and outlined Amy's shape from the photos.

A mechanical clunking noise from the street came through the screen on the open front door. Someone needs a new transmission, I thought.

Just after that there was a light tapping on the door.

"Mind if I come in?" Vicki peered at me through the screen.

"Hey, Vicki. No, come on it. Where's Floyd?"

Vicki opened the screen door and walked into the light. She was dressed for the weather wearing a white bikini top, low-rise cut-offs, and flip-flops.

"Sorry, what?"

"Where's Floyd?"

"He couldn't make it," she said vacantly.

I frowned. "He didn't say anything about getting together."

"Ain't that just like him." She sniffled and rubbed her nose with her hand.

"How's your cold?" I asked to be polite. I should have asked what drug made her nose run so.

"Oh, you know the old saying." She looked at me with a blank expression. "They're easy to come by and hard to get rid of." She smiled like a teenager lying to her parents and came closer, rubbing her hands together like they were cold. "What're you doing? Drawing?"

"Yeah, I'm starting a watercolor."

She saw the sketch on the coffee table. "You did all that with a pencil?"

"Yeah."

She sat down next to me on the couch, close, and reached across me to pick up the sketch. "Mind if I get a better look?"

"No, go ahead." I scooched over a bit. She kept coming.

Vicki said, "Floyd said you and Jimmy Dean was best friends growing up."

"We went to the same high school. Jimmy Dean and I were the same year. Floyd was two years ahead. We were all on the football team. That was what? Almost twenty years ago."

"Bobber?" Vicki looked at me beseechingly, taking my hand in both of hers like Scarlett O'Hara asking Rhett Butler to save Tara. Her hands were freezing. "May I ask you something?"

I just wanted my hand back, but I nodded.

"My, your hand is so warm. Mine are just like icicles. Can't you tell?"

"They are."

"Well, Jimmy Dean was telling Floyd about guiding and how important it was to get recommended by your fishing store."

"He doesn't need a recommendation to guide."

"Floyd told him that. But Jimmy Dean wouldn't listen." She looked at me. "So I was wondering if I could do something to help you decide."

She pressed my hand against her chest. I pulled it free, scrambled to my feet, and walked around the coffee table to the armchair and sat down.

"Oh, now, don't be so skittish. We're all friends here. I was just wondering."

"It's not my decision, it's John Ogle's." I looked at her from the relative safety of my armchair. "So, if that's all you've come for, I'd like to get back to my picture."

"My, that's a nice fish." Vicki picked up the photos of Amy and her fish and flipped through them. "Floyd used to catch fish like that all the time in Texas. He had his own guide business, too, you know." She picked up the frame and held it behind one of the photos like she was testing the fit. "Pretty sexy girl, too."

She stood up and held a photo so I could see.

"Is that out where we were?"

"That's the gravel bar just down from where we took out.

"I can see you're a breast man." Vicki reached behind her back with one hand. "Floyd's a breast man too." She pulled the string and her bikini top came loose. She lifted the top off and dropped it onto the coffee table. "See what I mean?"

"Vicki, does Floyd know you're here?"

Vicki came around the coffee table unbuttoning her cut-offs. She stood in front of me, stepped out of her flip-flops, and let the cut-offs drop down her legs to the floor.

"You like my new thong?" She turned slowly in front of me, like she was dancing on a stage, so I could get the whole picture. She seemed practiced.

"Very nice," I said, standing. "You tell Floyd he's real lucky to have a girl like you."

"You are such a gentleman," she purred.

She reached up to put her arms around my neck, but I spun her around instead.

"Oh!" She gasped in surprise, then again, slower, like she understood something. "Oh. Now that's what I'm talking about."

"Take off that thong and give it here," I whispered in her ear.

Vicki did as she was told.

"That was so hot," I whispered. "Why don't you do it again?"

I snatched her shorts from the floor.

"Do it again?" Vicki repeated blankly. "You're funning me, ain't ya?"

"No, get dressed." I got her top from the coffee table and held her clothes out to her. She snatched them angrily.

"What about my thong?" she asked. "It's brand new."

"I know," I said and put the thong in my pocket.

I stood at the door after she left until I heard the clunk of the transmission going into gear, then I took the thong from my pocket.

It was pink with a smiley face.

Chapter Twenty-Five

Second Thoughts

Monday was a scorcher, the kind of heat that makes every pore on your body ooze liquid and you melt into your shoes like the Wicked Witch of the West.

At work, I asked John about Jimmy Dean. Had he made his decision? I left out the part about Vicki. He said he was still looking into it and left it at that. I didn't press him. It was too hot.

When I got home that afternoon, I opened the windows to get a cross-draft going, then retreated to the back deck with the phone. Amy's window was open, so I knew she was there. I needed her advice.

"Hey, it's me," I said when she picked up. "How's the oven?"

While we talked, I took my pruning shears and lightly barbered my topiaries. The timer on my drip system went off and a gentle mist soothed my burning forearms. It gave me an idea.

"Reason I called, I need your thoughts on something, in return for which I will make you cool."

By the time Amy came over, I had rigged several runs of hose with mister heads in an arch across the top of my jasmine trellis.

"Stand here," I said, framing Amy in front of the trellis. Then I turned the water on.

"That feels so good." Amy giggled in surprise. "I feel like the coolest cucumber in the vegetable department."

I joined her in front of the trellis and we turned slowly like we were in a water rotisserie. There's something about water on a hot day.

"Okay, you've done your part." Amy took a seat in one of the Adirondack chairs. "What can I do for you?"

"Here's my problem, um." I stumbled, unsure whether to go on, afraid I couldn't.

"It's okay." She patted the back of my hand. "Take your time."

"It's, like, um, a question of etiquette."

She nodded, waiting for more.

"Say you wore something that was brand new, but belonged to someone else. And it didn't look like you'd worn it at all. But you wanted to give it back. Should you wash it before you give it back?"

"Just what are we talking about here?"

"A thong."

"Come again?"

"Well, because if you washed it, it wouldn't look new anymore, would it?"

"Have you and Floyd been exchanging underwear?"

In answer, I retrieved the thong, letting it dangle from my index finger.

"That looks like Kara's."

I nodded. "That's what I thought."

"Where'd you get this?"

I gave Amy a play-by-play of last night's adventure with Vicki. Her eyes got wider, then her jaw dropped.

"So, if I wanted to return this to Kara, what should I do?"

"You have to wash it. No question. Use the gentle cycle."

I frowned. I wasn't sure I had a gentle cycle.

"Here." Amy made a grasping motioned with her hand, took the thong, and headed across the yard. "I have a front-loader. It'll come out like new."

I followed her thinking I could learn something, unravel some mystery of femininity.

We climbed the stairs to her apartment. She unlocked the door and we walked in. It was like a pizza oven.

"I've got some stuff to wash, too," Amy said, making up a load and tossing the thong on top. She started the washer and set the timer on her cell phone. Then we retreated to the relative coolness of my back deck.

"You think she stole it?" Amy asked from the depths of a deck chair.

"She must have. Kara said it was the only one in the store."

"That doesn't mean anything, silly. She could have ordered it over the Internet or bought it from a catalog. She could have bought it in Portland for that matter."

"Oh." I started to sweat all over again. "I hadn't thought of that."

"You better find out." The timer went off and Amy stood up. "You may owe Vicki an apology. I'll put the load in the dryer."

I watched Amy until she disappeared through the backyard gate. The drip system came on again, but this time I hardly noticed. They tell you in training that when you're in a gunfight, your vision narrows to the immediate threat. That's what stress does. That's why they advise you to do after-action drills. I guess that's what happened last night in a way. My vision narrowed.

Amy came back and we idled around in the misters keeping cool until the timer for the dryer went off and she left again.

"Ta da," she said, returning with the thong. It was still warm.

"You're right," I said. "It looks like new, just like new." I was thinking maybe it wasn't too late for an after-action drill after all. "Come on, we're going shopping."

I put the thong in a plastic sandwich bag, locked the house, and we headed out to the lingerie store where Kara said she bought her thong. In the safety of my air-conditioned truck, with Amy smiling next to me, my heart stopped racing and I finally stopped sweating.

"Yes. It's one of ours," said the college-age girl behind the counter. "See the label?"

I nodded, seeing the label for the first time. Funny how a piece of clothing that tiny could have a label that big and me not see it. I must have been under a lot of stress. It made me a believer in after-action drills.

"Do you sell many of these?" I asked.

"Thongs? Are you kidding, we sell a ton."

"What about if I wanted to buy one like this?" Amy asked. "Do you have it in stock?"

"Pink with a smiley face?"

"Yes, exactly like this. Pink with a smiley face."

"I'm sure we do."

"Then I'd like to get one," Amy said. She turned to me. "Get out your wallet, big boy."

"They're right over here." The girl moved toward a rack of neatly stacked cellophane packages, talking as she went. "Here they are. Black with a smiley face. White with a smiley face. Pink, pink." She pursed her lips and frowned, flipping through the packages.

I started to feel a little better.

"Here it is. Pink with a smiley face."

She held out the package. Amy gave me an I-told-you-so look. I gave her an I'm-retarded look and took the package as I melted into my shoes again.

"It's your lucky day." The sales clerk smiled.

"How's that?" I asked.

"They're on sale, half price."

"Oh, good."

"Will there be anything else?" She walked back to the cash register.

I looked at Amy, then shook my head and sighed.

The counselor would say look on the bright side. Vicki gets her underpants back and Kara gets new ones. And they were on sale. How good was that?

I followed the sales clerk and Amy, looking meekly at the package of underwear, reading the advertising for lack of anything better to do. It read like some foreign language.

"What's lace-trimmed hipster?" I asked blankly, reaching reflexively for my wallet.

"Oh." The girl stopped and took the package. "Whoops. My bad. You wanted the thong, didn't you?"

We returned to the underwear stand. The girl started thumbing through the rows again, first one row, then another.

"Jill?" she asked a passing sales clerk. "These people would like to buy a pink thong with a smiley face. Do you know if we have any? All I'm finding is blacks and whites. And we have pink in the hipster."

I held up the sandwich bag for reference.

"No." Jill held the edge of the sandwich bag for a moment and we all examined the contents. "This is the only one. It came in the other day in a shipment of seconds." She dropped her hand. "A young girl bought it before I could even get it on the rack. She was with her mother. You're the dad?"

"Aunt and uncle," I fudged.

"I was putting the shipment out. That was the only pink one. I was going to put it aside for my niece, but your niece snatched them up. We had quite a laugh."

"Are they available through the catalog? Could I special order a pair?"

"Nope," Jill said shortly. "I've tried. They're completely out of stock. Sorry."

"Sorry about that." The first sales girl apologized. "I guess it's not your lucky day after all."

"That's okay." I smiled. "You've been a great help."

I felt like leaving them a tip.

Before we left the mall, I bought a nicer picture frame.

"What's that for?" Amy asked.

"It's a gift," I said, trying not to sound mysterious, but not wanting to say more.

"Oh," she said and let it drop.

I wanted to give Amy a present. At my skill level, it would take several generations to paint a watercolor of

Amy and her fish. I thought in the meantime I could give her one of the photos.

Chapter Twenty-Six

Hard Times

"You went shopping for a pair of girl's panties?" John winked at Bill.

"Don't answer that, Bobber." Bill played my legal counsel. "It could be incriminating."

Things were slow at the shop. I was the only entertainment.

Bill had stopped in on his lunch break to say what a fine time they'd had the other day and to get some fly tying materials. He mentioned his birthday was coming up and that he tied flies on a Thompson Model A vise he'd bought used from Methuselah. John took the hint and they adjourned to the back room where a discussion of vises somehow turned to me.

"Just kidding," Bill admitted helpfully.

"Seriously," Copper John looked up from the fly he was tying to catch my eye. "Are you locking your doors and windows at night? Taking precautions?"

"You think they'll go after my underwear next?"

"You know what I mean."

"Yeah, always. And I just installed a better lock on Amy's storage area."

Bill palmered hackle in front of the expertly tapered body he'd dubbed on the hook shank. He seemed to take naturally to the Renzetti vice John had him using. "You were a cop for forty years, John, what do you make of all this?"

John thought for a moment. "No telling."

"That the best you can do?" I asked.

Bill snickered as he finished his fly.

"I got to get back and see a client," Bill said, standing to leave. "I'll tell Carol about the vise. One just like this."

"I'll set one aside," John promised. "Happy birthday."

The shop door closed. A moment later it opened again. I expecting to see Bill returning for something he'd forgotten, but it was Jimmy Dean DuChien. He came into the shop, made it about half way toward us, then looked around nervously for customers. There weren't any.

"Hey Bobber. John." He nodded.

John nodded. I said, "Hey."

Jimmy Dean advanced a few steps further and stopped again.

"I'm calling it quits," he said.

I looked at John, then back at Jimmy Dean. "How do you mean?"

"About being a Copper John guide." He looked at me, then John.

"Up to you, Jimmy Dean," John said.

"Oh, I still want to," Jimmy Dean went on. "Ever since I found out Bobber here was a guide, I wanted to be one, too. I figured it'd be like old times. But it ain't turning out like I thought."

"How's that?" John asked.

"It's taking too long. Everything's hanging fire." Jimmy Dean waved his arms in frustration. "And these is hard times. The electrician business is slow. I had to sell my damn boat. Then you want to go down the river."

"So you took Ed Grissom's boat?" I asked. The flyer was still posted on the wall.

"Hell, Bobber, I don't know whose boat it was."

I could hear the dust falling on the cash register from where I sat, the shop got that quiet.

"Floyd done it," Jimmy Dean explained. "He was trying to get me through this rough spot I'm in. Besides, it was just sitting there and he knew I needed a boat. Hell, we brought it back when we was done. It ain't like we stole it."

I looked at Jimmy Dean. He was shifting his weight from one foot to the other. I couldn't think of what to say, so I just closed my mouth. Somewhere along the line, it had come open.

John was frowning at him.

"I'm old enough to know better," Jimmy Dean smiled at us. "I admit. It ain't like I'm a kid no more. But Floyd said it was the only thing to do. And bringing it back, there'd be no harm done."

I didn't know what to say. I was embarrassed for the guy. Men don't admit they make stupid mistakes, maybe to a counselor, but not to each other. Part of me admired Jimmy Dean for doing it.

"And, boss." Jimmy Dean raised his head and looked directly at me. "While I'm at it, there's something I got to clear up with you."

"What's that?"

"I know what happened the other night. Vicki told me. I'm ashamed for what she done."

"That's okay." It was all I could think to say.

"No, it ain't," he insisted. "I need to apologize. It was all a big misunderstanding. She thought she was helping me out, so she went ahead and did what she done."

"Sometimes good intentions don't go right," I said. I knew from personal experience. I didn't buy anyone Krispy Kremes anymore. "I need to ask you something, too. Just to get things clear."

"Anything, boss. We're buds, you and me."

"Vicki was wearing something that I'm pretty sure was, ah, stolen."

Jimmy Dean looked at me like he no longer spoke English.

"That thong? You talking about that goddamn thong?"

"Yeah, the thong," I said.

"Her and her goddamn thongs! I don't know where she gets them, if that's what you're getting at. She just comes home with them like that one she got Floyd."

"Floyd didn't give it to her?"

Jimmy Dean took a step closer.

"Boss," he said, lowering his voice. "You got to believe me when I tell you this." He looked at John, then back at me. "Fact is me and Floyd ain't nothing but a couple of dumb-ass rednecks. Hell, it ain't like we're keeping it a secret. But Vicki, she's got class. Floyd loves her, he really does. That's why he was wearing that thong, to make her happy. But truth is Vicki ain't nothing but a goddamn crackhead whore." He whispered the last three words. "I hate to say it that way, but it's the truth. She goes out sometimes. I don't know where she goes or what she's does. I ain't sure Floyd does either."

His eyes looked red, they glistened. I thought he was about to cry.

"I'm sorry," he said. "This ain't none of your burden. It's just that life is the shits right now."

I looked at John. "So what now?" I asked.

"I'm thinking to go in with Floyd. He's getting his own guide service going."

"I thought that didn't work the last time?"

"He fixed the problem," Jimmy Dean replied simply. "It'll work now. See, Floyd's a thinker. He can take something that ain't right and analyze it and make it work. Same thing with cars. He can't sit still till it's right."

"Who you bullshitting now?" I asked. No way I could let Jimmy Dean tell me that and not say something. "Every time Floyd thought something in high school it got him in trouble. And usually you, too, remember?"

"It's different now, boss. He's more mature. You'll see. He thinks everything out in advance."

He looked at John. "And he can put me on right away," he hinted.

John let it pass.

Jimmy Dean looked at us. "So I just come to apologize and I hope there's no hard feelings."

"That's okay," I said, not knowing what else to say. "It happens."

"Well, that's what I come to say," Jimmy Dean said, backing to the door. "I'll let you get back to business. I'd still be interested in guiding for your shop, though. In case Floyd ain't much fun to work for long term."

"I've got one more thing I need to get clear," John said. "Then I'll let you know."

Jimmy Dean closed the door softly. We watched him through the shop window as he walked across the small, sunlit parking lot and disappeared down the street.

"Hard times." I shook my head sadly.

"Maybe," John Ogle said, looking at me like I'd just passed gas at the dinner table. "But stealing is still stealing."

Chapter Twenty-Seven

Home Grown Forensics

"Oh, Mom, please!"

"Kara, you are not going to use that black dust in my house."

"But we have to dust for fingerprints."

"The answer is no."

"Kara, listen to your mother," Ken Kibble said flatly.

Detectives Kibble and Ogle and I exchanged glances. We knew when not to cross the line.

"Let's check the windowsill, maybe they left prints there," Amy suggested.

"Ken, do you remember which bucket we found under the window the other night? Maybe that has some prints on it."

Ken thought he could find the bucket, so he and I went to the garage.

"I've decided against a handgun," he told me as he rummaged through his 5-gallon bucket collection.

"It's a big step."

"So is divorce." He smiled weakly.

"What's plan B?"

"I'm looking at motion-detection lights. I think that's the way I'll go. I want to get an idea of cost first. And I can get a better system if I install them myself."

"With all the pruning you've done, that should do the trick. If you can keep the bad guys on the outside, you won't need a gun on the inside."

We found the bucket and joined the girls. A thin layer of black powder from the fingerprint kit covered most of the lower casing around Kara's bedroom window. They were gently pressing clear tape to the sill and lifting it off.

"We found prints!" Kara said.

Amy pointed to either side of the windowsill where the black powder stuck to the sill in noticeable patterns.

"They're latent," Kara explained. "That means we couldn't see them before we dusted, but they were there." She had obviously been reading the documentation that came with the kit.

"God! It looks like a whole hand, all four fingers." I looked more closely at the prints on the right.

"Most of them are smudged, but these are perfect." Kara beamed.

"We need to label them." Amy said. "It looks like whoever left them used the sill for support."

"It does! For balance when he was on the bucket," Kara exclaimed, then pointed. "See. Right hand here and I bet these smudges over here are his left hand."

"Well, you kids have fun," Ken said. "I'm going back in the house to learn about motion detection."

"We will," we all replied.

"And I hope you're going to clean that off when you're through," Ken said to Kara.

"We will. I promise," Kara answered for the team.

We dusted the bucket too, and lifted several prints. Most of them were smudged, but we decided it was important to be thorough. And we needed the practice. And who knew, they might come in handy.

"Your dad doesn't smoke, does he?" Amy asked.

"No. He used to a long time ago, but not anymore."

"Then I wonder how those got here." Amy pointed. On the ground next to the foundation were two cigarette butts. They had white filters.

"Here." Kara handed Amy a small plastic bag. "Put them in this evidence bag."

"Let's go back to Bobber's," Amy suggested when we were done. "We need to make a plan for what to do next."

"What about cleaning the black stuff off the house?" I asked.

Amy and Kara looked at each other.

"Would you do that for us, please?" Amy asked.

"Please! The hose is on the patio," Kara said helpfully.

Turns out Karen Kibble had the right idea: not in my house you don't.

It took forever to get the black crap off the windowsill. It didn't wash off just spraying it with water. Wiping it with a wet rag only pushed it into the cracks in the paint. I finally had to ask Ken for a brush and scrub it off. I was afraid that by the time I finished, Amy and Kara would have the mystery solved.

I didn't have to worry. When I opened my gate and walked into the back yard, they were standing in the opposite corner half hidden behind a couple of rangy rhododendrons.

"Why are you over there?" I asked.

"You said you couldn't find your shovel to help Ken?" Amy asked back.

"We're investigating a crime scene." Kara pointed at the ground.

"Yeah, it wasn't in the garage," I answered Amy. "What crime scene?"

I walked over to see what they were looking at. My shovel was leaning on the fence next to a mound of dirt maybe three feet across. I could see where the sprinkler system over time had worn away the dirt. The lower portion of a dog's leg was washed clean. It was Shaman.

We just stood there, all three of us. Nobody said a word.

"I think it's Shaman," Kara said finally.

"That explains the missing shovel," I said.

"And the missing dog." Amy looked at me.

"We should check the shovel for prints." Kara said.

"Absolutely," I said, returning Amy's look. "We need to settle this once and for all."

"We should," Amy said. She picked it up by the blade and we followed her to the deck.

She and Kara set to work.

"A fingerprint kit? You think this is funny? CSI: West Broadway?" We turned. Monica was coming across the yard. "I know what you're up to. You're destroying evidence, that's what. What?"

"We found Shaman," I said.

"He's dead, isn't he? I can tell. I knew it. You killed him."

"I didn't kill your dog."

She glared at me. I glared back. I don't remember seeing either Amy or Kara standing on the deck next to me. My peripheral vision was totally gone just like in a gunfight.

"Bobber couldn't have killed Shaman," Amy said.

We both looked at her.

"Why not? He hates Shaman. He hates me."

I opened my mouth, then I shut it before the words could get out. They wouldn't have done any good.

"When did Shaman disappear?" Amy asked her.

"When Robert left town."

"That's right. No Robert, no Shaman," Amy agreed. "But we know Bobber really did leave."

"So?" Monica asked.

"Now we know Shaman stayed here."

Monica's head jerked like someone had pulled a jar of honey off her nose. "Oh," she said slowly.

"Right." Amy nodded. "Why would Bobber leave town and not take the evidence?"

"Right. That's stupid," Monica agreed slowly. "Even for him."

"We have prints." We turned to Kara. "There's a lot of smudges, but I got three good ones."

She had lifted three prints from different locations on the shovel handle and put them on the cards from the forensic kit.

"You should work for the F.B.I.," I said.

"Now we have to get comparison prints from everyone we know," she said.

"That's stupid. If the killer isn't someone we already know, we still won't know who it is." Monica stopped, puzzled.

"We'll know who didn't do it," Kara told her.

"And the prints we can't identify," Amy said, "those will be the killer's."

Kara got out her inkpad and, one by one, took our fingerprints.

"I don't want to see Shaman," Monica said suddenly. Her eyes were filled with tears. "I want to remember him the way he was."

Frankly, that was the Shaman I didn't want to remember, but then I didn't want to see Monica cry either. Call me squeamish.

"I'll make him a coffin," I offered in a moment of weakness.

"A coffin won't change anything. My dog is still dead."

"You can give him a proper burial."

"A proper burial," she repeated. "That's it! We can have a funeral with drums."

I sighed. Don't ever do that again, I scolded myself.

Monica left to make funeral arrangements. I thought she might thank me, but she didn't. Amy and Kara left to collect more comparison prints from the neighbors. And I was left with Shaman.

I took some extra cedar fencing and made a nice looking coffin. Then I took a couple of plastic leaf bags, my shovel, and the garden hose out to wash the dirt off the corpse. The sprinkler system had helped preserve the body, but not much. It was still pretty ripe. I didn't spend a lot of time doing an autopsy. It looked like blunt force trauma to the head as they say on TV, but that was about all I could tell. I double-bagged him and put him in his coffin. Then I trimmed a heaping bunch of sprigs from my lavender plants and added those to the mix before I put the cover on and screwed it in place.

Death is always sad, even a dog's, even one you didn't like.

"I've been where you're going and couldn't get in. So I hope you have better luck with St. Peter."

It was as close to a prayer as I could get.

Chapter Twenty-Eight

Hot Night

In the shower, I tried to wash Shaman away, but the soap couldn't clean my memory. I toweled off and put on clean clothes, then retreated to the deck with the phone, the frame I'd bought at the mall, and the pictures of Amy's fish. The deck wasn't any cooler. It would be a hot night. I laid the three photo prints out above the frame and tried to decide which would look best framed, but all I could see was Vicki holding them the other night, telling me I was a breast man.

The more I studied the pictures, the more buying the picture frame looked like a waste of money. It was a nice fish, but the picture was more suited to a men's calendar than a personal gift.

I got a cold Corona from the fridge and drank about half of it. It didn't help; it was that hot. I rubbed the cold bottle across my forehead. I didn't know who was working with the Kibbles on their break-ins, but I had Detective Cadanki's business card, so I called him. It rang a bit, then flipped over to voice mail. I tried to talk but nothing came out. I couldn't think what to say. Hey, I caught Vicki wearing Kara's underwear, neener-neener. That was burglary, not the type of stuff Cadanki was interested in. So I hung up and realized I should have told him I'd found Shaman.

I thought about calling him back, but called the Calloway's instead. I wanted to know who was working Nancy's assault, thinking it might be Cadanki, trying to make some connection between all these pieces floating around in my mind. But no one answered there either.

I set the phone down and stared at the pictures. I shook my head. It wouldn't work. I had the receipt for the frame. I'd take the damn thing back and be done with it.

The phone rang. I thought at first it was Cadanki calling me back on caller ID, but it was John Ogle.

"Hey," John said. "Guess what?"

"What?"

"Ed Grissom's boat is back."

"How do you know?"

"How do you think? I called him and asked."

"Clever. You should be a detective."

"I was, it ain't that much fun."

"Did you tell him you know who took it?"

"Yes, I did." John sighed. He sounded weary, like he was remembering the old days, not the good old days, the frustrating old days.

"And?"

"He doesn't want to cause any trouble. He's just glad it's back. And he's got a story to tell his brunch group, so he's willing to let bygones be bygones."

"What about you," I said. "What does this do to the guide thing?"

"It doesn't change the fact that we could use another guide," John said.

"You know what I mean." I poked.

"I'm not going to rush to judgment, if that's what you're talking about." John sounded kind of stung. "Anyone can get in a bind and make a bad decision. Suppose some yahoo at Animal Control decided he had enough evidence on you? He could tag you with aggravated animal abuse in the fist degree, that's arrest without a warrant."

"I'd get out because of the over-crowding," I countered. "What are you going to do about Jimmy Dean?"

"I'm going to wait."

"You're waffling."

"I never waffled a day in my life," he shot back.

"Then what are you waiting for?"

"I'm waiting until I get my report."

"I gave you my report. You didn't seem that interested."

"Not your report. I know he can row a boat."

"Then what report are you talking about?"

"I got to thinking about those tattoos. They sounded an awful lot like prison tats."

"He got them in the army. So did Floyd."

"I'm not saying he didn't. I just want to know what I'm getting into," John said, trying to sound sage. "I still have friends in the business, you know."

"What business?"

"The FBI business. He's doing me a background check."

"FBI? Well, I guess you do have people."

"I told you I had people."

"I hope you treat them well."

"We need to talk about that." John coughed.

"Why?"

"I said you'd take him fishing."

"Oh, I get it. Just let me know when you get the report." I smiled and hung up.

I went back to looking at the three photos, trying to decide which one would look best.

"Such a serious look," Amy said, coming through the back gate. Even in a tank top and shorts she looked overdressed for the heat. "What are you thinking?"

"That your uncle is a crafty devil."

"Mind?" Amy moved to the fridge, lithe as a cat, and helped herself to a Corona. "You're not thinking of framing those photos, are you?"

"No, ma'am. That was just a passing brain fart."

"Let's go again. I'll wear a fishing vest."

"You'll probably want to destroy these." I handed her the photos. "In case you ever run for president or something."

She took each photo individually and tore it in half and then in half again. She took the pieces to the kitchen and put them in the trash. I followed her in with the frame.

"Wasn't there another photo? I thought you took four," she said.

"You're right. I think I did."

We went into the front room. I didn't bother with the lights; it was still too hot. We just sat on the couch in the deepening shadows, close together. It made it even hotter, but in a good way. I set the frame on the coffee table, picked up the camera, and turned it on. We flicked through the images together. I deleted each in turn: one, two, three, four. Amy's bare skin glistened in the light of the camera's LCD.

"I printed them all. Maybe it fell on the floor or something."

I got down on my hands and knees to look under the couch. Amy slipped to her knees and started feeling around the edges of the cushions.

"Anything?" she asked.

I reached up, felt her hip, and pulled myself up. "If you have a whole bunch of dust bunnies, is that a warren?"

She turned to me and I put my other hand on her hip and pulled her closer, our hips touching.

"Is it hot in here? I feel like I'm melting."

I watched Amy's lips move as she said the words. They were inches away and all I could focus on. When they stopped moving, I kissed them.

I probably should have done an after-action drill, but instead I kissed her again.

Chapter Twenty-Nine

Matchy Matchy

The phone rang while I was making breakfast for us.

"Karen and I are going to Portland for the day," Ken said. "Kara's staying here, but with all that's been going on, we don't feel good about her being by herself. Can she stay at your place?"

"Sure. Actually, this will work out great. There's more detective work for us to do."

"Detective work?" Amy asked between sips of coffee.

"The next episode of CSI: West Broadway." I placed two plates of scrambled eggs, toast, and bacon on the table. "Fingerprint forensics."

"Right. We need to match known prints to latents."

"That and your uncle said Ed Grissom's boat is back."

"The stolen boat?"

I nodded and gave her the short version of Jimmy Dean's visit.

"So, if we dust the boat," I concluded, "we may get more prints."

"But we're not looking for boat thieves. Besides, Jimmy Dean admitted he took it."

"Not latent prints, known prints. We need them for our library."

Amy looked doubtful.

"Come on, it'll be fun."

We cleaned the dishes, then lingered on the deck in the quiet morning sunshine over a second cup of coffee. Amy left to take a shower and get fresh clothes. I shaved and showered and put on a clean pair of brown cargo shorts and a white t-shirt. By the time I was done, Amy was coming through the gate. She was wearing brown cargo shorts and a white tank top.

"I guess this means we're in a relationship." I kissed her lightly on the lips. "Honey."

"I think it means mom and dad shop the twofer sales." Amy laughed and kissed me back. "Do you want to change or should I?"

"We haven't got time," I said, pulling the back door closed and nudging her toward the truck. "We have to pick up Kara. Besides, no one will even notice."

Kara was waiting for us with a small suitcase.

"Mom and I found it at St. Vinnie's. It's for the kit," she replied to Amy's inquiring look. "Nobody walks onto a crime scene with their kit in a cardboard box. It's amateurish."

She climbed into the backseat of the truck and put the suitcase on the seat beside her.

"Did you guys know you have the same clothes on?" she asked before I even had the truck in gear. "It's really freaky."

The sharp sting of Amy's knuckles hit my arm. I wondered how they could feel so sharp. She was a skinny girl. Maybe she had skinny knuckles?

I drove to the Copper John to get Ed Grissom's phone number.

John had already opened the shop. He said he didn't need me and liked the idea of dusting the boat. He also kept looking from me to Amy and back, an odd expression on his face, but he didn't say anything. Ed's sign was still posted by the door, so I used the shop phone to give him a call. He was going to his brunch session, but said we could stop by. The boat would be in his driveway unless someone borrowed it again before we got there.

As we drove cross-town Kara did most of the talking. She had overheard her parents arguing. She needed the release.

"All Dad said was that he bought a really cool motion-detection system. And Mom said we couldn't afford it and he would have known better if he'd thought to ask her first, but he didn't as usual."

I looked at Amy. Her head was turned. She was listening to Kara in the back seat.

"Dad said he would save money by installing it himself. That made Mom really mad because Dad's not too good at that kind of stuff. She actually swore. She said 'if you're so goddamn talented why don't you do more around the house.' So Dad said he just spent the whole weekend working on the yard. But Mom said if it hadn't been for you helping, it wouldn't have happened."

"That's not true," I said, looking at Kara in the rearview mirror.

"That's what Dad said. He got really mad, too. I thought he was going to throw something. I actually waited to hear something hit the wall. Mom just laughed at him and asked him exactly when was he going to install a security system. And Dad said he would make time. Mom laughed at that, too. She said it was too expensive for him to install anyhow. But Dad said it was designed to be self-installed. Mom said she didn't care. He wasn't going to install it. She said she would rather pay someone who knew what they were doing. Dad's supposed to find someone to do it."

"Is that why they're going to Portland?" I asked. "To pick up the system?"

"They said they were visiting a friend," Kara replied. "But I don't think they have any friends, at least not in Portland. I think they're going to see a marriage counselor."

"That's good," Amy said.

I nodded into the rearview mirror and left it at that.

Ed lived on the south side in a quiet neighborhood of older homes. The drift boat was in his driveway like he said.

"Is that the same boat?" Amy asked.

"I'm not sure."

It looked like the same boat, but from the truck, I just couldn't be certain. I felt rattled. I guess Kara's story did it. I was afraid of making another mistake. Like buying that stupid picture frame. I felt like Ken arguing with his wife. I felt defensive, ashamed of myself because of my faulty judgment. My breath quickened and my heart started to rev.

I felt Amy's hand on my thigh. "Park the truck," she suggested.

I took a deep breath and fought the panic back under the surface. I took slow, deep breaths. The familiar mechanical movements of breathing and parking my truck calmed me. That counselor had said indecision and panic attacks were symptoms of PTSD. I wondered if it was my own doubt, me thinking I had the symptoms, that brought them on. What irony.

We walked up the driveway to the boat, Kara in the lead with her forensic suitcase. It was the same boat. The floor was still littered with empty beer cans.

We started at the bow and worked to the stern, dusting the gunwales and other likely places where fingerprints would accumulate. When we were done with the drift boat, we dusted the beer cans. Many had latent prints, mostly smudges, but we did get several good prints, enough to make the effort exciting.

By the time we were done it was close to noon. We had a stack of maybe thirty print cards, each carefully logged in Kara's rounded, adolescent print. Three-quarters of the prints weren't any good. Either they were smudged already or they got smudged as we tried to lift them. We were still perfecting our technique. But a half a dozen were good prints, really good prints like a professional would do. All in all, we were pleased.

Before we left, I put the cans in a garbage bag and put the bag in the truck bed, not so much for evidence, but just to clean up Ed's boat from our fishing trip. I also got Ed's garden hose from the side of the garage and gave the boat a quick power wash, much to the disapproval of my CSI teammates. They wanted to dust-and-run so we could pick up lunch on the way back to headquarters.

When we got to West Broadway, Jimmy Dean's work van was parked in front of the house. It was towing an aluminum guide model drift boat. He waved as we pulled in the driveway. Kara hopped onto the deck with the forensic kit. Amy grabbed the lunch stuff and followed. I walked out to say hi to Jimmy Dean.

"What do you think?" He was grinning from ear to ear leaning out the driver's side window.

"Nice looking boat." I nodded my approval as I looked it over. The aluminum was shiny and the blue-on-cream paint job didn't have a scratch on it. The boat was brand new.

"I just stopped by so's you could see it before I ding it all up."

"They don't stay new for long."

"That's what Floyd said. He got it for me for joining his business."

"So you're really going to do that, hunh?"

"I done everything I could to get on at that shop of yours and it ain't happened."

"Good things take time."

"No they don't. Look at this boat here. That old man just took a dislike to me somehow. He was bullshitting me the whole time."

"That's not true, Jimmy Dean."

"Well if he wasn't, and it ain't happened, then it must be you," Jimmy Dean said slowly, looking at me, his smile gone. "That's what Floyd says."

"What does Floyd say?"

"That you been bullshitting me this whole time."

"I'm not a bullshitter," I shot back, returning his stare. "You ought to know that by now. So don't go sour because of Floyd."

"Floyd wouldn't lie to me."

"I'm not saying he's lying. I'm saying don't let him fill your head with some bullshit story."

"Floyd ain't like that."

"He was in high school."

"That coach wanted to keep him from going pro."

"There's your bullshit, Jimmy Dean, and you know it. Floyd got caught stealing. Coach had to throw him off the team. Floyd ruined himself."

Jimmy Dean looked at me, then looked away. "It don't matter anyhow. Floyd got me some clients and we're going down the Deschutes and party and have us some fun."

I shrugged and shook my head.

"Whose sour now?" Jimmy Dean asked and started his van like he was proving a point.

"I'm not sour," I said. "I just think you're making a mistake going in with Floyd instead of waiting on the Copper John thing."

"I ain't going to nigger down to no ex-cop no more. I'm tired of it."

"That's just Floyd talking."

"You shouldn't be so down on Floyd, boss," Jimmy Dean said, his face hidden by the shadows of the van's interior. He slipped the van into gear. "He's been trying to help you all along, you know."

"Oh yeah? Like how?"

"Let's just say you've had some problems assimilating into the neighborhood that Floyd took it upon himself to help you with."

"What do you mean?" I moved closer as the van started to roll. "You mean Monica's dog?"

"Figure it out."

189

"What do you mean?" I called, but the van didn't stop.

Chapter Thirty

Latent Prints

I watched Jimmy Dean's van turn right at the corner and disappear.

Floyd. That's when everything went to hell, when Floyd arrived. Floyd smoked. He had a Texas accent. That put him in the running as Monica's attacker. And the peeping tom smoked. It was Floyd all along.

I felt a light touch on my arm.

"That your friend, the fox?" Amy teased.

I nodded.

"Looks like he's going fishing."

"Down the Deschutes."

"For Uncle John?"

"No. For his brother. They're starting their own show."

"Good luck on that one," Amy scoffed. She took my arm and pulled me toward the driveway. "Come on, Kara's starving. We want to eat."

"He said something else."

"Yeah?"

"He said Floyd's been helping me out."

Amy stopped. We were halfway up the driveway. "Did he say how, exactly, he's been helping you?"

"No." We walked on. "He kind of left it to my imagination."

"And?"

"Well, Floyd smokes menthols. The butts are white. He talks with a Southern accent." I stopped.

"And?"

"So, I don't know if he took Shaman, but he could have attacked Monica. And he could be the peeping tom."

"Are you going to call what's-his-name?"

"I don't know. I need to think about it first."

"Bobber, this is serious."

"I know it's serious. All the more reason not to go off half-cocked."

"I think you should call."

We stepped onto the deck. Kara handed us each a submarine sandwich. She directed Amy to one chair and took the other. Two chairs and I still had no place to sit. I took my sandwich and sat on the steps.

Kara did the talking. I only half listened. I was wondering if Floyd had assaulted Nancy Calloway, too, and if or when I should contact the detective, Cadanki. I realized the answer was probably when.

"Come on, Amy," Kara said when we'd finished eating. "We have work to do."

"What about me?" I asked.

"Your job," Kara replied, "is to clean up so we have room to work."

"It would really help," Amy said with an assuring look.

I cleaned off the low table so they could spread the cards out, then picked up the lunch mess as they pulled their chairs together and concentrated on comparing fingerprints. I took the garbage to the can and returned. They were still hard at it, their heads together, like some kind of Vulcan mind-meld.

"How's it going?" I asked.

"I'm working on my window sill," Kara said.

"I'm trying to match the shovel prints," Amy said.

"Any luck?"

They shook their heads.

"It's really slow," Kara said. "We need a computer with pattern recognition."

The discussion turned to loops and whorls and arches, and the tedious process of trying to match an unknown print to a known print from the library. They lost me. Floyd kept coming to mind.

"I know I'm just the garbage man, but can I make a suggestion?"

The girls looked at me.

"Sort the library into loops and whorls and the other pattern first."

"Arches," they said in unison.

"At least that way you can compare an unknown print to prints of the same category instead of the whole library."

"That's really clever," Kara said. She sounded truly amazed anyone her parents' age could be so intelligent.

Even Amy was impressed.

"We didn't have computers when I was a kid." I shrugged. "If we couldn't play outside, we did jigsaw puzzles. That's how we did them, we sorted all the pieces, edge pieces first, then color pattern so we could find the piece we were looking for."

Kara and Amy sorted the library of known prints into whorls and arches and loops while I busied myself with the pot garden, all the while thinking of Floyd DuChien. Most of the pots were a little dry.

"You want to speed things up?" I asked, finished watering my plants.

"How?" Kara asked.

"Take a short cut."

"What short cut?" Kara demanded suspiciously, like I was breaking a rule.

"How many good prints do you have from the drift boat?" I asked.

Kara flipped through the unknown prints and came up with five. I looked them over. Three were from beer cans and could be anybody's. One was from the side of the boat I was sitting on and was probably mine. The last print was from the gunwale on the other side. There was a good chance it was Floyd's.

"Check this one," I said, handing it to Kara. "If I'm right, it should match the peeping tom's prints from your window sill."

"You know who it is, don't you?" Kara asked.

Amy eyed me, smiling.

"Colonel Mustard in the conservatory with the revolver," I replied shrewdly.

"Ow!" I said as two sharp fists jabbed into my biceps.

Kara and Amy poured over the prints. I waited. They moved the glass back and forth, pointing, talking in whispers.

"Well?" I said finally.

They looked at me. Amy shook her head and shrugged.

"Not even close," Kara said.

Chapter Thirty-One

Red-Handed

I probably shouldn't have built it up so. It was a shot in the dark. The print could have been anybody's. It was probably Ed Grissom's. But the girls were still disappointed. Sometimes you play a good game, but you still lose. Sad, but that's life. When it happened in high school, my dad wouldn't say anything. He'd just help me pack my football gear in the station wagon and drive home. What I didn't realize until much later, a year or so after he'd passed away, was that no matter where we played, the drive home always went past an ice cream store.

I felt bad about spoiling the fun, so I told the CSI: West Broadway team to pack the forensic gear, we were going on location. Kara's favorite ice cream parlor was over by campus. It featured huge scoops of homemade ice cream. It was also air-conditioned. Like seasoned politicians, we double-dipped and stayed long after we should have left.

It was a blistering mid-afternoon, the kind of heat that can only be quenched by total submersion in water. We drove back to West Broadway, got the girls' swimsuits, and went to Mount Pisgah. It was out in the country and a fork of the Willamette River meandered along one edge. There were lots of small, sandy beaches and little swimming holes to explore. We spent the entire rest of the day there, not talking about forensics or crime in the neighborhood, just swimming, sun bathing, and watching the other swimmers come and go.

I lay on my beach towel, eyes closed, feeling the hot sun bake the beads of river water off my flesh, my thoughts drifting near sleep. Amy and Kara splashed in the water, chattering like sisters, then flopped down beside me.

It was nearly dark by the time we left. We probably would have stayed even later, but Kara's cell phone rang. Her parents would meet us for dinner at the Mexican restaurant on our way home. They wanted to buy Amy and I dinner for babysitting Kara all day.

After dinner, it was dark, but still hot as a pistol. Amy and I followed the Kibbles back to West Broadway. I opened the doors and windows on a pass through the house as we made for the back deck. We took turns standing under the jasmine trellis like kids running through a lawn sprinkler.

We hadn't been doing it too long before I heard a sound like a vase or something had fallen off a countertop. It came from Monica's. I could see the side windows of her house in the gap between the back of my house and my garage. While I watched, a light flickered in one of the windows. It looked like someone was walking through the house with a flashlight.

"Monica?" Amy asked, standing beside me.

"Drum class." I shook my head. "Shaman would be barking his head off right now."

The flashlight flickered in the other window.

"Who then?"

"Don't know."

"Should we call the police?"

"They won't get here in time. We'll have to call them later. Come on."

By the time I opened the gun safe and handed Amy the shotgun, I had a plan. It was pretty simple, right out of training class: set a trap, force the burglar to surrender, call the police.

"You've got five in the tube. The chamber is empty," I told her as we went out the front door. I positioned her at the bottom of Monica's front steps. "If you see lights go on in the house that will mean I'm inside."

Amy nodded. "What then?"

"That front door is going to burst open. Step forward, yell, and rack a round into the chamber."

"But what should I yell?"

"Yell 'armed citizen, stop or I'll shoot.' That's what they tell you in training."

"Armed citizen, stop or I'll shoot," Amy repeated.

"Perfect. I'll come up behind him."

I undid the latch to the gate and moved into Monica's back yard. I looked at the windows along her house as I passed them, looking for one the burglar may have used for access. They were all closed.

The windows on the back of the house were all closed, too. I stepped onto Monica's back porch and reached for the screen door, then brought my hand back. Slowly and quietly, I racked a round into the chamber of my Glock. I'd almost forgotten. Then I tried the screen door.

It opened and I stepped forward.

I took a deep breath and put my hand on the back doorknob. It turned and I pushed the handle. The door opened slowly, like the door of a crypt, but made no sound.

I reached in, found a bank of three wall switches, and swiped them all. I winced at the brightness as the porch and kitchen lights came on. The third switch started the disposal grinding.

Left, right, no one in the kitchen, hallway straight ahead. I moved across, found another bank of switches and swiped them. All down the hallway to the front of the house lights went on.

I heard the shuffling feet before I saw them. Two guys in black entered the hallway from opposite sides, saw me, and took off down the hallway.

I raced after them. They pulled the front door open.

"Freeze, fuck-face!"

The pump on the shotgun racked a shell into the chamber.

The burglars turned back to me.

"Stop or I'll shoot." I raised my gun, then remembered the rest. "Armed citizen."

The burglars squared off in front of me. They had kitchen knives. They started to separate to come at me from either side.

Amy came through the door and poked one of the burglars hard in the back with the shotgun. "I said freeze, asshole."

"Down on the floor!" I shouted. "Drop the knives! Get down on the floor!"

"Down on the floor!" Amy kept poking the burglar with the shotgun. "Down on the floor!"

The two burglars hit the floor spread-eagle like they were skydiving.

I disconnected Monica's phone cord from the living room phone and hogtied one, then used some speaker wire I found next to her stereo on the other. I found her junk drawer in the kitchen, found a roll of duct tape, and wrapped their wrists and legs. Then I taped their mouths. They weren't going anywhere. They couldn't threaten anyone. They couldn't move and they couldn't talk.

I unloaded my handgun, then the shotgun.

"Take this stuff back to the gun safe, then call 9-1-1. I'll wait here."

Amy took the guns and ammo and went next door.

In the after-action silence, I realized I hadn't cleared the rooms in the house. Now I was unarmed. Suppose there was a third burglar. I grabbed a fireplace poker and checked each room like I should have just to be thorough.

Amy came back carrying her cell phone. "The cops will be here shortly."

I put my arms around her and looked deep into her eyes. "You're magnificent."

"I was so nervous, I forgot what to say."

"You made your point nicely."

Chapter Thirty-Two

Making a Case

John had just sat down with the paper when I got to the shop the next morning. I poured myself a cup of coffee. I could see the headline from across the room: "Broadway Bandits Busted By Matching Duo."

"Want some advice?"

"Like what?"

"Start watching the fashion channel."

He held the paper so I could see the photo below the headline. Amy and I stood arm-in-arm in front of Monica's house, frozen in the camera flash, looking disheveled, like the Bobbsey twins just back from their amazing safari adventure.

"You never know when someone's going to take your picture."

"Thanks, Coach."

John read the article out loud. The burglars were a couple of local twenty-something crackheads who had graduated over the summer from panhandling to burglary. The cop quoted in the interview talked about them on a first name basis. He made their criminal lifestyle sound oddly pastoral, like they were urban farmers of a sort, harvesting small electronics and cash from one neighborhood to the next as if it was some crop rotation program.

Around nine, Copper John regulars began streaming in. They'd all seen the Bobbsey twin picture. It was hard to miss on the front page. They wanted the details the newspaper had left out.

By quitting time, I was nearly horse and tired of hearing John tell Bobbsey twin jokes. I drove home mentally numb, my mind flashing images at random like an out-of-control slide show presentation: the two burglars coming at me, Amy with my shotgun to her shoulder, Jimmy Dean grinning, Floyd shooting his finger at me, fingerprint cards, customers laughing at John's Bobbsey twin jokes.

Maybe that's why I wasn't paying attention when I got home. I parked in the back like I do, locked the truck, and stepped onto the deck adrift deep in the white zone. All I wanted was a beer and some quiet time to think. And I had to call Cadanki, too.

I opened the deck fridge and grabbed a beer.

A woman sat forward in one of the deck chairs. My breath caught in my throat. I backed up thinking it was Vicki. Suppose she had a gun? I couldn't draw mine. I had a beer in my hand. I almost dropped it.

"I'm sorry," Karen Kibble said. "I didn't mean to startle you, but your back yard is so peaceful. I fell asleep."

"Karen," I gasped. "No, that's okay." I stood there for a moment, then sat in the other chair.

"I just want to thank you for what you did last night on behalf of our Neighborhood Watch program."

"How's that going?" I asked.

"We're still in the organizational phase. Actually, I've got to run next door. Gaia's leading us in a visioning exercise in a couple of minutes."

I nodded as she stood to leave.

"I also wanted to tell you Ken and I are getting a divorce. Kara and I will be moving to Portland in a couple of weeks. We found a place yesterday."

"I'm sorry." I stood up and shook her hand, not knowing what else to do. "I liked having you as neighbors and I'll miss Kara. There'll be no one to do our fingerprinting."

"Hopefully you won't need any more." She smiled and left.

About fifteen minutes later, Monica's drum squad started banging out a festive visioning tune, wailing as they went. It sounded like a mix of Comanche and banshee.

I was too spent to retrieve my ear protectors from the house, so I just sat there waiting for a vision. Nothing came to mind.

"Mayor here yet?" John asked, stepping onto the deck from the driveway. "After that write-up in the paper, I thought she'd stop by and give you a medal."

"Maybe she got mugged on the way over," I replied.

John grabbed a Corona from the fridge. "What's-her-name watching <u>Dances with Wolves</u> on her HBO again?" he asked, thumbing at the racket from next door.

I nodded as the back gate opened and Amy stepped into the yard followed by Kara with her fingerprint suitcase. They joined us on the deck just as the drumming stopped. I wished they'd come over sooner.

"Reason I'm here," John explained. "I was on the phone with Dick Granger."

Amy nodded like she knew who that was, but I asked, "Who's that?"

"My FBI guy. I called to see how he was doing on the report. He should have it in a day or two. Then we owe him a fishing trip."

"My time is your time," I said.

"And you must be Bobber's forensic expert." John put a hand on Kara's shoulder. "Is that your fingerprint kit?"

"Amy said to bring it, so I did."

"I swung by the station on my way over. I've got some prints for you."

"That's a little out of the way, isn't it, John?"

"Not the way I drive." John held up a couple of fingerprint cards. "From those bozos you two nabbed last night, Bernard Lamont Jessup and Douglas Thomas Hartman."

"How the heck did you get these?" I asked.

"I got people." John smiled. "I thought it might clear up some of your latents."

"Well," I said, "that's more help than the real police."

John, Amy, and I watched as Kara set up her gear and studied the prints.

"The fingerprinting is a good idea," John said. "Which one of you girls thought of it? I know it wasn't Bobber."

"Kara," Amy said. "It is a good idea. And adding known prints to the library is really helpful."

"That's the problem," Kara agreed. "We don't have a lot of known prints to compare the latents to."

I nodded my head, agreeing that we needed more prints for our library. It must have loosened something in my brain because I had an idea. It was so sudden and so unexpected that I snapped my fingers.

Amy and John looked at me, waiting.

"Just thought of something." I headed for the kitchen. I thought I had Vicki's prints.

In the kitchen, I opened the door under the sink and tugged the garbage container out. Vicki had handled the fishing pictures. Her prints would be all over them.

"Bernard Lamont Jessup's prints match a latent from the Calloway's backdoor," Kara announced.

I found the pictures under the breakfast garbage. They were in 2-inch squares. I'd forgotten that Amy had torn them up. Plus they were covered with eggshells and coffee grounds.

I went back onto the deck.

"Well?" Amy asked.

"Brain fart." I shook my head.

"I've got another match," Kara announced. "Douglas Thomas Hartman to Monica's back doorframe."

"That solves the burglaries," Amy said.

"Yeah, except for my dad's camera and my thong," Kara said. She was sitting at the low table, fingerprint cards spread before her. It reminded me of the coffee table in the living room. Vicki had been there, too.

I ran into the living room and lifted the morning's newspaper off the coffee table. Underneath it was the first picture frame. Even at arm's length I could see a thumb print the size of Texas on the glass where Vicki had held it the other night.

I brought it back to the deck and handed it to Kara.

Amy reached into the fridge and handed John and I each a beer as we watched Kara lift Vicki's thumbprint and card it.

"It's a tented arch," she said approvingly as she studied the print. "Our first tented arch."

"So what's so good about a tented arch?" I asked.

"Only five percent of all prints are arches," Kara said.

"It increases the probability of a good match," Amy explained.

"Yeah." John poked me with his elbow. "Don't you know anything?"

Kara thumbed through the unknown prints and extracted a single card.

I sipped on my beer. I didn't want to finish before Kara had made the match. I was afraid, if I did, somehow there wouldn't be one.

"I've got it!" she said like a client hooking into a big fish. She handed Amy the magnifying glass. "Take a look."

Amy looked at first one print, then the other. "Sure looks like it to me."

Amy handed the magnifying glass to me so I could look for myself.

I looked at the print from the picture frame. I could see the grooves and ridges of the print patterned like sharp, A-frame pup tents, one on top of the other. Then I looked at the latent print card. It looked the same to me.

I read the label. It was a print from my shovel.

Chapter Thirty-Three

Backyard Bondage

"Vicki buried Monica's dog?" Amy asked, frowning. "Vicki?"

"Vicki, your underwear gal?" John asked me.

"The one who stole my thong?" Kara asked.

"Hard to argue with a tented arch." I dropped the cards on the table.

"But why'd she bury him in your back yard?" John asked.

"Don't know," I thought about what Jimmy Dean had said. "Floyd's idea of a joke?"

"DuChien," Amy said, playing with the idea. "That's French for fox."

"He's clever, if that's what you mean," John said.

Personally, I was thinking DuChien might be French for elephant and this was Floyd's payback for getting him kicked off the football team. Regardless of what Jimmy Dean said, Floyd wasn't helping things.

"It's a shame he came back," I said.

"Jimmy Dean?" John asked.

"Floyd," I said. "Jimmy Dean was doing just fine without him."

"Blood's thicker than water," John said.

"It's still a shame."

"And how's that figure with the other two?" John asked.

"Hartman and Jessup." Amy supplied the names.

"Yeah, the Broadway bandits you busted," John said.

I shrugged.

We kept picking at it as we finished our beers and Kara packed up her kit, but came to no conclusion other than that Vicki and Hartman and Jessup were all crackheads.

"Do all crackheads know each other?" I wondered. "How does that work? Do they have a sign, a secret handshake or something?"

"They could buy from the same source," John said. "One of them could be the source for that matter."

Next door, Monica's drummers started pounding again, pulsing like a toothache in the sultry evening air. John and Kara left. Amy and I went inside. I opened the doors and the windows while Amy placed the fan in the front doorway to get a draft going, but the air was too thick with heat to move and we retreated to the deck again.

It was too hot to think and too noisy to talk, so we just sat in the deck chairs sweating. The thumping next door began to pulse, beating through the gathering dark like a giant heart. Maybe holistic drumming did have healing powers, I wondered, listening. When it finally stopped, the quiet seemed especially loud. The stars seemed especially bright. Maybe all the drumming had cleared the air. I hoped it had cleared the neighborhood malaise.

Then again, maybe it was just the heat. Or maybe all that banging had affected my senses.

I thought about turning on the kitchen light to give a little background lighting to the deck, but didn't. We just sat there. It was completely dark on the deck.

"God, I'm just exhausted," I said finally.

"Me too." Amy reached for my hand. "I keep wondering why, but think of it. Last night at this time we were catching criminals."

"Yeah, you're right. I wonder how Batman and Robin do it night after night."

"Maybe that's why they're super heroes."

The crickets stopped. A little while later, they started again.

"Funny how they do that," I said. "They all start and stop at the same time."

"Yeah. Does something disturb them and they stop?"

"Maybe they stop to listen."

"Listen to what?"

"I don't know. Other crickets."

"Maybe they just get tired," Amy said, unconvinced.

The crickets started again.

"Everyone really likes your mister," Amy said idly.

"I think I should patent the idea, the magic mister."

I went to the trellis. Amy followed me.

"What do you think about another row of hose?" I asked. I took the roll that was lying there and cut off a piece.

"Where?"

"Across the back. Right here. Stand there." I ran my finger across Amy's lower back. "Stand still, I want to measure."

"I can't, it tickles."

"I said stand still." I took the piece of hose, wrapped her wrists behind her, and tied her to the trellis.

"What are you doing, silly?"

"Stand still. I'm inventing."

I cut another piece of hose and tied one to the existing hose network at about the height it would go. I crouched and reached behind Amy, trying to fish the hose across her back from one hand to the other by feel.

Amy squirmed and pressed herself into my face. She smelled like coconut and baby powder.

After a while I forgot about the hose and lifted her tank top.

"What are you doing?"

I pressed my lips into the sweaty skin above her naval.

"Oh, Bobber," she said in one tone, then in another. "Suppose someone's looking?"

I pushed the tank top higher.

"Wait, I hear something," she said.

"Crickets."

"No, really. I heard something."

I undid the button on her shorts.

"What are you doing?"

"Looking for crickets."

I stripped off my t-shirt and pulled the front of Amy's tank top over her head. I undid my belt and let my shorts fall. Amy stepped out of hers.

She had locked her legs around my waist and the poor jasmine was shaking like in a windstorm when we heard the noise again. We stopped. We listened, motionless.

"What was that?" she whispered.

I listened, nothing. "Crickets," I whispered and started in again shaking the jasmine.

Another sound. We stopped. It sounded like the gate latch. We looked in that direction, frozen in place.

The flash from a camera lit up the deck like heat lightening.

Before we could move, the gate slammed. Footsteps crossed the alley. They echoed down the apartment house walkway. On 10th Street, an engine roared to life and the transmission clunked into gear.

"That's Floyd's van," Amy whispered standing, throwing off the hose on her wrists.

We pick our clothes off the deck and stood there as naked as Adam and Eve, holding them in front of us like fig leaves.

"It's Vicki," I whispered. "It's got to be. Her or Floyd."

"But why? Revenge for the other night?"

"Or just revenge."

We retreated into the darkness of the house leaving the back yard to the crickets.

Chapter Thirty-Four

Mug Shots

I opened the paper next morning half expecting to see our picture splashed all over the front page again, the photo from last night. Thank God it was a different photo. The headline was succinct: "Brew Pub Robbed, Brewer Beaten, Waitress Missing." The picture was from a high school yearbook, a headshot of a pretty blonde girl smiling. It was Fancy.

Amy read the article aloud while I fixed breakfast.

Someone had robbed Ray's brew pub last night, probably after hours as Ray and Fancy were closing it down. What actually happened was a matter of speculation at this point. Ray was in a coma, beaten there and left for dead. Fancy was missing and presumed abducted. Her full name was Fancy Ann Hollister. She was a senior at the University majoring in Business. She was well liked by her classmates. Her debit card had been used twice at ATMs shortly after the robbery to empty her checking account.

Just as we were finishing up, the phone rang. Amy picked up, talked a little bit, then replaced the receiver.

"Now we've got two things to do," she said.

"What besides find the picture?" I asked from the sink.

"That detective, Cadanki, just invited us to an exclusive viewing."

"Viewing of what?"

"Mug shots."

Amy didn't have any classes until afternoon, so I called John and told him I'd be a little late. I locked the house and we drove downtown to the police station.

The receptionist at the front desk paged Detective Cadanki.

Cadanki appeared almost immediately. He was younger looking than I remembered, with the nervous energy of an habitual coffee drinker. He introduced himself again, smiling and chewing gum with sharp, ferret-like bites. His eyes were unnaturally wide open as if he had new contact lenses, but I couldn't see them when I looked.

He led us back to a small room with a table and chairs, sat us down, and opened a binder he was carrying.

"I caught the Fancy Hollister case," Cadanki explained.

"It was in the paper this morning," I told him.

He scanned through the binder. "Notes from the Calloway case. I just want to check a few things. See if there's any connection."

I wasn't much help. My memory hadn't gotten any better. After about twenty minutes he shut the binder and we moved to a slightly larger room. Nancy Calloway was already there. She was looking through a stack of photos.

"You guys all know each other, right?" Cadanki asked.

"Yeah, hi Nancy," we both said.

"Hi Bobber, Amy. Long time no see." Nancy looked sad and worried both.

"I've got another batch over here just for you." Cadanki pointed to a table and a couple of chairs. "Take your time." He turned in the doorway. "No cheating." He smiled. "Just kidding." He worked his gum several quick bites and disappeared.

The stack of photos was face down. I flipped them over one by one, playing Russian roulette looking for a familiar face. I had one in mind. But we went through the whole stack and only recognized Hartman and Jessup and they were already in custody.

"What's the matter?" Amy whispered. "You look disappointed."

"I was looking for Floyd and Vicki," I whispered back.

"So was I."

Nancy looked up, wondering what we were whispering about. She smiled, then went back to studying her photos.

"Maybe I read too much into what Jimmy Dean said," I whispered even quieter.

"Maybe, but Vicki's fingerprints were on the shovel and she had Kara's thong."

"I'll tell Cadanki while we're here."

"Don't you dare."

I looked at Amy.

"Not until we get that picture back."

I nodded. "Gotcha."

Cadanki returned a short time later and we told him we'd struck out. Nancy said she'd struck out, too. She was disappointed that none of the photos looked familiar. I could tell she really wanted one to look familiar.

"I thought there might be a connection to the Hollister abduction," he said and looked at Nancy. "You're about the same age and height. Both have connections to the West Broadway neighborhood, that sort of thing."

"Sorry I couldn't be more help," Nancy said.

"No problemo. We have to turn over every stone." He smiled, working his gum three or four times in rapid succession. "Department policy. Thanks for coming in."

He walked us out to the front desk, thanked us again, and we left.

"That was a complete waste," I said, starting the truck.

"Civic duty," Amy replied. "Look on the bright side. We've got one item checked off our to-do list and it's not even noon."

I turned west on Eight Street. It was tree-lined and shady, big old shade trees.

"Any idea how to pursue the other one?" I asked.

"Call Jimmy Dean and ask him is he knows where brother fox is."

"Can't. He's fishing, remember."

"We can drive by his house. See if Floyd and Vicki are there."

"He was over on Friendly, but I think he moved when Floyd showed up."

"We could drive by anyhow," Amy said, not giving up.

"Why, if we know he's not there?" I asked.

We were passing through an area where the well-kept owner-occupied homes gave way to rentals and cheap apartments that nobody seemed to care about. Grassless yards were cluttered with last year's leaves and piles of junk, like blight on otherwise fair skin or rot on the fabric of society. The cars parked along the street looked abandoned. Some of them probably were.

"Well, maybe we'll just get lucky," Amy said brightly.

"Ever the optimist," I said automatically before I realized she was pointing down the street.

A dark panel van was parked askew, one tire up on the curb strip, in front of a rundown fourplex.

"Floyd's van," I said.

I pulled to the curb and parked. We were maybe five cars away.

"What now?" Amy asked.

"Check the van." I unbuckled my seatbelt and opened my door.

"Check it for what?" Amy asked, unbuckling her own seatbelt and opening the passenger door.

"Crickets." I walked down the street at a fast pace.

Amy followed, almost running down the sidewalk. "Crickets? What about crickets?"

I tried the driver-side door. It was locked.

"Try the sliding door."

"It's locked," Amy said.

The driver's window was down a bit, like a smoker would leave it. I looked in, but the van was too dark. I glanced up and down the street. I'm not sure why, it just felt like the right thing to do. I reached my arm in, pulled up on the lock, opened the door, and climbed in.

The back of the van was set up like a service vehicle with racks of pigeonholes from floor to ceiling on the driver's side. Aside from that, the interior looked like the inside of a pup tent after a bear attack.

Amy knocked on the slider and I two-stepped over the transom and cranked the door handle. The door rolled open, Amy got in, and I closed the door.

"This looks like Kara Kibble's bedroom," she whispered.

We started sifting through the van's contents, gently, like there might be rats or snakes. Amy held up a shoebox. It was full of iPods and cell phones. I found an envelope with credit cards, several dozen. I had started looking at the names when I heard a voice outside the panel door. Amy crouched as if to hide.

"I got you a present." It was Vicki.

"What, another damn thong?" Floyd didn't sound happy.

"No, not another damn thong," she mocked. "Something you'll really like."

"How do you know?"

"You'll see."

I put my hand on the door handle to steady myself.

"I don't want nothing but some cigarettes." Floyd was grumpy, impatient.

"It'll only take a second. It's right here in the van."

I held my breath.

"And smokes is right in that store. And getting them will only take a second. Then you can give me your present."

I could feel Vicki put her hand on the outside handle.

"It's worth it," she teased. "It's a picture of that girl you like."

"You already gave me the one where she's holding that fish with her titties showing."

"You ain't seen this one. It's her and that friend of Jimmy Dean's."

"So?"

"So you'll see. It might even be worth some money."

Vicki tugged on the handle once, twice, three times, but I held it in place.

"Shit!"

"What's wrong now?" Floyd whined.

"Never mind, it's locked."

"Well come on then, God damn it! You're just wasting my time."

I watched through the front window as they walked down the block to the little corner market.

We started pawing through the stuff in the van: a small flat-panel TV, a pile of men's clothes, a couple of CD players, an Xbox, an electric drill. The pigeonholes behind the driver's seat that should have been full of electrical parts were mostly full of women's underwear.

"Here it is!" Amy whispered. She held up an expensive-looking digital camera.

"Let's get out of here."

I locked the door behind us and we ran to my truck.

As we drove past the little store, Floyd DuChien came out tearing the cellophane off a package of cigarettes. He picked one out and handed the pack to Vicki. It was a pack of menthols. The cigarette in his mouth had a white filter.

Chapter Thirty-Five

Personal Pix

I parked the truck in the driveway and we went in the front door.

I opened the windows to let some fresh air in. Amy took a seat on the couch and turned the camera on. I could hear it making little boinking noises as she pushed the buttons.

"Here it is," she said, relieved. "The last one taken."

I nodded, looking at Amy. "What's wrong?"

"It's disgusting!"

"Vicki?" I sat beside her.

"No, not Vicki. The picture!" She rolled her eyes. "Guys are such morons."

"Let me see."

"No, I'm deleting it."

She hit the delete button. The camera boinked, and the picture was gone.

"Better see what else is there."

"That's creepy, it's like being a voyeur." She handed the camera to me. "You do it."

"If we watch a horror movie, will you hide your eyes then ask me what's going on?"

"Did Uncle John tell you that?"

I took the camera. The controls were like on my camera. The review function was a rocker, pressing one side reviewed from the end back to the beginning, pressing the other reviewed from the beginning forward to the end. I could never remember which was which, but I had a fifty-fifty chance of getting it right. I pressed.

The camera boinked.

"You pressed the wrong one." Amy sat beside me. "You're starting from the beginning.

"You said you weren't a voyeur."

"Well, if I wasn't, I wouldn't fit into the neighborhood."

The image that lit the LCD screen was Ken and Karen Kibble. They were leaning against a wooden railing. Behind them was Sahalie Falls on the McKenzie River.

Boink.

Kara petted a llama. Karen stood nearby smiling at the camera. The scenery looked like somewhere around Sisters, Oregon. The road there was up the McKenzie Highway. Sahalie Falls was on the way.

Boink.

Vicki was sitting on a beat-up couch. She was lighting a crack pipe for Douglas Hartman. Bernard Jessup was smiling at the camera as he waited his turn. Beer cans and a mostly-empty bottle of Jack Daniels littered the coffee table in front of them.

"Ah, now we're getting somewhere," I said.

Boink.

"Oh my God!" Amy exclaimed.

The camera's LCD showed Vicki in profile, nude from the waist up, giving somebody a blowjob.

Boink.

Vicki, smiling for the camera, lay naked on the couch. One leg dangled to the floor, the other over the back of the couch, a naked guy between them.

"Hartman," I said.

Amy nodded. "Jessup was probably taking the picture."

Boink.

The guy with Vicki was Jessup.

"There he is," I said. "They're taking turns."

"Holding the camera?"

"Holding Vicki." I felt the sharp sting of Amy's knuckles on my upper arm. How <u>did</u> they get so sharp?

Boink.

Two co-ed's in bikinis. They were down by the river near the footbridge to the stadium sunbathing while they studied.

Boink.

Amy's breath caught.

It was Fancy Hollister shot from across the street using the camera's zoom. She was delivering pints of beer to one of the sidewalk tables at the Duck Tail.

Boink.

Vicki was talking with Fancy on a sidewalk. It looked like they were somewhere in the neighborhood, but I couldn't tell where.

"Oh my God!" Amy whispered. "They were stalking her."

Boink.

A picture of a teenage girl in a messy bedroom. She was nude except for her panties. Her back was to the camera and she was bent slightly looking in a dresser drawer.

"That looks like Kara's room," Amy said. "Oh my God! That's Kara."

"It was taken through her bedroom window," I said recognizing the view.

Boink.

The first picture reappeared. Ken and Karen leaned against the wooden railing with Sahalie Falls in the background. It was a relief.

"Oh my God!" Amy said again.

I went to the kitchen and got the phone. I had Rick Cadanki's business card pinned to the corkboard by the refrigerator. I dialed the number.

"Violent Crimes, Cadanki. How may I help you?"

"Detective Cadanki, this is Bob Mulligan on West Broadway."

"That was quick," Cadanki joked. I could hear him working his gum. "Did you solve my case for me?"

"No," I said, "but I think I've found something that might help."

"What's that?"

"A camera. It was stolen from the Kibbles down the street on the Fourth."

"Cool. I'll transfer you to the property guys. They'll want to talk to you."

"Wait," I said before he had a chance to hit the transfer button. "There's more."

The line was quiet but I could hear gum crackling as it was chewed.

"There were pictures on it, pictures of girls, Kibble's daughter undressing in her bedroom, some college girls sunbathing, pictures of Fancy Hollister taken with a zoom lens."

That got his attention. "And where'd you say you found this camera?"

"I didn't say."

The phone line went quiet again. Amy came into the kitchen behind me. Cadanki chewed his gum three or for times in rapid succession, then stopped.

"Yeah, okay. I'll be right over." He hung up.

I followed Amy out to the deck. She handed me a cold Corona from the fridge.

Chapter Thirty-Six

The Profile

Cadanki was a good detective. By the time he left with the camera, he had pretty much wheedled all the relevant facts out of me. He knew the fourplex where the van was parked and asked to borrow the phone.

"Yeah, Cadanki here," he said into the mouthpiece. "I need some backup at a fourplex on West 8th and Monroe." He listened for a moment. "Is that the best you can do?" He listened. "I'm going right over. I'll meet them there. Tell them I'm the one with the badge." He hung up.

"I ask for backup," he answered my unasked question on his way out the door. "They give me Taylor and Smalley."

"Good luck," I said and locked the door behind him.

I retreated to the deck with Amy, but before we could get comfortable, John called from the shop. He said he had something to show me. He was alone in the shop, so I figured he was just bored. He wanted to close early and convinced me it was too late for lunch, even a late lunch, and we should go directly to happy hour hors d'oeuvres and cocktails. I gave in to police pressure.

Amy rolled her eyes as I hung up.

I grabbed her by the hand and pulled her with me into the kitchen. By the time John showed up we had a pretty good assortment of cheeses, crackers, shrimp cocktail, and crudités spread on the low table on the deck.

"I'm starving," John said, stepping onto the deck from the driveway.

"It's all yours, John." I swept my hand over the food display.

"I hope you don't mind." He smiled. "I brought my own cracker."

He pointed to a person following him, a military-looking man about his own age, but a bit taller and more muscular. The man was wearing a lightweight sports jacket with a wad of rolled papers sticking out of the right pocket. "This is Dick Granger. He's the guy I was telling you about."

Amy and I shook his hand. It was too early for martinis, so I made everyone gin and tonics.

We chatted a bit at first. Dick took his sports jacket off and laid it carefully over the back of his chair. On his right hip, he was packing a 1911 semi-auto in a worn leather holster with an FBI cant.

"Go head, Dick," John prompted. "Tell them what you found."

"John gave me a name to trace." Dick took the wad of papers from his jacket and read. "Jimmy Dean DuChien. I had an address on Friendly Street, a phone number, and the understanding that the person in question was a veteran."

He looked at John. John nodded that the information was correct.

"I started with his military records. The military doesn't like to release its records, but they will verify enlistment if you pester them. Which I did."

He looked at us, smiling slightly.

"Mr. DuChien has never served a single day in any branch of the armed forces."

"You mean he lied?" I asked.

"You hard of hearing?" John looked at me like I was embarrassing him.

"I'm saying I found no evidence he was ever in the military. If he told you otherwise, I think he was being less than honest."

"I see," I said, thinking John was right. I should get my money back on that training. It hadn't made me more aware. I was bending over being honest with Jimmy Dean and he was bullshitting me all along.

"So where was he if he wasn't in the service?" Amy asked.

"James Dean DuChien, alias James Dean, alias James Fox was mostly in and out of prison." Dick took a sip of his gin and tonic and read from his notes.

"Juvenile record?" John asked.

"Sealed," Dick Granger replied.

"What does that mean?" I asked. "Sealed?"

"It means some judge was trying to make a silk purse out of a sow's ear," John said.

"A judge sometimes orders a juvenile's records removed from the public record and held," Dick explained. "They usually do it to give the delinquent a second chance at rehabilitation if he's from a bad environment. But like John said, this appears to have been a waste of time."

"So you couldn't get his juvenile records," John prompted.

"I pieced together his early history through his family. That's what took me so long. Let's start with his daddy, James Duane DuChien: substance abuse, alcohol and meth mostly, spousal abuse, a few assault charges, petty theft. Pretty much a drifter type, manual labor jobs, in and out of jail, always small-time stuff. Mrs. DuChien wasn't much better. Alcohol and meth, welfare fraud, solicitation, and pimping. At one point, she had a couple girls working for her.

"All the people I talked to remember Jimmy Dean as an enterprising kid. He just picked the wrong enterprises: possession and sale of controlled substances, extortion, and receipt and sale of stolen property being his favorites."

He took another sip of his drink, letting the DuChien family portrait sink like sediment deeper into my mind.

"Tell them about the older brother," John said.

"Floyd." Dick nodded. "Substance abuse, alcohol, vandalism, burglary, shoplifting, petty crimes mostly, like the old man. Then there's menacing, battery, and a number of assaults. He's more the brawn of the two. Jimmy Dean's the brains." He looked at his documents. "And he doesn't like dogs."

"Who doesn't?" I asked. "Floyd?"

"Jimmy Dean."

"How do you mean?"

"Wherever the DuChiens moved, dogs disappeared." Dick looked at each of us in turn. "People I talked to put Jimmy Dean as their odds-on favorite."

"Why's that?" Amy asked.

"Two dogs have disappeared here, Dick," I said. "And we have a peeping tom."

"So I hear." Dick Granger looked at John, then back to Amy and I. "Jimmy Dean has a history of voyeurism. He may be your peeping tom."

"That explains that," Amy said.

"It might," Dick cautioned. "Remember this is all hearsay in a court of law."

"Tell them the rest, Dick," John said.

Dick went back to his notes and picked up where he left off. "They lived here in Eugene before daddy moved them to Texas. He died in a car wreck there about a year later. Alcohol was a factor. Here's an interesting note. Floyd got kicked off his high school football team. Stealing."

"That's not hearsay," I said. "It was at South. I was on the team when he did it. We knew someone was breaking into the lockers. Turned out it was Floyd. I was the one who told the coach."

"Floyd know that?"

I nodded. "That's when they moved."

"Good thing. He assaulted a kid in Texas who informed on him; same thing, stealing from lockers. That was his first adult arrest."

"Tell them about the guide service," John prompted.

"That's the contributing and pimping." Dick Granger ran his index finger through his notes. "The boys were big on the bass fishing scene in Texas, had their own guide business, very popular. Turns out it was a cover for a prostitution ring."

John looked at me and raised his left eyebrow.

"Jimmy Dean took the fall," Dick continued. "Pled guilty to a reduced charge, served his time, and came up here, probably to get away from Floyd."

"Floyd's here," I said.

"That's because he jumped bail in Texas."

"Floyd's talking about starting a guide service," I said.

"Yeah." Dick nodded. "John told me."

"He's in an apartment on West Eighth Street," Amy said. "We saw him this morning."

"Brother Jimmy is probably with him," Dick said. "They trashed the place on Friendly Street a couple of weeks ago and skipped out."

"You tell the cops you know where Floyd is?" John asked.

I nodded. "Cadanki's there now."

"I know Cadanki," Dick said to John. "He's pretty good at it."

"He went over to ask Floyd's girlfriend about a stolen camera," Amy said. "There was a picture of Fancy Hollister on it."

"That's how I know Cadanki. I'm the FBI contact on the Hollister case." Dick relaxed back into his chair. "I'll call him later, see what he's found out."

"See," John said, wagging his finger at me. "That's why I didn't let you rush me."

"I wasn't rushing you." I flushed.

"Say, John said a neighbor kid of yours was into fingerprints." Dick Granger pulled two cards from his papers. "The DuChien brothers'. For her collection."

"Recruiting for the bureau?" Amy asked.

Dick Granger smiled. "Doesn't hurt to try."

I called the Kibble's. Karen answered.

"Is Kara there?" I asked. "I've got some prints for the library."

"No, she's out with her father." Karen didn't sound happy about it.

"Can you have her give me a call when she comes back?" I asked. "Tell here I've got a definitive set of Floyd's fingerprints."

"Does she know who Floyd is?" Karen asked.

"She should. Floyd DuChien. Jimmy Dean's older brother, the guy who wanted to guide for the fly shop."

"Your electrician friend?"

"Yeah," I said, feeling odd about admitting it.

"Ken had him install our security system."

Chapter Thirty-Seven

Professional Job

"Karen, will you be home for a little while?" I asked. "I'd like to show it to some friends."

"Sure, I'll be here," she said, a little surprised.

"Great," I said and hung up.

"What's going on?" John asked. From the looks I was getting, I could tell he was speaking for the group.

"Jimmy Dean installed the Kibble's new security system."

"Nothing I have indicates he has any training as an electrician." Dick Granger held out his notes.

"Maybe he picked it up," Amy suggested.

"When? In between prison terms?" John scoffed.

"He's got a business van," I said.

"Could be a cover," Dick said.

"That's probably why his business is so slow." John looked at me. "He's doing more peeping than working."

"You don't know that," I said, still trying to match the Jimmy Dean I knew to the one in Dick Granger's profile.

We had eaten most of the hors d'oeuvres. I put the remnants in the big fridge in the kitchen. John and Dick were still speculating on the DuChiens. I tried to picture Jimmy Dean as the criminal they described. I thought of his big Texas smile and redneck charm. They weren't part of his personality; they were part of his criminal toolkit as false as fake ID. It made me angry.

It was a little after seven when I rang the Kibble's doorbell. The lights were on in the house, but no one answered. I knocked. Still no one came to the door. I tested the doorknob. It was unlocked.

I stood there for a moment, uncertain what to do, then poked my head in. The living room was a mess, like someone had been wrestling or fighting. The couch and chairs were pushed at odd angles. It looked like the other night at the Calloway's.

I was about to send Dick and John around back, when Karen walked into the living room.

"Bobber." She waved us in. "We're out back. Excuse the mess. The toilet stopped up and flooded everything. I told Ken it was acting funny, but as usual he refused to do anything until it was too late. We're letting things dry out. Come on in."

She led us to the patio. Ken and Kara were there.

"Got to love old houses," I said to Ken.

"Kara, I think Bobber wants to talk to your father. Let's do the dishes and straighten up in the living room."

"But Mom!"

"Do what I tell you."

"Karen said the DuChien's installed your security lights," I said after Kara had reluctantly followed her mom into the kitchen.

Ken nodded. "I've seen him around most of the summer. He was driving by, so I stopped him and asked for a bid. He said since I knew you, he'd give me a deal. And he did, a really good deal."

"Maybe too good," John said.

"This is Dick Granger, a friend of John's." I nodded to Dick Granger.

"Mr. Kibble." Dick shook Ken's hand, then gave him the Reader's Digest version of the life and times of Jimmy Dean and Floyd DuChien.

"Geez." Ken looked from Dick to me. "So you think they're criminals? I mean, they look a little down on their luck, but I knew the one was your friend, Bobber. That's partly why I gave them the job. Help them out. But criminals?"

"We're not talking youthful indiscretion either," John said. "We're talking lifestyle preference."

"I just can't believe it," Ken said.

We all looked at him.

"I checked their work. I did." Ken pointed around the yard. "They did a first-rate job. Your friend told me exactly what they'd do and that's what they did. He even put in an extra ground. And I tested everything before they left. Even Karen was satisfied."

I looked at the kitchen. I wanted to be sure Kara wasn't coming out. "One more thing, Ken. Amy and I found your camera this morning."

"Really? Thank God, I won't have to buy a new one. Where was it?"

"In Floyd's van."

239

Ken Kibble frowned.

"We don't know how it got there. We looked through the pictures. That's how we knew it was yours. One of them was Kara. It was shot through her bedroom window."

"That son of a bitch." Ken's knuckles whitened as he squeezed his hands into fists. "I don't care what Karan says. I'm buying a gun. I'll shoot that bastard if he ever sets foot on my property again."

"I'd be careful about making statements like that," Dick Granger said. "They have a funny way of coming back at you. I'd hate for that to happen."

"Ken, we don't know how the camera got in Floyd's van," I repeated. "Or who took the pictures."

"So what are you saying?" Ken looked at us, frustrated and annoyed at the same time. "I mean, the toilet's overflowing. I paid a crook to install my security system. Someone's taking pictures of my daughter. And you say don't get upset?"

"I talked to the police earlier," I said, trying to calm him down. "They went over to pick them up, Floyd and his girlfriend."

"How do you know it's no good?" Ken waved his hand angrily at the security lights. "The camera's been gone for weeks. Those pictures could be weeks old. Did you check the date stamps before marching over here with your accusations?"

I shook my head. I'd forgotten all about that.

"I thought not," Ken said.

He had a good point. I had assumed that since Fancy had been kidnapped from the Duck Tail Sunday, the picture of Kara must have happened after that. But it could have been taken any time since the camera was stolen. That was weeks. The security system was brand new.

"When did you have the lights installed?" Amy asked.

"Last week," Ken said. "Wednesday, I think. I talked to them and they said I either had to do it right away or wait until after some fishing trip."

"I can call Cadanki," Dick Granger said. "He'll have the date stamps on the pictures. But while we're here, Mr. Kibble, would you mind if we took a look at your lights?"

Ken went into the house, touched something on the wall, then stood in the doorway. Behind him, Karen was drying her hands on a dishtowel.

"Okay, it's armed," Ken said. "Move around."

Sure enough, as soon as we took a step, stadium-quality lighting exploded into life, chasing every shred of darkness off the patio and far out into the back yard.

"So what do you think now?" Ken asked. "Did I get my money's worth?"

The lights were big halogen barn lights, four of them across the back of the house and three more along the side of the garage nearest the yard. They were all on. They lit the back yard bright enough for a track meet.

Without the zebra plant, there was nothing to hide behind. A peeping tom would be in plain view.

"Is that the window where the picture was taken?" Dick asked walking toward it.

"That's it," I said, joining him.

He was looking down. At his feet were several circles cut into the soft bark-o-mulch. They were the rim size of a 5-gallon bucket.

"Can you shut the lights off for a minute, Mr. Kibble," Dick said. He turned to me. "You got a flashlight? I want you to trace the wiring. I'd do it, but my eyes aren't any good after dark anymore."

"I've got one," I said, thinking of my tactical flashlight, "but not on me." I'd left it at the house again.

Dick pulled a small light from his pocket. "Try this."

Jimmy Dean and Floyd had used standard outdoor wiring. At least they knew that much, I thought. They'd also done a good job of running the gray vinyl wire so that it was as inconspicuous as possible, another nice touch. The lights themselves were securely mounted under the eaves so they were out of the weather and relatively tamper proof. It looked like a professional job. I traced the wiring from light to light. The wiring went into the last light at the far corner of the garage. That should have ended it, but more gray wire came out, ran across the back of the garage, and disappeared around the other corner.

"What's this wire, Ken?" I asked.

He looked where I pointed. "Oh, that's the second ground wire. I'll show you."

We followed him back to the house. He got a screwdriver and unscrewed first the switch plate, then the switch from the switch box.

"Basically, it's an extra wire on the switch," he explained pulling the switch out so we could see where the wires attached. "It's this one. It prevents electrical shock from coming back up through the switch."

"That's not a ground, it's a 3-way switch, Ken," I said.

I flicked the switch on and went back into the yard. The security lights came on again, lighting the yard like a football stadium.

"You have a step ladder?" I asked.

"Yeah," he said and brought me a small aluminum ladder from inside the house.

I set it up where the Kibble's fence joined the garage at the corner. The gray wiring ran across the back of the garage, around the corner, and down the fence post. When I looked over the fence, I could see an electrical box a couple of feet down the post. It had a switch.

When I flicked it, the lights went out.

Chapter Thirty-Eight

Reason to Carry

When I got to work the next day, John was already there, mumbling as he pawed through our inventory of wading boots.

"You seen a size thirteen?" he asked. "I thought we had a size thirteen."

"Ain't seen it, John."

We kept pretty busy, mostly summer tourists buying flies for the McKenzie and other local rivers. The hot weather had really brought on the caddis hatch. Quill-bodied PMDs were working well, too.

I called Rick Cadanki around noon. He wasn't in, so I left a message. I wanted to update him on Ken's security lights. I also wanted to verify that he really did have everyone in custody that needed to be there.

When I got off the phone, in the absence of any paying customers, John had returned to pawing through the boot boxes.

"What're you doing?" I finally asked.

"Looking for boots for Dick for when you take him fishing. He's a size thirteen. I thought we had a size thirteen in stock."

"We did."

"I don't recall selling it."

"Neither do I."

"Well somebody did. I've looked high and low and can't find it." He was beginning to sound like Ken Kibble. "Either that or somebody stole it."

"I know a couple guys do security systems." I picked up the phone to make another call.

I watched John's ears for the first signs of steam venting. Instead, he grunted and stood up holding a boot box.

"Never mind, wise ass. Here it is."

I dialed the Kibble's. Kara picked up.

"Hey, I just called to see if your dad needs any help removing that switch."

"No, Mom made him hire an electrician. They're doing it now. Amy's here. She and Mom and I are going swimming."

"Oh yeah? Where?"

"Back to Mt. Pisgah. Wanna come?"

"I'll see what I can do." The shop door opened and I turned to see who it was. "Hey, I gotta run," I said and hung up. "Detective Cadanki, I didn't know you fished."

"Yeah, all the time." His sharp teeth worried a piece of gum. "I fish for bad guys."

"Having any luck?"

"No. With the overcrowding in the jail." He worked his gum a bit. "It's all catch and release anyhow." He stopped chewing long enough to show a quick, teethy smile. He stepped into the shop, his eyes darting over the walls like he was figuring trajectory angles in a crime scene.

John came over. He was pressing the boot box against his chest like it was the last life jacket on the Titanic.

"You're Ogle, right?" Cadanki asked. "Granger's friend?"

John handed me the box. "Don't lose it again." He and Cadanki shook hands.

"I need to chat with you guys in private." Cadanki jerked his chin at the only other person in the store, an old guy examining each package of dubbing on the fly tying rack.

"That's just Harry," John said loud enough for Harry to overhear. "Bobber won't let me to get a dog, so I got Harry instead. He's part of the scenery."

Harry flipped John the bird without turning around.

We went into the office. John and Cadanki sat down. I stood in the doorway where I could see the front door.

"Floyd DuChien is still at large." Cadanki worked his gum, looked for our reactions.

"What about Vicki?" I asked.

"Her too."

"What happened?"

"Don't know." Cadanki scratched the tip of his nose. "But here's my guess. They walk back from the store. Vicki goes to show Floyd the pictures. She can't find the camera. The red flags go up and they split."

"Ain't that the shits." John shook his head.

"So where are they?"

247

"Don't know." He reached into his jacket pocket, took out his notepad, and riffled through the pages. "You'd think a couple of rednecks in a college town would stick out more. Just kidding."

Cadanki found the page he was looking for.

"Vicki Sheenan hails from deep in the heart of Texas. Yee-haw, howdy partner. A doctor's daughter, former honors student, cheerleader."

"That doesn't sound like our Vicki," I said.

"There's more." Cadanki showed his teeth. He flicked to the next page. "She meets Mr. Floyd DuChien. He's out on bail at the time. A whirlwind courtship ensues after which time she drops out of school and goes to work fulltime for Mr. DuChien."

"What kind of work?"

"Call it sales." Cadanki wiggled his eyebrows. "Of sex and drugs."

"Where's Jimmy Dean during all this?" I asked.

"He was a guest of the state. Granger told you about the Fox Brothers guide service, right? Miss Vicki was the downfall. She was underage at the time." Cadanki worked his gum, flipped through his notes. "Here, you'll like this," Cadanki assured us. "I had a chat with your pals, Hartman and Jessup, aka the Broadway Bandits. They were a wealth of information. Native Eugeneians. They even belong to a cooperative."

"How's that?" John asked. "What kind of a cooperative?"

"A criminal cooperative," Cadanki bared his teeth at his little joke.

"Let me guess. They work for Floyd DuChien."

"Right on!" Cadanki pointed an index finger at me like it was a gun. "Granger said you were a quick study."

"Yeah," John agreed. "Dick was going to give you one of those McGruff Crime Dog badges, but he was all out."

Cadanki studied us like he was wondering whether to bet or fold. He decided to bet.

"Okay," he said, idly shaping his gum into a ball with his front teeth. "So I tossed that dive on West Eighth with Taylor and Smalley. They wanted to see how it was done. We found a few rounds of 9mm ammo, so we think Floyd's probably armed."

John nodded his head.

"Floyd might therefore be dangerous, so listen up, Mulligan. Granger says he can be vindictive and so far you've lied to him, played his baby brother for a fool, and tried to rape his girlfriend."

"Whoa, there." I tensed against the doorframe. "That's not what happened."

"I know." Cadanki raised his hand, chewing his gum slowly. "I'm just quoting the banditos quoting Floyd."

I leaned back. "Oh."

"I assume, Ogle, you have a firearm."

John nodded. "My service revolver. It's in the desk."

"Mulligan." Cadanki looked at me. "I could see you were carrying the other day. Like you are now."

"I have a concealed carry license."

"I know, I pulled your record." He held up his hand like he didn't want to argue. "My opinion? I think you're smart. That's good and bad."

"How's that?" I asked.

"It's good you can protect yourself."

"What's the bad part?"

"You might have to."

Chapter Thirty-Nine

House Call

I got religion in a hurry. I carried wherever I went and practiced dry-fire drills on the back deck. My guess was that Floyd and Vicki had skipped town. That would explain why I hadn't heard from Jimmy Dean about his fishing trip. He'd made his decision. Blood was thicker than water.

Saturday, I had a trip on the McKenzie. It was a good day for fishing, but not spectacular. #12 Caddis Pupae and #14 Comparaduns worked well. On the way back to the shop, I turned on my cell phone. I had one voicemail, probably John wondering where I was. I pulled into the parking lot at a country store to answer it.

It was from Rick Cadanki.

I called his number and he picked up on the first ring.

"Cadanki."

"This is Bob Mulligan."

"Mulligan, where are you?" He sounded both angry and relieved, like a parent getting a call from a late child.

"Walterville. I had a trip today."

"I'll meet you at the Copper John."

"You're the only one I know still makes house calls."

"No, there's one other guy does it," he said and hung up.

I stared at the dead phone. It didn't sound like he was joking, but I didn't know him well enough to tell.

A half hour later, I found out.

I had to park the truck and boat down the street and walk back to the Copper John. The place was surrounded by yellow crime-scene tape. Police cars parked at odd angles with their doors open. Uniformed cops and detectives milled in and out of the shop. An EMT unit sat off to one side, its lights flashing.

The closer I got, the faster I walked and the harder my heart pounded. A uniformed cop moved to stop me at the tape.

"Crime scene," he said. "Step back."

"I work here." I tried to push past. "I need to go in."

Cadanki spotted me and ran over. He nodded to the cop and raised the tape for me to duck under.

"What's going on?" I stammered. "Where's John?"

"Ogle's alive. He's at the hospital now. His friend from the other day wasn't so lucky," Cadanki said as we walked toward the front door. "Put you hands in your pockets. We're not finished dusting yet."

"What happened?" I repeated.

"Shooting," Cadanki said, worked his gum. "Looks like a robbery gone bad. The cash register's empty. Follow me. Be careful where you step."

He set off at a slow, studied pace.

"Looks like Ogle is at the cash register. The assailant attacks him with some kind of edged weapon."

I fell in behind. We marched along a route of foot-long blood smears.

"Ogle retreats to his office. The assailant follows still on the attack."

My heart beat in my ears like the sound of distant drums.

"Ogle makes it to his desk and reaches for his gun."

John's gun drawer was pulled out, the gun gone. In its place, only bloody prints like drying finger paint. On the wall, two eighteen-inch mandalas spattered in red.

The drums grew near, a familiar cadence. I couldn't place it at first, but then I did. I lay in the convenience store dying. The Black Watch marched behind me to the gates of heaven. Everything got dark, everything except the red mandalas.

"Hey." Cadanki put his hand on my arm and squeezed. "Stay with me. I need you to tell me, is there a safe in here?"

My eyes shifted reflexively to the small rug under the office chair.

"I need you to open it and check the contents."

He rolled the chair off the rug and I got down on my knees like I was going to pray. I folded the rug back, careful not to touch the blood. I lifted the floor panel, worked the combination, cranked the handle, and swung the door open on silent hinges. The inside was as peaceful as a sepulcher.

Cadanki's gum crackled in my ear as he chewed, his head almost resting on my shoulder as he peered into the floor safe. "So it looks like just the till money." He stood up. "And the gun."

I stood up, my eyes resting again on the slowly drying mandalas. "They shot him with his own gun?"

"Yeah." Cadanki admitted sadly, almost a sigh. "Looks that way."

He walked me out to my truck. While I unhitched the boat trailer, he called River Bend Hospital. John was in Intensive Care, but he was conscious. He wanted to see me. Cadanki put his hand on my shoulder as I opened the driver-side door.

"I got to finish up here," he said. "Then I'll be over. Drive carefully."

I sat in my truck, watching Cadanki recede in the rearview mirror. Sitting in the familiar interior felt novel, like I hadn't been there in a couple of years. On the way to the hospital, I tried not to think too much, but my eyes kept seeing blood.

Amy was sitting in the waiting room with Bill's wife, Carol. They were holding each other. Bill was with Dick Granger standing by the window. Everyone looked like they had been tear-gassed.

I shook everybody's hand and held Amy in my arms while her tears melted slowly into my shoulder. We hadn't been like that more than a few minutes when a nurse arrived in a rush of air like she was pneumatically activated.

"You must be Bobber," she said. "He's been asking for you."

She motioned for me to join her. We walked down the brightly lit hall. I felt like I was in a bubble. People moved on either side, but no sound, no noise, no contact, like walking into the kitchen of a busy restaurant with the audio off. I remembered, years ago, walking down the hallway to visit my dying father. There were a million things I wanted to know, but I couldn't think of any questions to ask.

"In here." The nurse flicked a thick curtain out of the way and pushed me gently through the opening.

Everything was white and silver and seemed to shine. John was lying in the bed; only his bandaged head and his skinny arms were visible, like there wasn't that much of him left.

"Hey," I said.

He motioned with his hand. I took it and sat gently on the edge of the bed.

"The bastard shot me with my own gun."

"Yeah." I nodded, remembering the blood mandalas. "Otherwise you could have got hurt."

"He came at me with a knife first." John stopped for a moment, out of breath. "It's tough when you get old."

"Who, John? Who did it?"

"You should get your money back from that class." John's lips twitched in a smile, but he was too weak to laugh. "What's-his-name, you're buddy's brother." Then he got serious. "Promise me you'll stay away from him, the both of them. You take care of Amy. Let Dick and that kid, Cadanki, handle the rest of it. Promise me."

"I promise, John," I told him, but it was a lie. I wanted to shoot Floyd DuChien on sight.

"Let them do it," he repeated like he could read my mind. "It's the only use you'll get from your tax dollars."

We sat there a moment. The room smelled faintly of chemicals and seemed oddly quiet for a place labeled Intensive Care.

"I think I'm done for." He looked at me, worry in his eyes. I didn't recall ever seeing that expression in them before. He looked old and frail.

"You'll be okay, John."

"I'm scared, Bobber." He gripped my hand in both of his. "All those years as a cop, it never bothered me. Now, I'm scared. Funny how that is."

"Hey, he only shot you twice." I smiled and squeezed his hands. "You'll be okay."

"I'm scared, Bobber. I'm scared I'll die."

"You'll be okay."

"You were shot. You've been there, where I'm going. What's it like?"

"Fish as long as your arm," I told him. "And they hit any fly you throw."

"I like that." He smiled. "I like that." He shut his eyes and seemed to relax a moment, then opened them. "Do I need a permit?"

I shook my head. "Nah. It's a private reserve. I know the guy at the gate."

"Hey," John said before closing his eyes. "You got people."

"Yeah, I got people."

He drifted off, so I let go his hand and backed away. My eyes burned. It must have been the tear gas.

Chapter Forty

Sunstroke

Cadanki was in the waiting room. He wanted to see John, but the nurse wouldn't let him wake John up. I told him what John had said.

"Your friend, DuChien." He clicked his ballpoint pen like it was the button on a detonator. "Is a real pain in the ass."

I was going to tell him Floyd wasn't my friend, that he was my friend's older brother, that I didn't even like him, that he was a bully in high school, but all I said was, "Yeah, he is."

John never woke up. He died Sunday evening.

Monday morning Amy and I went down to the shop. The place didn't look that bad until you noticed the dried blood. Then, it looked like a butcher shop.

"I can't do this," Amy said, wiping the tears from her eyes. "Take me fishing, Bobber. Please, let's just go fishing."

I looked at her like she was speaking Farsi. But I guess I speak Farsi too, because I understood. I could accept that John Ogle had died, that his spirit had left his body, but it was still too present at the Copper John. It would leave soon enough. I didn't want to rush it.

As I locked the door, I wondered if the Copper John would ever open for business again.

I towed the boat with my truck. Amy followed in the shop truck with the extra trailer. I could see John's old "Gone Fishin'" sign in the window as we left. We swung by my house. I checked my fly box for Elk Hair Caddis and threw the rest of my fishing gear in the back of the truck while Amy got her swimsuit. We made some sandwiches, then packed the cooler.

"Do you think Kara would be interested?" I asked.

"I'll call her." Amy picked up the phone and pushed the Kibble's speed dial number. "Kara, hi it's Amy. Want to boat the McKenzie?"

I could hear Kara squeal from across the kitchen.

"Ask your mom." A moment later Amy said, "Oh, that's too bad. Maybe next time." She listened. "Yeah, we can go to Mt. Pisgah. Yeah, next week."

"She has to go to Costco with her mother," Amy said, hanging up.

We were half way out the door when the phone rang.

"Maybe Karen changed her mind?" I looked questioningly at Amy.

She picked up the phone. "Hello?" She listened. "He's right here." She handed the phone to me. "Detective Cadanki."

I took the phone from Amy and held my hand over the mouthpiece for a moment. I looked at her remembering my promise to John about Floyd DuChien, about letting Granger and Cadanki handle it. I'd still shoot him on sight. She smiled at me unaware.

"Yeah?"

"Mulligan, I just want to say how sorry I am."

"Thanks."

There was silence on the other end of the phone line. Then I heard the chewing start.

"I also want you to promise me you won't do anything stupid."

"Like what?"

"Like anything that would make use of your concealed carry permit."

"Like shoot Floyd DuChien?"

"That would be a good for instance."

"Then are you going to shoot him?" The anger rose in my voice. I couldn't help it. "Because he needs to be shot."

"Couple things, Mulligan." I could hear him working that damn piece of gum again. "Because you were Ogle's friend. One, don't talk like that, especially now, especially to a cop like me. Two, the citizens of this fair city pay me to find the bad guys, and I'll find this one. Three, and you didn't hear me say this, I hope I get the opportunity."

I didn't say anything, thinking John was a cop; Cadanki is a cop. I bet he would. Then I said, "I appreciate that. Anything else?"

"Just that we found out Floyd's van was stolen, so were the plates. Big surprise."

"But you haven't found him?" I asked.

"No, but it's not because we haven't been looking. He either knows how to disappear or he skipped town."

"Seriously?"

"Seriously. I'm thinking he's up in Washington. He can't go back to Texas."

I thanked Cadanki again and hung up.

"Who's going to shoot Floyd DuChien?" Amy asked right away.

"Whoever finds him first," I said, then, remembering Cadanki's advice I added, "Just kidding."

"Sure. What else did he say?"

"Just that Floyd stole the van," I said as we grabbed the cooler and headed for the truck. "Cadanki thinks he left town."

"What about Jimmy Dean?"

"He didn't say."

"What do you think?"

"I think if Floyd's still here, I may get my money's worth."

She looked a question at me that I didn't answer.

We dropped the shop truck and its trailer off at Armitage Park and drove upriver to the Bellinger Landing boat ramp. It would give us a longer float and more time to fish and enjoy the bright, sunny day.

The McKenzie did not disappoint. It ran cold and clear, turning from Doug-Fir green to turquoise and white as we slipped passed the occasional rapids that gated our passage like a slalom course. And all the while, the sun overhead smiled on our upturned faces and warmed our shoulders like the hand of the Heavenly Father.

I picked one of my favorite holes for lunch. It had a nice place to beach the boat, a flat rock by the river to picnic on, and a long, wide eddy line that you could undo like a zipper one fish at a time. It was John's favorite spot.

As I watched Amy work the water, my thoughts drifted into their own eddy and circled there in the quiet backwater.

I didn't know how long it took to get to heaven, but I was sure John Ogle would get there. Once he stopped putzing around the shop. John was a good man; he'd get in. I was glad for that. I realized I wasn't mad at St. Peter anymore. I don't know why. I just wasn't. I don't know when it happened. It just did. Where that anger went, I didn't know. It just went. It got absorbed somehow in my life like my pot garden absorbed water from the magic misters.

I was glad I had the chance to talk with John in the hospital. I did that right. Dying is a lonely experience. Even though there are people and activity all around, they don't concern you. Dying is a personal affair. I hoped what I said had eased John's way through it.

I watched Amy fish, backlit in gold by the afternoon sun.

"St. Peter," I whispered. "I'm sorry I called you a dickhead. A friend of mine is coming your way. He's a good man. I'd appreciate you letting him in. I'm sure you'll hit it off. I know you both like to fish." Then I said, "It would mean a lot to me if you let him in."

By the time I packed the boat, we had caught most of the fish in the river, swam side-by-side like Tarzan and Jane, and baked like cookies on the flat rock. Life was good again.

Amy was rowing when we got to Barclay's.

"This is where the infamous thong incident happened," I said, pointing.

"This is the place, hunh?"

"BLM is going to put one of those historic markers here just so's everyone will know."

"You want to stop and take a couple of pictures?" Amy made like she was going to turn the boat and pull into the eddy. "Before they restrict the access."

"No, I forgot my thong."

"Well, shucks then."

We slid passed the opening to the back eddy, Amy keeping the boat in the current just outside the eddy line.

I was smiling at Amy when I noticed something far back in the still water of the back eddy. It was a drift boat. What caught my attention was the splashing of the oars, like someone was learning to row in the quiet water.

"What's the matter?" Amy asked, turning her head to look in the direction I was looking.

"I must have sunstroke." I wondered if it was a stress reaction, but knew it wasn't. "That looked like Vicki rowing Ed Grissom's drift boat."

Chapter Forty-One

Barclay's

We took out at Armitage. I wanted to call Cadanki right away, tell him I'd found Vicki. Floyd would be there, too. But my cell phone was in the other truck. Amy hadn't brought hers. So we loaded up the boat and gear and scooted back up river. The road went right passed the turn-off to Barclay's. I kept thinking Floyd was there and about what John had said. It kept repeating in my mind like a drum beat. Stay away, take care of Amy. let Granger and Cadanki handle it.

I watched the gap in the guardrail draw near. Floyd was right there. All I had to do was drive in, pop him center mass with a couple of rounds, and one in the head for good measure, and it would be over. I could take him by surprise. He'd be dead before he hit the ground.

My hands tightened on the steering wheel until they ached. Sweat burned my eyes. My heart raced until it hurt to breath. I rubbed my chest and turned to Amy. She was looking out the window, her arm pushing against the airflow, enjoying the ride.

My foot stayed pressed to the gas pedal and we sped past the opening. Let Granger and Cadanki handle it. That was John's wish. I took a deep breath and glanced at Amy again. Then I put my arm out the window into the caress of the warm, summer air.

By the time we got to Bellinger, it was late afternoon.

I picked Ed Grissom's name out of my contact list and made the connection.

"Hello, this is Ed."

"Ed, this is Bobber from the Copper John."

"I'm so sorry to hear about John. They catch the bastard who did it?"

"No," I said, "but they're working on it. That's actually why I'm calling."

"Oh, is it?"

"Yeah," I said. "You still got your drift boat?"

"Sure do, sitting in the driveway."

"Oh."

"You sound disappointed."

"Sorry," I apologized. "Ed, would you mind checking just to make sure?"

"I suppose so, if it's important."

"Yes, it is, very."

The line went quiet. I could hear Ed walking and a door opening, then he walked back and picked up the phone.

"Son of a bitch!" he cursed into the phone.

"Gone?"

"Yup. Again."

"Thanks, Ed. I'll be in touch. I got to make another phone call."

I opened my contact list and this time picked Cadanki's name.

"Gone?" Amy asked.

I nodded.

"Cadanki."

"This is Bobber Mulligan, you got a minute?"

I heard him say something in the background. "Now I do," he said, coming back on the line.

"I think I know where they are." I told him what I'd seen at Barclay's Hole and that I'd already checked with Ed Grissom about his boat.

I could hear Cadanki working his gum, like he was thinking about it. "You ought to be a cop," he said at last. "Where you at?"

"Bellinger Landing."

"Here, I'm going to put a guy on. You tell him how to get to Barclay's Hole."

"This is Sergeant Stevens of the Lane Count Sheriff's Department."

I told him how to find the old dirt road off McKenzie View Drive that lead down to the campsite at Barclay's Hole. Then he asked how to find it coming upriver. I told him that, too. When I was done, he put Cadanki back on.

"You working for the county now?" I asked him.

"Kind of. Couple fishermen spotted a floater. Thought I'd come out and take a look."

"Fancy?"

"It crossed my mind." He chewed. "Been in the water about a week."

I held my breath.

"But it's not her." Cadanki stopped chewing. "You still there?"

"Yeah. So you're on the river too, then? Where abouts?"

"Marshall Island. Know where that is?"

"On the Willamette downstream from here."

"Hey, hear that?"

I listened to the roar of a big sled boat gunning its engine. I imagined the Lane County Sheriff's search-and-rescue boat heading upstream for Barclay's.

"That's the mounties on their way. They dispatched a couple of cruisers for good measure."

"I don't think Vicki saw us, so they should be there when they arrive."

Amy was nodding her head.

"This is good." His gum cracked like he was chewing the bones of a small animal. "This is the way it's supposed to be. They got nowhere to go, nowhere to hide. They can't run and they can't swim."

"I'll be glad when this is over," I said, looking at Amy. A quiet life in a quiet neighborhood sounded pretty good.

"You and me both," Cadanki said.

I put the phone in my pocket and hugged Amy. "Hey, you hungry?"

"Starved."

"Let's go upriver to Milly's."

"That the pie place Uncle John raved about?"

"His favorite. We can have a farewell cheeseburger and a slice of homemade pie."

We switched the boat to my truck, left the shop truck and other trailer behind, and followed 126 upriver to Milly's Pie Palace. Milly entertained us with stories while we ate and it was nearly dark by the time we picked up the shop truck at Bellinger Landing and continued on toward town.

As we approached Barclay's, even at a distance, I could see commotion. There was a lot of traffic, most of it parked in either direction along the shoulder of the road. A small parade of vehicles trickled through the bottleneck. Down below, closer to the river, the stand of oaks was lit like a three-alarm fire with flashing red lights.

I joined the parade. Amy was behind me in the shop truck, her face lit by my brake lights. When we got to the break in the guardrail where the dirt road took off, there was Rick Cadanki, standing on one side of the road. He was talking to a Lane County sheriff on the other side. They were both using flashlights to look into the passing cars. His jaw worked relentlessly. I wondered if he was actually chewing a small chunk of rubber. He saw the truck as I approached.

"Hey, how many cops does it take to arrest a redneck?" I asked him.

"Sixteen." He chewed and nodded at Amy. "If it's a girl. Don't know yet for a guy."

"What do you mean?"

"We got the girl, Vicki. DuChien wasn't there."

"What about Jimmy Dean?"

"He's on some fishing trip."

"Right, the Deschutes." I remembered. "So where's Floyd if he isn't here?"

"He figured we'd be looking for his old van, so he went off to steal a replacement."

"Peachy."

"We've been checking vehicles as they go by, but he'd have to be stupid to come back here now."

"So what are you guys still doing here?"

"We need the overtime." He looked at me and bared his teeth. "Just kidding. We got to work a crime scene when we find one. It's policy, even for the County sheriffs."

"What crime scene?"

"Fancy Hollister. They drugged her up and had her handcuffed inside an old trailer. Vicki was guarding her until Floyd got back." Cadanki read my mind. "She'll be fine once the drugs wear off. They were going to drug her for a couple weeks, then turn her out, make her a prostitute."

He leaned into the window and scanned the inside of the truck. "Habit," he explained when he saw my frown. "You packing?"

"Yeah, why?"

"Just making sure," he said. "One in the chamber?"

"Yeah," I lied.

"Good, there's a problem when you don't carry with one in the chamber."

"Oh yeah? What's that?"

"It doesn't go bang when you need it to."

Chapter Forty-Two

Funeral Deal

John's funeral was Wednesday. It was the first time I had seen Amy in a dress. She looked beautiful, even in black. I wore a suit from my previous life. After two years of freedom, the tie around my neck felt like a mustang's first halter.

Barney, the funeral home director, was a long-time customer. He fixed John up personally and his care showed. I complimented him on the job. It was the first time I had seen John in makeup. He looked like a perfect wax impression of himself. But that's the best Barney could do. He couldn't bring John back from the dead. Although the likeness was there, the soul was gone.

Working at the shop, seeing John's friends come in one at a time, I never got a good count. Seeing them at the funeral, all in the same room at the same time gave me a different perspective. John had people all right.

Bill, his lawyer friend, saw us and came over. He shook Amy's hand, then mine. "Are you available this afternoon? There's something we need to discuss."

"Your Deschutes trip coming up?" I asked, trying to remember the schedule.

"No, that's later. The fall Caddis hatch," he replied. "This has to do with John."

I looked at Amy, then back at Bill.

"I was John's attorney."

"Oh, you're that Bill!" Amy said. "Uncle John talked about Bill, his attorney, but I didn't realize that was you."

"I handle estate planning, wills, probate, that sort of thing." Bill smiled. "John named me his executor."

He handed us each a business card.

"For his will?" Amy asked.

"For his entire estate."

Bill looked at me. I nodded, not knowing what else to do.

"It's my obligation to settle his estate."

He stopped and waited for us to say something. We just looked at each other then back at him.

"Can you to stop by the office after lunch, say around two o'clock? I'd like you present when I read his will."

Amy nodded and looked at me again.

"I'll make sure," I said.

We left the funeral home for the Catholic church. Patrick, a guy I recognized from the shop, said the mass. I didn't know he was a priest. I had only seen him in waders. I think he cut some parts out for John's sake. I was glad he did.

After that, we went to the graveyard for the finale.

Amy and I stood at the grave listening to Patrick. Dick Granger came and stood on one side, chest out, straight as a flagpole, like an honor guard. Rick Cadanki stood on the other. He looked nervous, his eyes darting in all directions like he was expecting someone to pull a gun.

"We got to talk," he finally said when the service was over.

I looked from him to Dick Granger. Dick nodded to a spot off to one side.

"We had a little chat with your friend Vicki," Cadanki said, indicating himself and Dick with a flick of his finger.

"If we go light on her, she'll help us out." Dick Granger cut to the chase.

"I'm happy for you guys, but what does that have to do with me?"

"We need your cooperation." Cadanki looked at me. He wasn't chewing his gum.

"I get the same deal as Vicki?" They didn't laugh. Neither did Amy for that matter. "What kind of cooperation?"

"Surveillance," Dick explained.

I didn't get it.

"You, genius." Cadanki chewed his gum, stopped once to show his teeth, then continued. "We want to keep you under surveillance for a couple days."

"If the DuChiens stay in the area, they may try to contact you," Dick said.

"You mean try to hurt him." Amy gripped my arm as she looked at Granger.

"Not Jimmy Dean," I said.

"Why not Jimmy Dean?" Cadanki asked.

"We're friends. I was trying to get him on at the Copper John."

"You didn't," Granger said.

"And look what happened," Cadanki said.

"That was Floyd."

"You've seen their profiles," Granger said. "They're not that different."

"It's been Floyd all along." I ignored him.

"You willing to bet on that?" Cadanki asked.

"Jimmy Dean was doing all right before Floyd showed up," I said, but I was running out of steam.

"Yeah," Cadanki said, "like he was turning his life around."

I glared at him, but he just kept chewing his goddamn gum. That made me even angrier. I was angry because he wouldn't let up. I was angry at the DuChiens for coming out of the past to wreck my quiet life and take John's. But I was most angry at myself for not stopping the slow parade of events that had led to John's death, angry I hadn't shot Floyd and ended it.

"It's just for a couple days," Dick prompted quietly. "Then we'll let you go."

I looked at Amy. She smiled and took my hand.

"It couldn't hurt," she said.

"So how does it work?" I asked. "You guys follow me around twenty-four seven?"

"Yup," Cadanki chomped on his gum. "Just like on TV."

"It's pretty simple," Dick Granger said. "Most of the time you'll be one of two places, at home or at the store."

Cadanki counted them off on his fingers like it was a big number.

"We'll stake those out."

"Suppose I'm on the river?"

"We can coordinate that with the County patrol boat."

I looked at Amy. She smiled and shrugged.

"What happens if nobody comes?" I asked just for argument.

"That will tell us they've left town," Cadanki answered.

Granger looked at me. "But we're pretty sure one of them will contact you."

I looked back at John's grave. The hole was there, but I couldn't see the bottom. People were milling around saying their last goodbyes. I felt like I was jumping into something way over my head. In training, they teach you to look for a second exit when you walk into a room. That way, if you need to leave in a hurry, you've got plan B.

"Okay," I said, "but on one condition."

Cadanki and Granger shot each other glances.

"If you guys aren't around, I have the right to defend myself."

The two men shot each other another glance.

"That's fair." Dick Granger nodded.

"Just don't shoot him in the back." Cadanki smiled and snapped his gum.

Chapter Forty-Three

Where There's a Will

"Well what next?" I asked as we drove slowly out of the cemetery. It wasn't even noon yet so we had time to kill before the meeting.

"Change out of this dress and have some lunch."

I drove back to my place. The turn off Polk onto West Broadway made me think of the good old days when all I had to worry about was my house being burnt to the ground. I parked in the driveway. Amy took her heels off, jumped out, and ran over the deck and across the back yard to her apartment.

I stepped onto the deck, intent on pulling lunch stuff out of the kitchen refrigerator. Instead I loosened my tie, pulled a Corona out of the deck fridge, and sank into my Adirondack chair.

"Change of plans," Amy said, coming back through the gate in shorts, flip-flops, and a sleeveless t-shirt. "I've been invited to go shopping with Kara and her mom."

I frowned. I felt a little wounded, like I'd been shot with a small caliber slug of loneliness.

"I think they need me to referee," she explained as a car honked from the street. "It's Kara's birthday this weekend. We're shopping for her present."

I glanced reflexively at my watch. "Will there be time?"

"Yes, if you pick me up at Valley River at 1:45." Amy backed across the deck. "Kara worked it all out. I'll meet you by the cigar store. You know where that is. I'll cook you dinner," she said over her shoulder as she stepped onto the driveway and disappeared behind the house.

I finished my beer and decided it was easier to buy lunch for one than to make it. I got in the truck and started driving, but couldn't decide where to go. And all the while I could feel that slug of loneliness working inside. It must have been a hollow point; it was expanding. When I parked the truck, I was in front of the Catholic church. It was the second time in one day. I felt almost religious.

The door was open, so I just walked in. The place was empty and so quiet it hurt my ears. The only sound was the slow cadence of my footsteps as I walked down a side aisle to the candle stand.

I knelt down and stuffed a five into the moneybox, lifted the flame off one candle, and lit a new one, one of the big ones.

"St. Peter," I whispered. "Can I ask a favor? John's always wanted a dog. Can you introduce him to Shaman?"

I looked around, suddenly embarrassed that someone would hear me, but the place was empty.

"And could you give me a sign?" I stopped, too self-conscious to continue. It was a silly idea. "Please hook John up with Shaman," I said and left it at that.

I stood up like I was ending a phone call and retraced my steps to the front door. As I turned the knob and pushed it open, a dog barked. I left the church convinced St. Peter and John were both laughing at me.

I was about to put the truck in gear and head home when my cell phone rang. I fished it out of my pocket and flipped it open.

"Mulligan, Cadanki. Where you at?"

"On my way home. I was running an errand. Why?"

"Our seniors-on-patrol volunteers spotted a guy looks like he's casing vehicles for a new ride. We're going to check it out."

"So?"

"Might be somebody you know."

"Floyd?"

"Maybe."

"Where?"

"Don't worry. This is across the river at the mall," he said.

"Amy's there with the Kibbles. I'm supposed to pick her up."

"No problem. Most of the time these things don't pan out. Give me fifteen, twenty minutes. You can pick her up then."

We hung up and I started home.

I drove one block, then turned on Washington and took the bridge over the Willamette to the mall. The parking lot at Valley River Center is pretty big. As I drove around it, I saw a couple of patrol cars moving slowly down the parking aisles, but I didn't see Floyd DuChien. I parked in the front by JC Penny's, racked a round into the chamber of my Glock, put it back in the holster, and stepped out. My funeral suit would be enough of a disguise to fool Floyd if he was still around.

I started at Penny's and worked my way from store to store looking for a familiar face. I wasn't sure who I wanted to find. Amy, Kara, and Karen or Floyd DuChien.

As it got closer to 1:45, a bad feeling started working on me. The closer it got, the worse it was. I couldn't find Amy anywhere.

I was at the cigar store at 1:40. Amy wasn't there. I bought a couple of cigars just to kill some time. It was 1:45 on the nose.

"Must be hot out there," the guy at the counter said, eying me.

"It is today."

"I can't stand the heat."

"Yeah, neither can I."

He put the cigars and a small box of matches in a plastic bag and ran my card through his machine. Amy still wasn't there. It was 1:50.

I walked out of the shop and looked both ways, unsure what to do.

"You look lost," she said, coming out of the crowd at me. "Hello, it's me."

"Jesus Christ," I sighed. I'd looked right at her and not seen her. I was picturing her in her black dress. She had changed into shorts.

"Come on," she said, grabbing me by the arm. "We've got to get going or we'll be late."

We were a few minutes late anyhow, but Bill was gracious about it. He led us into his private office and closed the door. The air conditioning felt good, so did sitting in his leather armchairs. For the first time that day, I felt safe. I was able to catch my breath.

He sat on the edge of his desk and got right to business. He was the executor of John's estate, he stated for the record, although no one was taking notes. John's personal estate consisted of his house, some investments, and a small number of personal items. Everything else was tied to the business. He owned the Copper John and everything in it free and clear. Everything: the building, the contents, the lot the store sat on.

"He has instructed me to liquidate the entirety of his personal estate with the exception of one item." Bill looked up, summarizing what he was reading from the will. "10% of the liquidation amount, whatever it turns out to be, will be donated to Trout Unlimited. Another 10% will go to the Federation of Fly Fishermen. In both cases, the money is stipulated for use in local conservation projects. The remainder will go to you, Amy. You are his only surviving relative."

Amy nodded, expressionless, like she hadn't understood a word.

"Bobber." Bill looked at me. "The remaining item he left to you, his service revolver."

"The one in his desk drawer at the shop?"

"Yes, that's the one."

"I know who has it," I said. "I'll get it back."

Bill smiled, missing my point, but Amy looked at me like I had suggested lunch with the devil.

"Now as for the disposition of his business assets." Bill came to a full stop and looked first at me, then at

Amy. "He requested all the physical assets, namely the lot, the building, the inventory, the truck, the boat and trailer, as well as the value of any good will associated with the Copper John name be given equally to the two of you."

Chapter Forty-Four

New Management

Thursday morning I unlocked the door to the Copper John like I'd done a hundred times before. Amy followed me in. For lack of any solid thought to hold onto, my mind flooded with emotions, like I'd slipped off a rock into too-deep water.

"I thought I'd work for John a couple of years," I said. "I needed some down time. Get a little distance, a little perspective. I think John knew that. He hired me anyhow. Then I'd be ready. I'd feel like managing products again."

"This wasn't in my plans at all." Amy stood by the till and looked back and forth across the shop.

The shop was quiet and as lifeless as a sepulcher.

"So what next?" Amy asked finally.

I shrugged, trying to concentrate, but all I could see was dried blood. I couldn't tell if the dried blood was everywhere I looked or I was just looking everywhere there was dried blood.

"It's a good business," I said, wanting to give her an accurate appraisal. "Year round, trout in the summer, salmon and steelhead in the winter. Good mix of products, too, different price points, something for everyone. We did a lot of guided trips. Then John did a couple of group trips each winter for bonefish, someplace where it was warm. He was sharp. He knew his customers and how to market to them."

"You were in marketing. Could you run the shop?"

"I could," I answered her, "but not by myself."

"If you had one or two people, could you do it?"

"I suppose so." I looked at Amy slowly. "Why? What's going on?"

"Just an idea. Nothing set in stone or anything."

"Out with it."

"We could hire Kara. She and I could work in the shop while you guide."

"Kara Kibble?"

"Yes Kara Kibble. How many other Karas do you know?" If she were closer, I'm sure she would have slugged me with her sharp little knuckles. "She needs to get out of the house. Like you said, get a little distance. Her parents are driving her crazy."

"That's what parents are for."

"Not this kind of crazy," Amy said. "They're rehashing their entire marriage in front of her, hateful, divorce things, the kinds of things kids shouldn't hear. She needs to get away."

"You think this will help?"

"I hope a little. It will give her a place to go that's safe. And she trusts us." Amy looked at me. "Do you know why you couldn't find us at Valley River yesterday?"

I shook my head. "Were you buying underwear or something?"

"Because we weren't there. We were in Springfield at Best Buy."

"I thought you went clothes shopping?"

"Kara didn't want clothes. She wanted a police scanner."

"Really? Cool!"

"She wants to be a forensic scientist," Amy said. "That's you're doing."

"Corrupting a minor."

"So, I was thinking if you ran the shop and did the guiding, Kara and I could be employees. I'll finish my degree about the time Kara graduates and leaves for college."

"What then?"

"I don't know. We'll cross that bridge when we come to it."

"Well." I looked at Amy, knowing we'd already made the decision. "Let's get started then."

I filled the mop bucket with warm water from the sink in the utility closet. I added some chlorine and disinfectant and I started in on John's office with a big sponge. Amy gathered all the blood-spattered bags of fly tying materials and started cleaning the dried blood off the plastic.

By the time we stopped for lunch, the floor and inventory were good as new. After wiping, then scrubbing, then wiping some more, the walls where blood spatter had dried had gone from near black to pink, but they stubbornly refused to go any further. So we decided to take everything down and paint the shop.

We decided on submarine sandwiches for lunch because the sub shop was next door to the paint store.

"You know," I said, kissing Amy on the cheek as we surveyed the store's brush selection. "It feels good to build something up. All summer it's felt like everything's been falling apart."

"I know. I think I'm going to enjoy this." She slipped her arm around my waist.

"How many paint brushes do we need?"

"Hang on, I'll find out." Amy pulled her cell phone out and picked Kara from the contact list. She was home and available. Amy said we'd pick her up on the way back. "Three."

It took the rest of the day to move furniture and inventory away from the walls. I patched the two bullet holes in John's office. I'd never plastered over a bullet hole before and wondered momentarily if it required a special plaster, but the stuff I had worked. It wasn't until Friday morning that we opened the first can of paint. There was a lot of trim work to cut in around the windows and doorframes, so we started there. After a while, I switched to rolling the walls while the girls continued on the trim. We had the radio on and I could hear their voices occasionally over the music.

Eventually, I rolled my way into John's office, all the while worried that the new paint wouldn't be enough to cover the pink stain from the mandalas. The plaster had worked fine, but I couldn't shake the feeling that the paint would fail and the stains would be permanent. I did the other three walls before I did that one. Delaying didn't help. The uneasy feeling just kept getting worse.

The whole thing started with two missing dogs. Then there were two robberies. Two women had been assaulted; two bums in the park and two burglars. And the DuChien brothers, there were two of them. They'd come back like a bad stain.

I kept staring at the pink mandalas, my breath coming in quick, shallow gasps. What if the paint didn't cover the two stains? What if it couldn't? My mind raced through the litany of twos: two dogs, two robberies, two women, two bums, two burglars, two DuChiens. I couldn't hear the music in the other room. I couldn't hear the girls talking. I couldn't hear anything at all and I couldn't see anything but the two pink mandalas.

I felt like I was on the firing line. I snapped the roller up and punched it forward like I would my handgun. It didn't go off. There was only a hissing noise like something frying and the stains had disappeared. I took a deep breath and relaxed from my shooting stance.

"What are you smiling about?" Amy asked as I came out of the office.

"I'm done rolling," I said. "How are you two doing on the trim?"

The phone rang and I picked up. "Copper John's."

"Cadanki. Just checking in. You doing okay?"

"You're checking in?" I asked. "You're asking me if I'm doing okay? You're supposed to be watching. You're supposed to know. You were going to watch me twenty-four-seven, remember?"

"Look out your front door, to the right, about half a block up the street. That's it. What do you see?"

"A white four-door Dodge Ram pickup." As I spoke, the driver side window slid down.

"We call it an unmarked vehicle." Cadanki spoke into his cell phone, looking at me as he did so. He chewed his gum a couple of times. "Clever, hunh?" He bared his teeth in a smile, then the window slid up and he disappeared behind the tinted glass.

"Who was that?" Amy asked, handing me a brush and a yogurt container with paint in it.

"McGruff the crime dog," I replied. "He's ready to take a bite out of crime."

Chapter Forty-Five

Tour of Duty

I lay on my side. Moonlight streamed through the window. It washed blue and white across Amy's naked skin, like a watercolor. I marveled at the shadows created by the smooth contours of her body, the dark stubs where the faint breeze touched her nipples, the flash of light from her eyes.

"What do you think?" I asked, running a finger slowly down her breast, watching the shadow it made in her skin.

"You mean about us?" She held my hand still over her heart.

"No, should I shave my chest?"

I blocked the fist that came shooting out of the darkness like a meteor.

"Of course about us. That's really what we've been talking about since dinner."

"But we haven't really, have we?" Amy's head rustled on the pillow. "We've talked about everything else: Uncle John, the shop, the DuChiens, Cadanki."

"Yeah, even Cadanki." I sat up against the headboard. "So we should talk."

"About us."

"About us. I don't want us to just happen. I want us to decide and make us happen."

Amy didn't say anything. She lay perfectly still, only her eyelids moved. They blinked twice, slowly.

"I feel like I'm back in Iraq," she said.

"Like a war zone?" I asked slowly, unsure of her meaning, afraid what the meaning might be.

"In Iraq, you're scared most of the time, even when you don't think you're scared. Fear is what drives you. It makes you do things you normally wouldn't do."

"Cadanki and Granger will get Floyd sooner or later. We could wait if that's what you mean." I touched her forehead with my hand.

"No." Amy sat up, turned to me, and kissed me hard on the lips. "That's not what I'm saying. Not at all." She kissed me again. "In Iraq, you go charging into places you'd never go in real life, but you go because you're part of a team." She held my face in her hands, searching it for understanding.

"The other night at Monica's."

"Yeah." She sighed in relief. "I liked being part of that team."

"So did I," I said and kissed her.

We slipped down on the bed. Her cool blue skin glistened above me. And we worked with each other to release the tension of the past few days. After it was over, I sat up on my elbow next to her again, her body still glistening, and ran my finger down her stomach.

"I love you Amy Ogle," I said, looking directly into her flashing eyes.

"I love you Robert Mulligan." She returned my vow.

We didn't say anything for a while, then we started talking, making plans for the shop, real plans this time. And we made a plan to move Amy's stuff into the house and spend Saturday fixing up our new life. Then we were quiet for a while again, each thinking our own thoughts.

"Kara's such a cute kid," Amy said. "She invited me to her party tomorrow night. She's having a combination birthday sleep over and going away party. She's moving to Portland with her mom."

"Aren't you a little old for a pajama party?"

"Apparently not."

"Don't let them pump you for information about you know what." I indicated our naked situation.

"My lips are sealed."

I kissed her.

"Your lips aren't sealed," I said.

We stopped talking and fell asleep. When I woke up, Amy was already up and putting the coffee on. We shared the shower, dressed, then she took the coffee pot and cups to the back deck while I retrieved the Saturday paper. It was still early.

"You know, you could train a dog to do that," she said, handing me my coffee.

"I'm already trained. Besides, what would the neighbors think?"

We looked through the paper, each taking different sections, reading aloud what we thought was interesting. It didn't take that long to lose interest.

"Just out of curiosity," Amy asked, sipping the last of her coffee. "What kind of dog would you get?"

"Oh, something terribly incorrect. Like a pit bull."

"People resemble their dogs, you know."

I felt like celebrating, so I made huevos rancheros. We were both starving. Amy made a second pot of coffee. We were enjoying the last of that on the deck, planning the move from Amy's apartment as I tinkered with my pot garden when Ken Kibble poked his head around the truck.

"Can I ask a favor? A couple of favors?"

"Ask away Ken. I'm feeling good."

"Can I borrow your truck? I need to take a load of furniture to Portland."

"That'll take most of the day." I frowned, looking at Amy.

"I'll pay for gas," Ken said quickly.

"Oh, it's not the gas. We were planning to move some stuff ourselves."

"But we're only moving across the alley," she said. "We don't really need the truck."

I thought about it. "It'd probably be easier as a matter of fact." I turned to Ken. "The truck is yours." I tossed him the keys. "What's the second favor?"

"Can you watch Kara while I'm gone? Karen will be in and out."

"Sure. She can help us move."

Ken left with the truck, promising to send Kara down. By the time we had washed the breakfast dishes, she was there and we headed across the back yard to Amy's apartment. Kara went first, so I got to watch Amy's butt as she climbed the stairs to her apartment. Kara stopped on the landing. Amy stopped beside her; she moaned.

"What's wrong?" I asked, coming up behind them.

The door to Amy's apartment was open. The doorframe was splintered, the part that held the deadbolt was laying on the carpet where it had fallen.

I pushed past the girls, conscious that my gun was back at the house and my house was unlocked and vulnerable, wishing I was more aware, reminding myself when things happens, they happen just that quick.

The apartment looked like a dollhouse that had been thrown into the closet by an angry parent. The furniture was all topsy-turvy, Amy's clothes were everywhere.

I turned to Amy, wanting to give her a hug, but she waved me off.

"It's okay," she said, looking at Kara, then at me, then away as she wiped a finger at the corner of her eye.

I stepped further into the apartment.

Sometime yesterday, between the three of us painting the shop and me watching the moonlight paint Amy's skin blue, someone had had their own painting party. They'd used a can of red spray paint to write words like "bitch" and "cocksucker" and "wanted: crackhead whore" on all the walls.

Amy and Kara came in. Kara remained by the door, working her hands in front of her. Amy sifted quietly through the mess, recognizing one piece of clothing or another, holding it up like she was going to make a pile, but she didn't. Everything she held up was ruined. It looked like whoever it was had sat on the living room couch with a knife watching TV and, piece by piece, shredded all of Amy's clothes.

Chapter Forty-Six

Good Advice

I called Cadanki like I was ordering room service. He came quickly. He only had to drive around the block. He walked through the door of Amy's apartment and looked over the carnage thoughtfully as he took the paper off a new stick of gum, rolled it into a cylinder, and stuck it in his mouth.

"My first wife." He chewed briskly. "She used to keep house like this."

He spent about an hour, mostly with Amy, going through the apartment room by room. He wrote down all the hateful words and took pictures as well. He asked if she had lost any personal information, credit cards that type of thing. She hadn't. They were in her purse at my place. He asked if she owned a gun. She did. It was also at my place.

He looked at me like he was trying to do math in his head.

The manager of the apartments came by to see what was going on. Cadanki went after him. No, he hadn't heard anything. The apartment next door was vacant, had been all summer.

After a while, we told Cadanki we were going back to my place. The manager said he would get the doorframe fixed pronto. We looked around for something to take with us, but there was nothing to salvage.

"Mulligan, wait up," Cadanki called as we headed down the stairs.

The girls went on. I watched the tops of their heads as they walked down the sidewalk between the apartments, deep in their Vulcan mind-meld.

"I'm not liking this," Cadanki said, standing by me on the landing.

"You think it's Floyd?"

"He's on the short list. You got anybody else in mind?"

"Jimmy Dean," I said.

"I thought he was your friend."

The heat burned up my neck like a heretic's fire.

"He used those same words," I said. "He came to the shop to apologize and he used those same words. He called Vicki a 'crackhead whore.'"

Cadanki slowly chewed his gum. He seemed to be considering me rather than what I'd just said. "Jimmy Dean was fishing, remember, when Ogle got killed? It was Floyd."

"I know who murdered John Ogle," I said, the words clipped with anger. "I want to know who did this."

"Look, Mulligan, I checked him out on those missing dogs. He came up clean."

"What about his profile?"

"Okay." He shrugged like I'd caught him in a lie. "He was at least as clean as the two sex offenders in the area."

"What does that mean?" I frowned at him.

"No evidence."

"You dropped it, is that what you did?"

"No evidence." Cadanki shrugged again and started chewing. "No reason to pursue."

"That's your idea of police work?"

"Department policy," he said. This time he wasn't joking.

"So what now?"

"If I wanted to keep an eye on Miss Ogle, I gather I can do that from in front of your house?"

"We're business partners," I replied, offended by his insinuation. It was a stupid thing to say. "John left us the shop."

"Granger told me. He's looking for something for when he retires, case you want to sell."

"Why don't you look for who did this and let Dick Granger do his own retirement planning?"

Cadanki bared his teeth. "We'll keep on the surveillance," he said, backing toward the broken doorframe. He stopped in the doorway. "Oh, in the interest of full disclosure, they released Miss Vicki."

"What?"

"D.A said the theft charge wouldn't stick and there's not enough evidence on the kidnapping. He needed the bed."

I stared at him like he'd just shot a large caliber hollow point into my forehead.

"I'm so happy he got his fucking bed back."

Cadanki shrugged. "Just thought you should know."

"Here's an idea, Cadanki. Why don't you stop following me around and follow Vicki. She could lead you to Floyd. You've got evidence on Floyd, don't you?" I glared at him.

He looked bored. "You got a real knack for this type of thing." He stopped chewing long enough to show his teeth. "Her folks bought her a one-way ticket back to Texas."

"Great! You know, Cadanki, in the interest of full disclosure, I was at a handgun training class when Shaman disappeared."

"Go on." Cadanki nodded. I couldn't tell from his look whether it was because he'd heard what I'd said or because he already knew.

"Part of their spiel was you couldn't rely on the police. You have to protect yourself."

He came toward me, close, backing me into the railing.

"Way things are going, Mulligan," he whispered in my ear. "That would be good advice. Like I said, just don't shoot him in the back."

I slid sideways and looked at him. He just chewed his gum. I shook my head and went down the stairs hoping the afternoon would turn out better than the morning.

Chapter Forty-Seven

The Lesson

"Where's Kara?" I asked.

"She went to get the keys to her mom's car."

I looked a question at Amy as she sat, eyes closed, her face smiling into the morning sun. "How come?" I asked finally.

"She got her permit. I thought she could take me shopping for a few things."

"Are you okay?" I said, kneeling, holding her forearms in my hands.

"No, but feeling violated doesn't do any good."

"Not into the Kubler-Ross thing?"

"It's too wimpy," she said. "I like just two stages of grief: suck-it-up and revenge."

"That would be the Kubla Khan model."

I was going to kiss her, but she was still smiling at the sun. I sat down in the other chair.

"So," she said finally, sitting forward and looking at me.

"You guys can drop me off at the shop. I suppose someone needs to run the business."

Her eyes opened wide. "The business! I completely forgot about the business."

Kara came back with the keys to her mother's Volvo.

"Mom wants us to pick up some things for the party tonight," she said, holding out a list.

"Yeah, like pajamas," Amy replied.

I went into the house and unlocked the gun safe. I slipped my holster into my waistband, loaded my handgun, did a chamber-check-mag-check, and holstered it. It was all habit now. I put a short-sleeved shirt over my t-shirt as a cover garment.

Amy came in behind me, loaded her gun, did a chamber-check-mag-check, and zipped it into the concealment pouch of her shoulder bag.

"I think we're ready for the day," I said.

"I think we are." She hefted the bag, then slipped the strap over her shoulder.

It was only a little past our regular opening time when I got to the shop. I told the girls I'd see them back at the house. I'd drive the shop truck until Ken and Karen returned my real truck.

Business was slow like it usually is on a Saturday. The few customers that came in mostly wanted a place to hang out, delaying some household chore. The last one left a little after noon. I walked around straightening things up. Out the front window, I could see the white four-door Dodge Ram pickup, Cadanki on the job. I replayed our conversation and felt bad about what I'd said. None of this was his fault.

I did a little paperwork hoping it would make the time go by. It didn't. I thought about getting a dog. That didn't help either. What was making me restless was Cadanki. I needed to apologize. A casting lesson in the parking lot would show there were no hard feelings. That would make me feel better, kill time, and provide entertainment as well.

I squinted at the brightness as I stepped out of the shop, then started across the street at an angle. Heat rose up my legs from the hot blacktop. As I approached the truck, I could see movement on the driver's side. The engine started and the window slide down revealing the shady interior.

"Hey." I stopped at the door. "How about a casting lesson?"

In answer, a fist twice the size of a large snake's head came rocketing through the window and landed on the side of my nose.

I staggered back, someone laid on their horn and hit their brakes. I felt the hot metal of a car fender bounce to a stop behind me. I pitched forward of the fender. They called me a stupid idiot and went on down the street cursing.

The fist came out of the window again. This time it grabbed me by my shirtfront and pulled me against the door.

"Hey, Bobby, how they hanging?" It was Floyd DuChien.

I tried to ignore the pain long enough to focus my eyes. His hair was darker, like it had been dyed, and cut short. His breath stank of beer.

"What's the matter?" He slipped his sunglasses off. His eyes were bloodshot, the pupils dilated. "Don't remember me?"

I didn't say anything. I just hung there, dangling from where he was holding my shirt, trying to get it together. I could feel the blood dripping down my face to my chin. I could taste it in my mouth and throat.

"I hear you're running the show." He shook me to make sure I was listening. "Thought I'd stop by, see if you had any openings."

"I got one," I said. "It'd be perfect for a shitbag like you."

Bang! His other fist hit me on the side of the head. Now he was head and shoulders hanging out of the truck window and hopping mad.

"Bobby, you don't know when you're licked, do you?" He reached back into the truck and pulled out a large knife. He placed the blade against the side of my face. It felt cool and razor sharp.

"What do you want, Floyd?" I looked at him. It hurt to focus that close.

"Oh, I want to slit your throat, but I want an apology first."

"Apology for what?"

"For not letting sleeping dogs lie so to speak." He grinned at me.

"What are you talking about, Floyd?"

"That neighbor lady and her dog. We was just funning you, but you couldn't let it go."

"You did that?"

"Well, Jimmy Dean took the dog. That's how bad he wanted that job. It was me thought to kill it and bury it in your back yard. Clever, hunh?"

"You're crazy, Floyd."

"Crazy like a fox, Bobby."

"No, just crazy."

"See. You just can't let it go."

"And Nancy Calloway? Was that you or Jimmy Dean?"

"Oh, that was pure Jimmy Dean. He always liked window shopping, even as a kid. Then, if he liked what he saw, he'd go get himself some. He was on that most of the summer except when some damn dog messed him up."

When you train, they tell you never to give up. Never surrender.

"Jimmy Dean called your girlfriend a crackhead whore," I said.

Bang! He punched me in the side of the head with his knife hand.

"You're a real fuck-head, you know that, Bobby? You just can't let it go."

"Yeah." I shook my head, trying to stay focused, but between the ringing in my ears from Floyd's headshots and the adrenaline pounding through my chest like a drumbeat, it wasn't easy. "That's always been a problem."

"Well, I aim to fix that," he hissed, pulling me closer, tightening his grip on the knife. "Hey, Bobby, Jimmy Dean said you took a gun class. You learn anything?"

"One thing." I felt along my right hip.

"Yeah? What's that?"

I stuck the barrel of my Glock in his ear. "Never bring a knife to a gunfight."

"Whoa, Bobby." The tension in his grip relaxed. "Don't go getting no hardon. I was just funning, see if I could get a rise."

301

"Drop the knife, Floyd."

Floyd released his grip and the knife clattered to the ground.

I jerked the truck door open, pulling Floyd with it, then I reached over him and pushed the window switch on the door panel.

"Goddamn, Bobby, don't cut me in half," Floyd said as the window pressed against his upper chest, locking him in place.

I heard someone moan and looked into the backseat. Taylor and Smalley were bound like mummies with silver duct tape. They were motioning to set them free.

I went around to the passenger side, shut the truck engine off, and took the key from the ignition. Then I got out my cell phone and dialed Cadanki.

"Cadanki."

"Hey, this is Mulligan. I'm sorry I got mad at you this morning. Come over to the shop. I've got a present for you. And while you're here, you can pick up Curly and Larry. I won't be needing you guys anymore."

Chapter Forty-Eight

Pajama Party

Dick Granger came late to the party. By the time he walked into the shop, Cadanki had already left for the jail with Floyd, patrol cars from various area policing agencies were descending like flies at a picnic, and Taylor and Smalley were being treated in the parking lot by the EMT for epidermal trauma where Cadanki had yanked the duct tape off their mouths.

He wanted to know what had happened so I told him the story just like I'd told it to Cadanki.

"What'd Cadanki say?" he asked, surveying my black eye and the tail of blood that ran down my shirt.

"He said, 'most people would have ducked.'"

"Yeah? What'd you say?"

"That I was too busy looking at the knife."

He grunted and looked around the empty shop. "It's too bad about John." His eyes continued to move through the store. I had no idea what he was seeing. "I'm glad it's over," he said finally.

"What about Jimmy Dean?"

"I'm not worried. We'll catch him eventually. Floyd was the bad one."

I touched a hand to my cheek. My face was beginning to hurt like hell.

"You want a ride home?" he asked.

I did. The cop cars cruising slowly past the shop eliminated any chance of customers.

"Hey, how much to go down the McKenzie?"

"Free for you," I told him. "The shop owes you a trip, remember."

"Can I take someone with me?"

"Sure. When?"

"How about tomorrow? Do it before something else goes wrong."

"Works for me," I said. "We supply all the gear and lunch. I'll bring pop and water to drink. Bring beer if you want it. There'll be room in the cooler."

"Pop is fine. I'll bring a thermos of coffee. Cadanki doesn't drink."

"Cadanki, eh? I didn't know he fished," I said. "For trout, that is. He did say he fished for bad guys. I think he was being funny."

"No he wasn't. That's why I'm taking him. He needs a hobby."

"You mind if I bring Amy?" I asked. "She needs the experience. She can work the boat while we fish."

"Sounds like a plan."

I got a few things together for tomorrow and locked up. If Granger suspected I didn't believe him about Jimmy Dean, he didn't say anything.

Amy was at the house when we got there. When she saw me, she wanted to stay, but all I wanted to do was lie down, so she left to help Karen and Kara with the party. They'd gotten only half their chores done and were running desperately late.

I took a shower and a couple of ibuprofens and lay on the couch with a damp towel over my head. I don't remember falling asleep, but when I pulled the towel off my head, it was dry and the daylight was almost gone. I turned on the light and checked my face in the bathroom mirror. Pit bulls have smaller patches around their eyes. I wondered what Amy would think if I got a matching puppy.

The deck beckoned. I found a plate of leftover lasagna in the fridge and took it out. What I could see of the pot garden in the kitchen lights looked happy. The yard was dark and quiet. Monica was at an overnight group hug somewhere in the Cascades, annoying the native fauna with her precision drum team. The night was mine. The only sound drifted down the alley from the Kibbles. They were playing some yard game, about thirty of them, but I knew it was only five or six.

I sat in the dark, listening, not wanting to move. At the far end of the yard, I watched for shadows passing down the alley along the fence. Eventually, the party went inside. I heard the screen door slam.

My fingers rubbed gently across my bruised cheek as if to conjure some significant revelation. Where was Jimmy Dean? Would Kara's party attract him like splashing attracts a shark?

I thought about calling Cadanki, but didn't. He had Floyd in custody and Granger wasn't worried about Jimmy Dean. I settled back in my deck chair and tried to feel safe.

But I couldn't relax. It didn't matter that Floyd was in custody or how Granger felt. Jimmy Dean was still out there, and my friend, Jimmy Dean, was a shark. Floyd had said so. That was enough for me.

I got my handgun from the safe and made ready. On the deck, I practiced the four-step draw sequence. The soft glow of the night sights reminded me of airport landing lights. Then I set off through the deep shadows, alternately moving and stopping along the side fence I shared with Monica, staring across her dark yard to the Kibbles.

I slipped through the gate without rattling the latch and glided silently down the alley, all the time watching for movement in the shadows. When I got to the Kibbles, I stood on tiptoe and looked into their back yard. A squared-off finger of light poked the darkness. It came from Kara's bedroom window. I stepped toward their gate to get a better view.

"Hands on the fence," a voice behind me said. I felt something poke me in the center of my back. "Now!"

I leaned forward against the fence. A foot kicked my feet apart and a hand patted me down. It found my handgun and removed it.

"Hands behind your back, one at a time, right one first."

I did as I was told and felt the cool metal of handcuffs grip my wrists.

A hand spun me around.

"I thought that was you," Cadanki said. He spun me back around and unlocked the cuffs.

"Then why'd you cuff me?"

"Floyd wasn't enough practice." He chewed. "Besides, my taser's in the shop."

He unloaded my gun and handed the magazine to me. I put it in my pocket. Then he gave the gun back with the slide locked open. He touched my chin gently, turning my face into the light. "I hear we're on for tomorrow."

"Yeah."

"Good." He chewed, appraising my black eye. "I like a tough guy."

"You think it's a good idea?" I asked. "Tomorrow, I mean."

"You're bringing your girl, right? Granger's bringing me." Cadanki wagged his head and shrugged. "I'd say we're good until Jimmy Dean finds out about his brother. That's what's really going to piss him off. Now, go home. Leave the night shift to me." He gave me a send-off push down the alley. "And lock your door."

I eased the slide forward, holstered my gun, and retraced my steps, all the while thinking I had it right, Cadanki was fishing for sharks. The thought made me smile. On the deck, I grabbed the dirty dishes for the dishwasher.

I heard the hammer cock before I felt the gun muzzle press against the back of my head.

"You're up late," Jimmy Dean said behind me. "You seen Floyd?"

"No," I said back.

"You ain't bullshitting me are you, boss?"

"No, why?"

"Because he went looking for you." He pushed me toward the kitchen door.

"Sorry. Haven't seen him."

Jimmy Dean nudged me into the kitchen and locked the door behind us. He lifted my handgun half out of the holster.

"They work better loaded," he said and slipped it back. "Even plastic ones. They tell you that in training class?"

I set the dishes in the sink and turned. If he was close enough, I could rush him. But as I turned, he backed away.

"What happened to you?" Jimmy Dean looked at my swollen face and black eye.

"Ran into a door."

"You sure it wasn't Floyd you run into?"

"I told you I haven't seen him," I said. "And what are you doing with John's gun?" That's what he was pointing at me, John Ogle's .38 Special.

"Floyd got it for me."

"When he murdered John Ogle." I took a step forward.

"Self defense, boss." Jimmy Dean raised the revolver to face level. "He was fixing to shoot Floyd, so Floyd shot him first."

"He robbed him and stabbed him with a knife."

"Floyd was just trying to straighten thing out to avoid hard feelings, but the man wouldn't listen."

"That why he's looking for me? To straighten things out?"

"He's got a bone to pick 'cause of Vicki," Jimmy Dean said, lowering the gun to my chest as he backed toward the living room. "You ain't never apologized for snitching him off that time. He forgave you that because of me. But then you go and snitch on Vicki and get her arrested."

"She's a thief," I said, pointing my finger at his face. "She's been stealing from my neighbors and you know I don't like that."

"You turned her sour." Jimmy Dean raised the gun again. "She come out and she didn't want to do nothing no more. Floyd had to let her go."

"Was that why you trashed Amy's apartment, revenge?"

"We was looking for a new girl and Floyd was kind enough to give her an audition. Only she wasn't home, so we had a little fun was all."

"You keep away from Amy." I took a step forward.

Jimmy Dean backed a step and waved the gun. "Don't think I won't shoot you, boss."

"Floyd isn't here," I said flatly, "and you shouldn't be either. There's a cop just down the alley."

"Oh, I know that." Jimmy Dean chuckled. "I seen you down there in my old spot window shopping. See anything you like?"

"Did you hear what I said?"

"Boss." Jimmy Dean stepped forward. "I could whip you and burn your whole house down before he got here."

The backdoor knob wiggled. We both turned to look.

"Think so?" I asked.

"Mulligan, you in there?" Cadanki knocked on the door.

"You better not be bullshitting about Floyd," Jimmy Dean whispered and disappeared into the living room.

I unlocked the backdoor. Amy and Cadanki came in. They were laughing like Cadanki had said something funny.

"Just checking," he said.

"Yeah, thanks."

He saw my look, looked through the dark living room at the open front door, then took off at a run.

Chapter Forty-Nine

Payback

Sunday morning Amy and I met Granger and Cadanki at the Copper John. It was the first time I had seen either of them out of sports jackets and slacks. They were wearing blue jeans and short-sleeve shirts. Granger looked retired. Cadanki looked out of place. He had a small satchel and with his sunglasses on, he looked like a safe cracker.

The cooler water in the upper McKenzie would have been better fishing, but the boys wanted to stay close to town. I didn't really care where we fished as long as Amy was with us. So we left Granger's car and the shop rig with the extra trailer at Marshall Island and headed for Armitage. The mouth of the McKenzie was usually good and there were some nice holes on the Willamette. Stevens and two deputies were putting in when we got there. It crossed my mind it wasn't an accident.

As Amy pulled us neatly into the current, Cadanki took a handheld radio from his satchel, turned it on, and adjusted the frequency.

"Put it away, Cadanki," Granger ordered. "We're fishing today."

"Yeah, but if the fishing's slow, we can pester the county guys."

"I said, put it away."

Granger looked like he'd throw the radio overboard, so Cadanki put it away.

"Cell phones don't work that well either," I said, turning mine off. "I usually just turn mine off. Saves the battery."

Amy turned hers off, but Granger and Cadanki nodded politely like I was speaking a foreign language.

With Amy rowing, I concentrated on getting Granger and Cadanki into some trout. Granger hadn't fly fished in years, but he got the feel back right away. Cadanki had never fished before, so the mechanics of a fly rod were a mystery, but he enjoyed flailing the line around.

Small hatches of Pale Morning Duns spotted the river. I had Amy beach the boat on a long tongue of bar run just up from the mouth. Granger fished a dry fly, Cadanki an emerger. They caught a couple of cutthroats and Cadanki got a nice rainbow.

The Lane County boat motored silently past like it was stalking something on the river's edge. The sheriffs nodded as they went by. That was all it took for the shoptalk to creep back into the fishing trip.

"Too bad catching bad guys isn't as easy as catching fish," Cadanki said, looking at Granger as I released the rainbow from his line.

"That's because Mulligan's doing all the work."

"Hey, Mulligan, could you teach Taylor and Smalley to fish?" Cadanki asked.

"No," I said, "but anybody else."

They thought that was funny.

"I wish somebody'd catch Jimmy Dean DuChien," Amy said.

"I almost had him last night," Cadanki said.

"Sounds like a fish story." Granger nudged me with his elbow. "The one that got away."

"I'm getting closer."

"So is he," I said. I meant it as a joke, but nobody said anything after that.

We moved further down river. Amy slipped the boat over a riffle and pulled into the eddy. Just below us was a snag that had fallen sideways into the river during the winter. The branches bobbed slowly in the current like some mechanical device.

Granger fished the pocket water at the head of the eddy with a dry fly. I tied a small dropper fly onto Cadanki's nymph and showed him how to mend line into the current. That way, he could let the slowly passing water move his nymphs downstream without casting.

"If you feel anything, set the hook," I said.

Granger shouted. I grabbed the net, Amy got the camera, and we raced upstream. It was a beauty: a native rainbow, a female probably twenty inches in length. Amy told him to hold the fish up so she could take a picture.

"A little higher," she said looking my way. "That's it."

She took a couple more pictures, then I released the fish while Granger tried in vain to wipe the grin off his face.

"Hey, Cadanki," he called. "Did you see that?"

"Wait till you see this one!" Cadanki called in response.

I went downstream to see what Cadanki was into.

"Don't let him get into that snag," I warned.

Cadanki reeled line. The fish followed a few feet, then turned into the current and slid downstream.

"Oh-oh," Cadanki said as the fly line passed the snag.

"Don't give up."

But after a few tugs, it was clear the only thing on Cadanki's line was the snag.

"Reel in," I said. "Maybe we can save the fly."

As we got closer, I could see something long and light-colored draped across the front of the snag. A light-colored beach towel or a strip of Tyvek, I thought. That kind of stuff blew into the river all the time. It was in about five feet of water, too deep for me to wade to. I couldn't see Cadanki's fly line.

"Can you see it?" Cadanki asked.

"Not yet." I gazed into the water, but the broken surface made a bad window. I waited for it to clear. It didn't look like either a towel or a strip of Tyvek.

"What is that?"

"I don't know." I squinted into the wrinkled water. "It looks almost like a body."

Before I could say more, a yard-wide boil of water rose straight up like the lens of a magnifying glass. I thought for a moment I would see myself lying there in the convenience store, but the face wasn't mine. "It's Vicki."

Chapter Fifty

The Truth Will Out

That put an end to our fishing trip. Cadanki called Stevens on the radio and got the county sheriffs there; then Amy, Granger, and I left. Cadanki stayed with Vicki.

We tried fishing, but neither the bright July sun nor the native beauty of the Willamette could erase the image of Vicki staring at us through the gin-clear water.

I switched seats with Amy and pushed the boat down stream. Marshall Island seemed a long way away.

"John told me you got shot somehow," Granger said. "Is that true?"

"Yeah. That's why I came back to Eugene. I wanted to find a quiet life in a quiet neighborhood."

"He's pretty much kissed that idea goodbye," Amy assured him, looking at me.

Granger grunted. "What was it like?" he asked. "If you don't mind me asking."

"You know, Dick." I watched the birds flit along the riverbank blackberry vines. It all seemed so long ago. "It doesn't hurt as much as you'd think. They manage all the pain with medication." What the meds couldn't manage was the gnawing shame that I'd been so willing to trade life for death. Maybe that's why that counselor didn't work so well. He believed in the shame, but I couldn't get him to believe in St. Peter.

"How'd it happen?" Granger half-turned to look at me.

"Innocently enough," I said. "I was buying doughnuts. A couple bad guys walked in to rob the place, a couple good guys tried to stop them. I was in the middle."

Amy and Granger were both looking at me now.

"You want to hear something funny? Nobody could tell who shot me. Everybody was shooting 9mm and all the hits passed through."

My sense of humor didn't liven up the mood any and when we finally reached the boat ramp everyone was glad the trip was over.

Vicki was supposed to be safe in Texas. John took off to find out why she wasn't.

Amy and I retrieved the truck and trailer we'd left at Armitage, drove to the Copper John, cleaned the gear, and put it away. The voicemail light was blinking on the shop phone, but I figured it could wait till tomorrow.

By the time I turned off Polk onto West Broadway, it was late afternoon. A couple of patrol cars were parked in front of the house. Off to one side, Mrs. Batty and the Calloways were standing on the sidewalk. Nearer the house I could see Cadanki and his two stooges milling around.

I parked across the street.

"What's going on?" I asked as Amy came around the truck and we crossed the street together.

"Someone just shot your house," Mrs. Batty said, pointing with her cane.

I looked at the front of the house. It didn't look any different until I realized all the glass from the picture window lay like crystal snowmelt on the windowsill.

"A dark van." Tim Calloway waved his arms. "It came roaring around the corner, parked right there, fired a bunch of shots, and roared off."

"We called the police," Nancy said. "They came right away."

"Turn your cell phone on, Mulligan," Cadanki said from the front steps. "Somebody might want to call you sometime."

"Sorry." I reached reflexively into my pocket. It was still off from the trip. "What happened?" I asked him.

"Someone let the cat out of the bag," Taylor said.

"DuChien read the paper before we did." Cadanki nodded at the paper still rolled on the front steps.

I reached for it, shook the bits of broken glass off, and unfolded it.

"What?" Amy asked coming up behind me.

I held up the front page. The headline read, "Fishing Guide Captures Fly Shop Owner's Murderer." The subhead read, "D.A. to seek death penalty."

Amy hugged my arm, her head resting on my shoulder. She didn't say anything; she just stayed like that.

"Mind if we go in, look around?" Cadanki asked.

I unlocked the front door and Cadanki, Taylor and Smalley followed me in. Amy stayed outside talking with Mrs. Batty and the Calloways.

"Did Granger ever find out about Vicki?" It felt strange to speak.

"She got as far as San Francisco," Cadanki said. "She switched her ticket and flew back to Eugene. One of the taxis saw her get into a dark van with a bad transmission."

I nodded. It was simple enough. "You know last night Jimmy Dean said Floyd had to let her go. I thought he meant let her go to Texas."

Cadanki stopped chewing long enough to purse his lips and nod. "Check your voice mail," he said.

I dialed the mailbox and put the phone on speaker. I had four messages. The first two were hang-ups.

"I called twice to see where you were," Cadanki said.

"Fuck you, boss." Jimmy Dean had left the third message while we were on the river.

The fourth message was from yesterday. A reporter said he wanted an interview for a story he was doing. I didn't bother to write down his number.

"I count six holes," Taylor said to Cadanki.

"How about you, Einstein?" Cadanki asked Smalley.

"Six." Smalley looked at Taylor.

I looked around the living room. Except for the bullet holes in the walls and the broken glass from the front window, nothing else seemed damaged.

We walked out to the sidewalk. Karen Kibble was there talking with Amy.

"Do you need your truck tomorrow?" Amy asked. "I promised I'd help Karen move and she was thinking maybe tomorrow."

"Sure," I said looking to Cadanki. "I'll be in the shop."

"Where they moving?" Cadanki asked.

"Portland," Karen answered him. "We have to make two trips. We'll pay for gas."

"A hundred miles each way." Cadanki stopped chewing his gum like he was thinking, then nodded. "Okay, here's what's going to happen: Taylor and Smalley will watch out front tonight. Miss Ogle spends all day tomorrow driving up and down I-5. She's out of the action. Mulligan, you open the store as usual. Taylor and Smalley will tail you. I'll relieve them."

"You want me to wrap them in duct tape before you get there?" I asked.

"Every bit helps," Cadanki said, not sure whether I was joking or serious.

"Look, fellas," I said, "no offense, but this surveillance stuff hasn't done that much good."

"Yeah." Taylor nodded at my black eye and jerked a thumb at my house. "Like you're doing better by yourself."

Cadanki put his hand up for silence. "We need you to work with us on this, Mulligan. You're in obvious danger. So, yeah, we can't guarantee your safety, but we can make hurting you more difficult."

I looked at Amy. She nodded agreement.

"You got some plywood to nail over that window?" Cadanki asked.

"I do," Tim Calloway said. "I'll help you put it up, too. No problem."

"You better get started then," Cadanki said. "It's getting dark."

"So you guys are out front, who's watching the back?" I asked.

"Neighborhood Watch volunteers." Cadanki bared his teeth. "Trust me, Mulligan, it's for your own good." He pushed Taylor and Smalley out of his way.

Amy cleaned up the glass while Tim and I cut the plywood. We started nailing it into place over the vacant window just as the drums started banging in the back yard.

"Hi-a-wath-a, Hi-a-wath-a," Tim chanted, nailing in time with the drumming.

"They're holding an all-night vigil to protect us from evil spirits," Amy said, returning from dumping the broken glass in the garbage can. "They said there's a meteor shower around midnight, too, in case we were interested."

We sat out front talking for a while, me, Amy, Tim and Nancy, and Mrs. Batty. Karen left early to finish packing. It was fun to enjoy the warm summer evening like nothing had happened. The only distraction, aside from the drumming, was the police car parked across the street. When it was good and dark, everyone said their goodbyes, I waved to Taylor and Smalley, and Amy and I retreated into the house.

"Thus ends another day in paradise," Amy whispered as I turned the deadbolt to lock the front door.

Around midnight, we went out to the deck. Monica and her drum corps sat on blankets in a circle in the middle of the yard, their drums thumping softly like an ancient heartbeat.

Amy and I sat with our deck chairs together looking at the stars.

"There's one!" I said, pointing into the night sky.

"There's another one," Amy said a moment later.

After a while, we didn't bother to talk. We just watched the meteor shower. I found it disturbing at first that there was no pattern to it. The tiny streaks of light went off totally at random. It made me uneasy until I realized I had been seeing each streak as a muzzle flash and expecting return fire.

Chapter Fifty-One

What Tomorrow Brings

The next morning, I watched from the front door as Amy drove the truck the hundred feet to the Kibble's. Taylor and Smalley watched from across the street. A half dozen people came out to greet her and load the truck. I relaxed a bit, safety in numbers.

I went inside where Taylor and Smalley couldn't see, swept my shirttail back, did a chamber-check-mag-check, and reholstered. I wanted to make sure there was a round in the chamber. Then I locked up and walked across the street.

"You want to watch me walk to the store, call me a taxi, or give me a lift? Your choice."

They looked at each other reluctantly. I knew what they were thinking. They wanted to watch me walk to the store except they'd have to roll along behind me at three miles an hour for twenty minutes.

Smalley got out and helped me into the back seat. At the store, he helped me out.

"Mind if I ask you a question?" I asked.

"Shoot."

"How'd Floyd get the drop on you two the other day?"

"I knew it," Taylor sighed and sank lower in the driver's seat.

Smalley glanced over both shoulders. "Okay, so I was texting someone. It was personal. I felt the knife on my throat and that's all she wrote."

"You do know his brother is really mad right now, right?" If Smalley were a piece of paper, I would have crumpled him up and, OMG, thrown him in the street in front of the shop. "I mean really, really mad. And he could show up at any moment. You do know that, don't you?"

"No problem."

"Yeah, Cadanki took his cell phone," Taylor said.

"Oh, good for Cadanki," I said. Then I poked Smalley with my finger like it was the barrel of my handgun. "Fuck the both of you. If you aren't going to help, stay out of my way."

I crossed the parking lot, unlocked the door, flipped the "Gone Fishin'" sign around to the "Open" side, and slammed the door shut. Taylor and Smalley backed their car around and parked across the street in the shade of a big maple tree.

I didn't expect much business. It was the dog days of summer -- another reason not to own a dog. All I wanted was one customer, Jimmy Dean DuChien. If he walked in, I'd shoot him, bang, right in the middle of the shop.

Then I thought how poetic it would be to march him into John's office, stand him by the wall, and shoot him with John's gun. Twice.

Good thing I don't know much. A steady stream of customers wandered through the door, none of them Jimmy Dean. A couple guys came in with fliers for the bulletin board. I was helping an older gentleman select a fly rod, so I told them to drop them on the counter and I'd put them up as soon as I was done.

About twenty minutes later I rang up the sale, almost $1600 worth of rod, reel, extra spool, and two lines. John would be proud. I loaded the spools with backing and put the lines on them for the gentleman before he left. When I was done, I looked around the shop. It was empty, but after that sale it didn't matter.

I took the two fliers over to the bulletin board. The first was an old aluminum drift boat for sale. I could tell from the photo it was well used, but the price was fair. The picture on the second sign also showed a drift boat. This one was a brand new aluminum guide model with a blue-on-cream paint job. It was Jimmy Dean's boat. The flier was labeled "Stolen."

I called the number on the flier, but nobody picked up. I had my hand on the shop phone to call Cadanki, but my cell phone went off.

"Bobber?"

"Speaking."

"Hi, Karen Kibble."

"Hey, Karen, how's the move going?"

"Great and thanks for the truck. It makes things so much easier. I just wanted to see if Amy had stopped by on her way to the house?"

"No," I said, starting to tense. "Was she going to?"

"No, but if she did, I wanted her to buy you lunch before she left with the second load."

"Oh." I relaxed. "She's probably over at your place loading then." I looked at my watch. "If I close the shop, I can catch her, help with the load, then have lunch with her before she goes back."

"That sounds good. We're eating now. I know she's probably starving."

It wasn't that I wanted a free lunch. As long as Jimmy Dean was running around, I wanted Amy with me if she was in town. I locked up, flipped the sign, and left in the shop truck.

I could see Taylor and Smalley in the rearview dutifully tracking me to West Broadway.

My truck wasn't parked in the Kibble's driveway like it should have been and my heart started to accelerate. I stiffened and leaned over the steering wheel. Then I saw the truck in my driveway. I sighed in relief and relaxed into my seat. Amy was probably picking up something for the trip back. Maybe she was making me lunch.

I parked in the street, walked up, and tried the front door. It was locked. When I opened it and walked in, everything was just like we'd left it that morning.

"Amy," I called, but there was no answer. I took a deep breath. "Amy?"

I pulled my gun and pied around the doorway. The living room was empty. It looked normal. I moved through the rooms, clearing them one by one. They all looked normal, too, except the bedroom.

Scrawled across one wall in red spray paint were a bunch of swastikas and cuss words. On the wall above the bed were the words "crackhead whore."

Chapter Fifty-Two

Bad Timing

I holstered my gun and called Cadanki.

"Jimmy Dean's got Amy."

"Where you at?"

"My place."

"I'm on my way."

Time does funny things when you're under stress. I thought it would take Cadanki forever to get there, but by the time I stepped out the front door, he was pulling into the driveway. Maybe it just took me forever to back out of the house.

He looked up at me, gave me the hi-sign with his chin, and sent Taylor and Smalley to check the Kibble's and Amy's old apartment building.

"You touch anything?" he asked, pushing past me and going up the front steps.

"No." I followed him in.

"Then how did you get in?"

"Just the front door. I unlocked it and opened it."

"I got the techs coming over. Keep your hands in your pockets."

He stood in the living room and looked both ways like he was crossing a street. "You check the back door?"

"No."

Cadanki went directly to the kitchen and stood in front of the door. He pulled a latex glove from his coat pocket and stretched the glove over his hand, letting the cuff snap against his wrist.

"Always wanted to be a proctologist." He wiggled his eyebrows twice and bent to examine the dead bolt. The door was unlocked.

"Came in through the front, left through the back," he said, standing. "Which room is yours?"

We went to the bedroom.

"That's right, your friend's an electrician."

I wanted to grab Cadanki and shake him. "He's not my friend."

"He's still an electrician." Cadanki pointed to a cable tie lying on the floor near the bed. "My guess is he was already in the house. You come home for lunch?"

"Sometimes." I shrugged.

"What are you doing here now?"

"I was going to make Amy lunch."

"He was waiting for you, but Amy showed up instead. Looks like he followed her in and caught her here."

"But she had her gun."

"Sometimes guns aren't enough." Cadanki looked at me, then went back to working the room. He nodded at the open closet door. "He probably heard her coming, hid in there, and jumped her from behind."

All I could do was squeeze my sweaty hands inside my pockets.

"They haven't been gone too long." Cadanki pointed a latex finger at a spray painted swastika. "The paint's still wet."

We turned at the sound of footsteps entering the house.

"Gentlemen, you're going to have to vacate the premises," said the crime scene tech. "You, too, Cadanki."

"Didn't they teach you about contaminating a crime scene?" he chided Cadanki as he escorted us out the front door.

"I didn't get that far," Cadanki replied.

"What now?" I asked, feeling a little abandoned as Cadanki got in his car.

"Did Amy have a credit card?"

"Visa."

"You said you came home to make Amy lunch?"

"Yeah."

"You had lunch?"

"No."

"Have some lunch. I'll round up Taylor and Smalley, then get on the credit card. We may be able to track him that way."

Cadanki caught my look as he started his car.

"Eat lunch," he said firmly. "It'll help you think. If you think of anything, call."

I watched him drive down the street and round the corner onto Polk. Not knowing what else to do, I went back in the house to see about lunch.

"Sorry, sir," the crime scene tech said. "You can't come in here."

"Then can you move your vehicle so I can get my truck out?"

"The red one in the driveway? No. I haven't gone over it yet."

I crossed the street to the shop truck and started the engine before I realized I didn't know where to go. I wanted to find Amy, but I didn't know where to look. Cadanki wanted me to get lunch, but I wasn't hungry. I thought about going to the church, but praying wouldn't bring me any closer to Jimmy Dean.

Instead, I drove to Armitage Park. Maybe it was just reflex, one of those muscle memories the trainers talked about. I parked were I could see the river and watched as the blue-green water slide by like life itself.

I was looking for inspiration, but all I saw was Jimmy Dean. He was leering at Kara Kibble saying, "DuChien, that's French for 'the fox,'" the words repeating in my mind like a bad jingle. Clever like a fox. The fox brothers had outfoxed me all summer. They'd played the law the same way, always one step ahead. They'd raid the henhouse, then disappear, then popped up again to take another chicken.

I started the truck and called Cadanki as I headed out of the parking lot.

"Think of anything?" he said before I said a word.

"He's hiding."

"Yeah, but where?"

"That place on the river, Barclay's," I said. "He called it the Fox Hole."

I closed the phone and drove to the opening in the guardrail that led down to the campsite. A wave of fear washed over me. I was glad I hadn't had lunch. From where I sat, the oak grove looked abandoned.

It was surprising the change only a few weeks had brought. Massive tangles of blackberry vines encroached into the open space between the trees and intertwined in large mounds. I turned the truck onto the road and moved slowly down the grass-covered tracks. When I got to the bottom, I started across the flat toward the oak grove and the river. What had looked like blackberry vines and shrubs from the highway were actually a series of tarps and netting that camouflaged a camper and a couple of dark vans.

I pulled to a stop where the track ended at the oak grove and turned the truck off.

"Hey, Boss," Jimmy Dean said from behind me even as I felt the hard muzzle of a gun press against my ear. "Welcome to the Fox Hole."

Chapter Fifty-Three

Better Prepared

"You're a little early for business, boss," he said, pushing his gun into my ear. "I ain't had a chance to train my new whore. But if you wait, I'll get her fixed up. You can watch."

I turned and looked directly at him. I made a point of it. In training, they say you have to control the situation.

"This isn't a business call," I said, talking like we were sitting on my back deck. Talking wasn't shooting. I didn't want any shooting until I could get my gun out, that left talking. "I came to get Amy."

"Oh, did you now." He straightened his shoulders. It was a twitchy, nervous movement like he was on something. "Admit it, boss. I outfoxed you on that one."

"Funny." I looked at him calmly. "That's been your problem all along."

"What's that?"

I didn't answer. I just looked at him.

He stood there, sweating under the hot sun. He wiped his forehead with his gun hand, then took a quick step forward like an animal threatening to charge. "What's that?"

"You think you're clever," I said. "You're not even as clever as Floyd."

The door of the camper rattled like something had fallen against it.

"You can't bullshit me, boss," he said, backing toward the camper. "That's your problem. You think you can bullshit me."

"I'm not bullshitting you, Jimmy Dean," I said. "You read the paper. Floyd's in jail because I put him there. That's what a clever fox your brother is."

"You fucker, you." The camper door rattled again. Someone was kicking it. Jimmy Dean backed toward the camper, thought better of it, and came back to the truck. "God damn you!"

The camper door burst open, pushed by a pair of legs bound at the ankles with cable ties.

"Better hurry, Jimmy Dean," I chided him. "Looks like the chickens are escaping the hen house"

"God damn it!"

Jimmy Dean sprinted toward the camper.

I yanked my door open and followed behind him. I had my gun out and up, but was running to fast to shoot.

Jimmy Dean reached in the camper and pulled Amy out by the arm. She balanced in front of him, her legs strapped together, hands behind her back, while he held his gun to her head. She looked at me, made her eyes big, and rolled them toward Jimmy Dean.

I had my gun up. I had a head shot. It would bring him down.

"Mexican stand-off, boss." Jimmy Dean grinned at me. "What's it going to be?"

I looked down my night sights at Jimmy Dean DuChien's head.

"Armed citizen, stop or I'll shoot."

"That don't work out here," Jimmy Dean pressed the muzzle of John's service revolver against Amy's head.

She gestured with her eyes again. Do it.

My finger tightened on the trigger.

"You going to shoot me, boss, or are you bullshitting again?" Jimmy Dean stuck his head out like he wanted to check my gun. "You got it loaded this time? I'll blow her fucking head off."

I pressed the trigger back to the handle.

I didn't hear my gun go off, but when the sights came back on target, a small hole dotted Jimmy Dean's forehead. A puff of red moved slowly off behind him and Jimmy Dean dropped straight to the ground.

I did my after action drill, looking to each side. A cop car was roaring down the grass track raising a cloud of dust.

Without Jimmy Dean behind her, Amy wobbled. I holstered my gun and sprinted forward, grabbing her before she fell, and cut her free.

"Nice shot," she said, rubbing the tie marks on her wrists.

I kissed her and hugged her to me.

The cop car skidded to a stop behind us. For a second, nothing happened as the cloud of dust it was trailing caught up and passed by.

"Eugene Police," Cadanki shouted. "Hands on your head. Hands on your head."

I did like he said. So did Amy.

Granger came up behind me, slipped my Glock from its holster, and unloaded it.

Cadanki squatted and felt Jimmy Dean's neck for a pulse, looked at Granger, and shook his head. He stood and took a couple quick chews. "You ought to shoot in the league."

Granger sat us in the cop car and asked us questions, writing down what we answered while Cadanki searched the oak grove. When he was done, I took Amy to the shop truck. It was the only place she felt safe.

A second police vehicle came down the trail. That was followed by the EMTs. They talked to Amy and had her sign a statement refusing treatment. A county sheriff arrived, then another. Pretty soon the oak grove was covered in publicly owned vehicles.

"If there's nothing else, I'm going to take Amy home," I told Cadanki.

"Good idea. We can use the parking. This is turning into a real inter-agency cluster-fuck."

He walked me to the truck. "How'd you know to come here?" he asked.

I thought about it a minute, looking off in the distance. "I didn't really," I concluded finally. "But I couldn't give up."

He looked off in the distance, too, like he could see what I was looking at.

"You and I are a lot alike," he said, holding the door open, then shutting it for me. "You ever get tired of fishing for trout, you could be a cop."

"You mean a fisher of men?" I stuck my hand out the window and we shook. "I'll leave that to you and St. Peter."

"We'll probably have some questions. I'll be in touch." He tapped the door twice. "Buckle up. Hate to see you get a ticket after all this." He stopped chewing long enough to smile.

I watched him recede into the background as I turned the truck around and headed home.

THE END

About the Author

Charlie Fernandez divides his time between Eugene, Oregon and Phoenix, Arizona. He is a contract technical writer who likes fly fishing, handgunning, and house remodeling. He also likes martinis and character-driven mysteries. He is an NRA- and IDPA-certified range safety officer and a CERT (Community Emergency Response Team) trainer. *Night Sights* is his first published novel.

Made in the USA
Middletown, DE
29 October 2022

13761485R00195